# CLUNY BROWN

*Margery Sharp*

Little, Brown and Company · Boston
1944

PRINTED IN THE UNITED STATES OF AMERICA
BY H. WOLFF, NEW YORK

*TO*

GEOFFREY CASTLE

# CLUNY BROWN

## By MARGERY SHARP

SOMETIMES I wish that every reader might receive books as your committee of judges do—I mean in bundles of proof-sheets, with no neat binding and bright colored jacket and publishers' fanfare. Of course it would be very inconvenient, and the luxurious customer would wonder how anyone could endure reading under such conditions—and on those highly glazed galley-proofs that dazzle and bloodshot the eyes. But at least you have the fun of starting at scratch; you know nothing about the book beforehand, nothing at all; and sometimes you have the full and perfect thrill of joyful discovery. No one has told you just how or why or in what respect the book will be delightful.

For that reason I honestly try, in writing reviews of novels, not to say too much in detail. I hate to deprive the reader of any instant of the blissful forgetfulness — or the painful identification—that fiction can give. I wish I could just say here, you will lose your heart to Cluny Brown, and leave it at that. I wish you could have seen your committee (middle-aged people with many cares) grin at each other when her name came up. "Cluny Brown!" said one, "I haven't enjoyed anything so much in I don't know when."—"Cluny Brown!" exclaimed another; "I always had a special feeling for tall girls."—"Of course I wouldn't say she's terribly important," said a third, "but as I think about it, maybe she has Social Significance, too." —"I don't care if she has or not," was the consensus; "we couldn't possibly get along without Cluny Brown."

In a world that is grim with pain and fatigue, so innocent a comedy has its own service to perform. You will think with love, and pity, too (for her heart is very unshielded), of tall, gawky, long-legged Cluny, aged twenty. She came from Paddington, a most unglamorous region of London; she was an orphan and lived with her uncle, Mr. Porritt, a resolute and conscientious plumber. When we first meet Cluny (her real name was Clover) her stout-hearted uncle is worried about her. He has raised her from childhood, and she has become very useful; she answers his telephone and this is important in a plumber's business. Jobbing plumbers deal mostly with emergencies. But what is queer about Cluny, the thing quite outside Uncle Porritt's purview in the England of 1938, is that Cluny doesn't seem "to know her place." One day she went to the Ritz and had tea, just to see what it was like. Another time she stayed in bed all day Sunday, drinking orange juice and relaxing (trying to pretend she was a Persian cat) because she had read something to that effect in an evening paper. Although (to Uncle Porritt's eye) she was "as plain as a boot," she had actually been followed on the street. But when she took the bag of tools and went off on a plumbing job herself, and found herself chased by a lecherous old heterophile with a studio apartment and a Chelsea bathroom and Martinis, Uncle Porritt and the other Uncle (a railway porter) got serious. Cluny must learn her place in society. She must go into domestic service. Which was easy enough in the world of England, 1938. Although entirely "untrained" (as the reader will quickly see), she finds herself that much desired creature, a Tall Parlormaid, in the beautiful old house of Friars Carmel down in Devonshire.

You may guess (and you will be right) that lean, long-thighed, loping Cluny, with her deep voice and black eyes and pony's-tail of jagged black hair rising above her nape, makes an unusual parlormaid in that ancient English mansion. She has no conception of the things that Aren't Done. The housekeeper, Mrs. Maile, and the butler, Mr. Syrett, have never seen anyone quite like her; but maids are at a premium, and at least Cluny has the long reach which enables her to wait at table without breathing in the ears of the sitters. Those who remember something of English country houses in old days, the sacred baize door that divides the domestic quarters from the rest of the house, the brass cans of hot water, the morning tea in bed, the dressing gong, the easy life of animals and the hard life of servants, will enjoy amusing and accurate reminiscence in the description of Friars Carmel. But all this is only byplay. Margery Sharp quickly and shrewdly complicates her plot with several important people. My own special homage goes frankly to the housekeeper, Mrs. Maile; if there is Social Significance in this delightful book it comes richest when the other housemaid had a bastard, but (as Cluny reports) "Mrs. Maile overlooked it." The action begins when young Andrew, the son of the house, brings as guest to Friars Carmel the exiled Polish author, Belinski. And there is another guest, the incredibly beautiful Betty Cream. A far-away literary agent in America exerts mysterious power; the Polish author gets a royalty check and invitations to lecture; he has somewhat overstayed his welcome in Devonshire and before his departure there is a celebration with champagne. But what happens, and how it affects the history and love-life of our adorable Cluny I will not divulge. In a story of this sort much depends upon the illusion of surprise; it may be that in this case surprise is attained by rather drastic means. But that is for you to decide, not for me to suggest. The book is delicious in charm and humor, and in a deeper feeling, too, for the brave, joy-hunting cockney child who broke through the patterns all her friends tried to impose. The sympathizing reader will repeat to himself that outraged refrain, "Who do you think you are, Cluny Brown?" And every girl who has suffered by being a little taller than her sisters will read this book with enchantment.

CHRISTOPHER MORLEY

In accordance with a suggestion made by a number of our subscribers, this monthly reprint from the Book-of-the-Month Club *News* is printed in this format so that it can be pasted, if desired, to the flyleaf of the book.

# CLUNY BROWN

# Chapter 1

THINKING of Cluny Brown, Mr. Porritt, a successful plumber, allowed himself to be carried past his 'bus stop and in consequence missed the Sunday dinner awaiting him at his sister's. It was not much loss. The food would be all right, for Addie had her virtues, but she was too much of a harper. At the moment she was harping on Cluny Brown.

Paying an extra penny, Mr. Porritt got off the 'bus at Notting Hill Gate. There was still ample time to return to Marble Arch and proceed as usual down the Edgware Road, but a spirit of independence moved him to turn instead into Kensington Gardens. He hadn't been inside the Gardens for more than a year — not, in fact, since the day of his wife's funeral, when he went on a long dogged tramp through all the London parks getting his mind used to the fact that Mrs. Porritt was no more. It took some doing — they had been married twenty-six years and never a hard word; but somewhere along the road Arnold Porritt came to an interim agreement with Providence. He would go on as before, doing his duty as a plumber, and his duty by Cluny Brown, and if at the last he and his Floss were not reunited, he would make trouble. Mr. Porritt was a man with a strong sense of justice.

The day, for February, was uncommonly mild. Hardy persons sat on seats outside the Orangery, their faces to the sun, their backs to brickwork that had faced the sun for three centuries; it was always warmer there than anywhere else in the Gardens. After circling the lawn Mr. Porritt too set his foot upon this terrace; since no bench was entirely vacant, he chose one accommodating a solitary lady. To Mr. Porritt's eye she was no longer young, and could never have been attractive; the glancing eye of the lady noted Mr. Porritt as definitely quaint; and each would have been extremely surprised to learn the other's opinion.

The lady had a book on her knee, but Mr. Porritt had left his paper in the 'bus, and was thus defenceless against the well-known effects of proximity in a public park. Within five minutes the desire to confide in a stranger became irresistible. He uttered a preliminary cough, and remarked that it was uncommon mild for the time of year.

"Deliciously," said the lady. Her voice, and that one word, assured Mr. Porritt she *was* a lady, a fact which her hat and make-up had caused him to doubt.

"Makes me wish my niece was here," said Mr. Porritt.

"Yes, children love the Gardens," agreed the lady affably.

"She's no child," said Mr. Porritt.

The lady gave him an encouraging look. She was waiting for a young man who she intended should become her lover, and thought it would be rather piquant to be discovered in conversation with any one so quaint, so unexpected, so altogether out-of-her-picture as Mr. Porritt. Even as she smiled fragments of dialogue were forming in her mind — "*But people always talk to me!*" she would say. "*I feel like that man in Kipling who sat still and let the animals run over him.*" Or was Kipling just a little bit — dating? "*Like that man in the jungle,*" perhaps — and leave his provenance vague. . . .

"She's twenty," pursued Mr. Porritt. "An orphan. My wife's sister's. Sometimes I don't rightly know how to handle her."

"Twenty is a difficult age."

"She ain't exactly difficult. It's more — " Mr. Porritt frowned. He pondered, he cogitated, groping as he had so often done before after the root of the trouble. Cluny Brown was good-tempered, willing, as much sense as most girls —

"Is she pretty?"

"Plain as a boot."

"Attractive?"

Mr. Porritt, who thought he had answered this question already, merely shook his head; and the lady smiled. She was plain herself, but no one could call her unattractive. (Mr. Porritt could have, of course, but the question was not likely to arise.)

"Then perhaps she has an inferiority complex?"

"Not her," said Mr. Porritt. He knew nothing about complexes, but any idea of inferiority was so wide of the mark that it suddenly showed up, by contrast, the very thing he had been after. "The trouble with young Cluny," said Mr. Porritt, "is she don't seem to know her place."

At last it was out, Cluny Brown's crime; and her uncle could never have put into words — not even to a stranger, not even in a park — the uneasiness it caused him. To know one's place was to Arnold Porritt the basis of all civilized, all rational life: keep to your class, and you couldn't go wrong. A good plumber, backed by his Union, could look a Duke in the eye; and a good dustman, backed by *his* Union, could look Mr. Porritt in the eye. Dukes of course had no Union, and it was Mr. Porritt's impression that they were lying pretty low.

"But what is her place?" asked the lady, looking amused.

Mr. Porritt thought this a remarkably foolish question: any one looking at *him,* he considered, should at once recognize his niece's place. But he had a fine answer ready, a proper bomb-shell, which he was by no means unwilling to explode.

"I'll tell you where it ain't: it ain't the Ritz," said Mr. Porritt; and astonished himself all over again. For that was what young Cluny had done, only a day or two before: she had gone and had tea at the Ritz, all on her own, to see what it was like. Two-and-a-tanner it cost her, and not even bloater-paste. Told him herself, making no secret of her daftness, no idea, it seemed, she'd done anything out of the way. Mr. Porritt was pleased to see that his new acquaintance (for all *her* daftness) looked properly taken aback. "And that's Cluny all over," he finished, in gloomy triumph. "Just no idea what's what."

"Cluny?" repeated the lady.

"Cluny Brown. Short for Clover," explained Mr. Porritt. He paused, to see whether a tall young man, just then approaching, meant to sit down on their seat. But the lady (who had observed the new-comer a moment in advance) leaned forward with increasing animation.

"Do you know," she said rapidly, "I think your niece sounds exceptionally charming. You mustn't suppress her, you must help her to develop. She may be a really special personality."

Then she turned with a start, and saw the young man smiling down on them, and Mr. Porritt at once realized it was time to take himself off.

II

"Who the hell was that?" asked the young man, sitting down.

The lady made a comical face.

"I haven't the faintest idea. People always talk to me in

parks. I feel like that man in the jungle who sat still and let the animals run over him."

"One of these days you'll find yourself assaulted."

"My dear, you know I only attract the respectable."

They both laughed. The young man looked after the diminishing figure of Mr. Porritt and shook his head.

"The old rip! Did he tell you his wife doesn't understand him?"

"Not at all. I've been hearing all about his niece, a young person named Cluny Brown, short for Clover, who went to tea at the Ritz."

"Darling, you're wonderful!" said the young man. "What a line! But why the Ritz?"

"Because she doesn't know her place."

"How shocking. Shocking Cluny Brown! I'd like to meet her."

This being out of the question, the lady was able to say that she would too; and then feeling that Cluny had been talked of long enough, and was even becoming a nuisance, demanded to be taken to lunch.

## III

It was half past two when Mr. Porritt walked into his brother-in-law Trumper's house in Portobello Road. The open front-door, and a trowel stuck in a border, showed that Trumper had started a bit of gardening and given it up. Within, the narrow hall smelt strongly of linoleum and brass-polish, and Mr. Porritt, sniffing appreciatively, did his sister justice. She knew how to keep a house. Neat as a new pin. A place for everything, and everything in its place. Mr. Porritt hung up his cap and went into the front room, and there sat Trumper, shirt-sleeved, reading the *News of the World*.

"Got here," said Mr. Porritt.

"Thought you'd bin run over," said Trumper.

"Wrong 'bus," explained Mr. Porritt.

"Had your dinner?"

"Snack," said Mr. Porritt.

He sat down and removed his boots, placing them neatly on the lower shelf of a bamboo whatnot. The top of the whatnot bore a chenille mat, a brass tray, a brass pot, in the pot a fine rubber plant; the whole standing just where it ought, plumb in the centre of the bow-window.

"You left a trowel outside," said Mr. Porritt.

"Aye," agreed Trumper. "Where's young Cluny?"

"In bed."

"What, ill?"

"No, she read a piece in the paper," said Mr. Porritt; and remembered his own paper left in the 'bus. He now wanted it, because this was his time and place for a good read. It was also Trumper's time and place, and the minute he finished Addie started in, and it was wonderful how nothing annoyed people more than taking their Sunday paper. Mr. Porritt remembered a very striking illustration of this from his own experience: it was when his wife's sister turned up with the infant Cluny, and her husband dead, poor chap, and nothing for it but to take them in and give them a home; and both he and Floss agreed on it, glad and willing, and Cluny's mother behaved just as she ought, except for one thing: she would take the Sunday paper before Mr. Porritt had done with it. He never said a word, but just that one habit so irritated him that he gradually took a dislike to her. For a while he even bought two papers: it was worse. She wanted to read them in bits, piece here and piece there, swapping and muddling the sheets until you couldn't even find the football. And yet she was a nice woman in her way, and when she died, of pneumonia, Mr. Porritt felt sorrier than he expected. . . .

"I see Eden's gone and resigned," observed Trumper. "I s'pose he knows what he's at."

"If you ask me, we'll have trouble with Mussolini yet," said Mr. Porritt, "and that Hitler. I don't trust 'em."

"Nor me. What this country ought to ha' done — "

In another moment they would have been embarked on a good, meaty, masculine conversation; but the door opened, and in bounced Addie. She was four years junior to her husband, and five to Mr. Porritt, but one would never have guessed it, because she didn't hold with making yourself look young. She held with looking neat and clean and hard-wearing, and in this she perfectly succeeded.

"There you are!" she exclaimed — running her eye over her brother as though to make sure that he was all there indeed. "What happened?"

"Wrong 'bus," explained Mr. Porritt.

"Had your dinner?"

"Snack," said Mr. Porritt.

"Where's Cluny?"

"In bed."

"What, ill?"

"No," said Mr. Porritt patiently. "She read a piece in the paper, about how it rested the nerves and toned the system to stay a day in bed eating oranges."

For a second Addie Trumper stared, speechless. Her jaw tightened. Her eyes snapped. Both her husband and her brother unconsciously braced themselves.

"My stars!" cried Addie Trumper. "Who does she think she is?"

There it was again, the inevitable question that Cluny Brown seemed always, and so unnaturally, to provoke. For what could be plainer than the answer? — her father a defunct lorry driver, one uncle a plumber, her late mother that plumber's sister-in-law, her other uncle a railway porter (Great Western) — how could any one doubt who Cluny was? How could there be any doubt as to who she thought she was? It was obvious. And yet if Mr. Porritt had heard that question once, he had heard it a thousand times. He even asked it of himself. And neither to himself, nor to Addie Trumper, could he give an answer.

"What young Cluny needs — " stated Mrs. Trumper, drawing breath — "I've said it before and I'll say it again — is to go into service. Good service, under a strict housekeeper. You mark my words."

But Mr. Porritt did not intend to be browbeaten.

"And I've told you, I can't spare her. I've got to have some one for the phone when I'm not there."

"What you *want* with a phone — !"

Mr. Porritt and Trumper exchanged brotherly glances. Of course a plumber had to have a telephone: half the calls, and all the urgent ones, came by phone. It was one of the reasons for Mr. Porritt's success — you could get hold of him. People rang up at midnight, or even later, and even if Mr. Porritt did not turn out, his solemn professional tones brought comfort, and if he said he'd be round first thing, they seldom bothered to get any one else. Of course he had to have a phone . . .

"And by the same token," said Mrs. Trumper, turning on her husband, "you've left a trowel in front." Then she snatched up the *News of the World* and bounced out.

It was a few moments before the atmosphere settled down

again. The two men lay low, like fish at the bottom of a stirred-up pond. Mr. Porritt looked apologetically at his brother-in-law, and slowly reached for his boots.

"No need to go," said Trumper kindly.

"Better," said Mr. Porritt.

"You stick to what you think's fit. Young Cluny's a help to you, you find her keep, it's no business of Addie's."

"Aye," said Mr. Porritt. He finished lacing his boots nonetheless. "But I don't mind telling *you*: I'm worried." He paused. There was that tea at the Ritz; there was something else, something he hadn't mentioned even to the lady in the park. "She's been followed," said Mr. Porritt.

Trumper whistled.

"Followed? Cluny?"

"Twice," said Mr. Porritt, "in the past week. First time she told me of, second I saw for myself. In the High Street, outside a shop: Cluny and this fellow talking together. He made off fast enough when he saw me."

"I'll lay he did," said Trumper appreciatively.

"Cluny says she's looking in this window, looking at hats, when up this fellow comes, asks her is there anything she fancies. Cluny says no, she's just having a free laugh. Then *he* says, maybe if they moved along to the West End, maybe they'd find something better. That was when I come up."

"She'd never have gone."

"So she said. She said there was a piece she wanted to hear on the wireless. But what beats me is *why*. You wouldn't call her pretty —"

"Plain as a boot," agreed Trumper heartily. For a while they both pondered. "This other time — was it the same chap or another?"

"Another. Fellow outside the cinema."

"She shouldn't hang about so much."

"What's a lass to do?" argued Mr. Porritt defensively. "Can't she look into a shop-window? Maybe — I didn't tell you, but I was mentioning young Cluny to a lady — maybe we're treating her wrong. Maybe she didn't ought to be threaped down, but encouraged to develop, like."

"Not her," said Mr. Trumper firmly. "Whoever told you that didn't know Cluny."

This was so true that Mr. Porritt could not dispute it. But for a moment his silence was stubborn. The lady's earnestness, just before they were interrupted, had made an impression on him: his attitude towards his niece had become as it were more elastic than ever before. He was ready for some sort of action on her behalf, if need be for some sort of shake-up in the solid routine of their common life. At the back of his mind there germinated a notion that perhaps Cluny might learn to type.

"All this foolishness about oranges," added Trumper obliquely.

"She paid for 'em. And I don't mind telling you," said Mr. Porritt, in a sudden admission of weakness, "nonsense or no nonsense, worried as I am, it's a real comfort to know she's safe home in bed."

He spoke (as always) what he believed to be the truth.

# Chapter 2

THAT CLUNY BROWN was not in bed, nor even at home, was due to sheer conscientiousness, a quality for which she rarely got credit. The piece in the paper laid great stress on complete repose, drawn blinds and no phone calls. Cluny had drawn her curtains, but she couldn't stop people ringing up a plumber, and when shortly before three the bell began to go, she reluctantly (but conscientiously) swung her long legs out of bed and ran barefoot downstairs.

"Hello?" said Cluny, in her deep tones.

A man's voice answered her — urgent, curt, harsh with that sense of injury common to all in trouble with their water-supply.

"Is that the plumber's? I want some one to come round at once — "

"He's out," said Cluny.

"Can't you get hold of him?"

Cluny reflected. It wasn't the weather for burst pipes, and for no lesser calamity did she intend to disturb her uncle's Sabbath.

"No, I can't," she said.

"Good God!" cried the voice passionately. "This is intolerable! This is unheard of! Isn't there any one else? Who are you?"

"Cluny Brown," said Cluny.

There was a short pause; when the voice spoke again it was in quite a different key.

"She was only a plumber's daughter — "

Cluny, who had heard that one before, rang off and went back upstairs. She got into bed and lay down again and relaxed according to the directions, joint by joint all the way from her toes up to her neck. "*Now pretend you're a Persian cat*," said the piece in the paper; but Cluny, whose imagination was precise rather than romantic, felt more like one of the long green or crimson sausages hawked about the streets to keep draughts from under the door. It probably didn't matter . . . What did matter was that hardly had she achieved this desirable state when the phone rang again. "Let it," thought Cluny; and proceeded to the next stage, of completely emptying her mind. Only she couldn't, because of the telephone. It went on and on, until at last there was nothing for it but to get up and answer it again.

"Miss Brown?" said the voice. "Please accept my apologies."

"Is that all you got me out of bed for?" cried Cluny indignantly.

Again there was a pause; and Mr. Porritt, had he been listening, would have sympathized with the caller. When you rang up a plumber you didn't expect — well, you didn't expect Cluny.

"Good heavens!" exclaimed the voice solicitously. "Are you ill? Shall I bring you some grapes?"

"It isn't grapes, it's oranges."

"What is?"

"The cure. But I'm not ill." (Having gone so far, Cluny felt she had better clear the whole thing up.) "You stay in bed twenty-four hours drinking orange juice, at least I suppose it's the same if you suck them, and the whole system is wonderfully toned."

"You sound better already," observed the voice.

"I feel better," agreed Cluny.

"You don't feel well enough to come round and see what's the matter with my sink?"

Cluny hesitated. As a matter of fact, she felt very well indeed. Standing there in her cotton nightdress, in a draught, her bare feet on the bare linoleum, she felt quite extraordinarily well, all over, except for one spot on her upper lip which was rather sore from sucking oranges. Could it be that the cure had worked already? And if so, ought she not to do her duty by the trade, and perhaps get a new name on her uncle's books? A sink didn't sound serious; stopped up, most likely, and no one with enough sense to unscrew the bend . . .

"I'll give you ten bob, as it's Sunday," lured the voice, "and you can take a cab. Ten-A, Carlyle Walk, Chelsea. Are you coming?"

"O.K.," said Cluny; and conscientiously reached for the order-book, to put it down.


II

The correct costume for a young lady going to fix a gentleman's sink on a Sunday afternoon has never been authoritatively dealt with; Cluny had naturally to carry her uncle's tool-bag, but as an offset wore her best clothes. These were all black, being part of her mourning for Mrs. Porritt, and the circumstance was not, at this stage in her career, without importance. It explained for example how she had got a table at the Ritz. Unusually tall, thin as a kippered herring, Cluny in a plain black coat looked very well. From the back she looked elegant; it was only her face spoiled it from in front. But in twenty years Cluny had got used to her face, and now, dabbing on the powder, could contemplate it without resentment: thin cheeks, big mouth, big nose, not a spot of colour: a short face from brow to chin, wide-angled at the strongly-marked jawline; thick black hair, which she cut herself whenever it grew below the shoulder, and tied behind, well away from the nape, so that it stuck out like a pony's tail. "Lucky Uncle Arn's short-sighted," thought Cluny philosophically; and then ran downstairs laughing, for it had suddenly struck her that maybe the Voice was looking for a bit of fun, and if so he wouldn't half get a shock when he saw her.

## III

Ten-A turned out to be not a house but a studio, built over a mansion-garden in the palmy days of Victorian art. Since then the mansion had become a block of flats, and the studio a garage, now turned back into a studio by Mr. Hilary Ames. He was not an artist but liked giving parties. He was giving a party that evening, and it was therefore particularly necessary that his sink should be unstopped. But Cluny's malice was also half-justified: the quality of her deep voice, the incongruity of her occupations, had tickled his fancy. This was not difficult to do: Mr. Ames's fancy was for young women, and rather easily stimulated; but Cluny was right also in foreseeing a slight shock at first sight. She arrived, knocked, was admitted, and surprised upon the gentleman's face an extremely mixed expression.

"Now then, what's the trouble?" asked Cluny benevolently — standing over him rather like a young policeman. She was considerably the taller, and the first thing she noticed about

Mr. Ames was the small bald patch on top of his head. For the rest, he was fiftyish, plumpish, and had on a canary-coloured pull-over which had cost six pounds, and which Cluny thought made him look like a tiddlywink.

Mr. Ames for his part took one look at Cluny's nose and dismissing all frolicsome thoughts at once led the way into a small malodorous scullery. The sink brimmed with greasy water, some of which had slopped upon the floor, but nothing seemed to have burst and there was no smell of gas. Cluny set down her bag in a competent manner, removed her good coat, and handed it to Mr. Ames. She might have been Arnold Porritt in person.

"Can you put it right?" asked Mr. Ames anxiously. (Just as they all did.) "I'm expecting some friends about six, and I can't have this mess."

"They'd smell you a mile off," agreed Cluny cheerfully. "Got a coat-hanger?"

"Certainly," said Mr. Ames, looking surprised. "Do you need one?"

"Not here," said Cluny, "but you might put my coat on it." As soon as he had withdrawn to do so she undid her suspenders and rolled her stockings below the knee. (They were her best.) Then she rolled up her sleeves, hitched up her skirt, and got down to it. It wasn't difficult: all you had to do was loosen a nut, unscrew the joint, and let the foul water run out into a pail. In this instance the stoppage was considerable, but by working at it with a bamboo Cluny satisfactorily ejected the last gobbet. Then she turned the taps full on for a good sluice down, and to make a job of it scrubbed down the sink itself with Vim. Opening the back-door, Cluny further emptied the pails into a patch of derelict shrubs, and took in a couple of milk-bottles which happened to be on the step. It was at this moment that Mr. Ames returned, and it was a moment of peculiar significance. Cluny's tall thin figure, dark against the sunlight, was admirably balanced between the pail in one hand and the bottles in the other; as she turned her head the ridiculous pony tail of hair showed in a bold calligraphic flourish. She looked like no one on earth but Cluny Brown, and at the same time, stepping in with the milk, she looked as though she belonged intimately to her surroundings. For no reason that he could seize Mr. Ames thought suddenly of a blackbird at a window.

"There you are!" said Cluny. "Clean as a whistle!" She set down pail and bottles and looked at him. Mr. Ames looked back, and there was a short silence.

"If you don't think it's worth ten bob—" said Cluny uncertainly.

"Of course I do . . ."

"And the taxi was three-and-six. But I needn't take one back."

"We'll call it a pound, and all square," said Mr. Ames.

But Cluny would not. She took the note, but produced six-and-six in change, and began to repack her kit. In a few minutes she would be gone; Mr. Ames realized the lapse of every second, but the rapidly increasing pressure of his dishonourable intentions, acting like a mild concussion, held him speechless. For the first time in his life he didn't know how to begin. And yet there was one move so simple, so obvious, that Cluny herself advanced it in the most natural way.

"Can I have a wash?"

"Good God, yes!" cried Mr. Ames.

All his aplomb returned as he led her to the bathroom. It was the very place to arouse, as he now urgently desired to do, her wonder and admiration; he had confidence in his bath-room, and he was not disappointed. Before the enormous amber-coloured bath, the amber-tinted mirrors — the oiled-silk curtains and innumerable shiny gadgets — Cluny in turn was bereft of speech. She gazed and gazed, till her eyes were like pools of ink.

"Nice?" prompted the owner.

"Heaven!" breathed Cluny.

"I like it too," said Mr. Ames, "though my friends say it suggests a love nest." He made a practice of introducing this term into conversation with new young women, to see their reaction. Cluny's was unexpected.

"I do wish Uncle Arn was here!"

Slightly jarred, Mr. Ames asked why Uncle Arn.

"Being a plumber," explained Cluny. With a professional air she examined the taps, the waste, the snaky hand shower; the yellow rubber cushion and fish-shaped ash-tray aroused an emotion more purely æsthetic. Laying the silkiness of the curtains against her cheek, she almost purred. "It's as good as the films!" she sighed at last. "Can I really wash here?"

"Of course you can. Have a bath," said Mr. Ames.

He lit a cigarette while Cluny considered. The situation was unusual, owing to the fact that she really did need bathing; Mr. Ames, with his wider experience, was naturally more struck by this than Cluny. He felt he had never advanced this gambit in more favourable circumstances, and that it was a good omen.

"You *are* kind . . ." said Cluny.

"Not in the least. I'll get you a towel."

But Cluny Brown had not yet made up her mind; in the Porritt-Trumper circles of her upbringing one did not take baths as lightly as all that. One planned them ahead, with due regard to when the boiler would be on, and who else wanted one; above all, after bathing, one assumed clean underwear. Cluny naturally had no change of linen with her, and this put her off. She also felt she could have almost as good a time in the hand basin.

"I'll just wash," said she. "But thank you all the same."

"Much better have a bath," said Mr. Ames.

"Do I hum?" asked Cluny anxiously.

Then Mr. Ames made his mistake. He should have told her the truth, that she did indeed smell pretty foul. But he wasn't used to people who took their truth neat.

"Good heavens, no."

"Then I'll just wash," said Cluny. "Run along."

There was no key to the lock, but this did not worry her, because of course Mr. Ames knew she was inside; removing the upper part of her dress Cluny sluiced herself vigorously in the lovely hot water and worked up a glorious lather of geranium-scented soap. (Mr. Ames, quietly reopening the door, saw nothing of her but her long, thin, ivory-coloured back; and Cluny, her eyes full of suds, did not see Mr. Ames.) The sweet spicy scent enchanted her, it easily over-rode the last of the cabbage-water, and she readjusted her dress with well-founded complacency. Her nose was of course shiny again, but by some fortunate chance the toilet appliances included a large bowl of powder. Cluny was never one to spoil the ship for a ha'p'orth of tar. When she returned to the studio Mr. Ames, mixing cocktails, smelt her before he saw her.

He did not immediately speak. A moment was repeating itself (Mr. Ames was a connoisseur of such moments). As he had been struck before by the peculiar intimacy of Cluny's entry by the back-door, so now he was struck by the intimacy of her entry from his bathroom. He gave her a long look; then the ice clinked in the shaker as he set it down.

"Cocktail or tea?" asked Mr. Ames.

"Cocktail," said Cluny promptly.

He handed her the small ice-cold glass — the first cocktail of Cluny Brown's experience. It was a dry martini, and it went down her ivory throat in one long ripple.

"Good God!" exclaimed Mr. Ames. "You don't drink it like that!"

"Beer you do," said Cluny simply.

Strangely moved by this unsophistication, Mr. Ames made her sit down on the divan and waited with almost paternal anxiety for the effects. There seemed to be none. To his enquiry how she felt Cluny replied that she felt fine, and asked for another to drink it properly. Mr. Ames poured her a small one, and one for himself, and under his guidance Cluny tried again, taking delicate sips, and setting the glass down, between times, on a low coffee table. The divan too was low, very wide and soft, backed by a pile of cushions: Cluny settled comfortably back, happy in the belief that as cocktails were so much more relaxing than orange juice, so no doubt they superiorly toned the system. Mr. Ames leaned on one elbow and watched her. It was by now incredible to him that he had ever thought her plain: he could see only the extraordinarily fine texture of her white skin and the extraordinarily clean cut of the lids over her long black eyes.

"What about your party?" asked Cluny suddenly.

"You're staying for it."

"Do you think I ought?"

"Positive."

"Thank you very much," said Cluny.

Mr. Ames took a firm hold on himself. His desire to make

love to her was by now extreme, but time was against him. At any moment some of his friends might arrive — the Drake woman, for instance, who always came at least an hour early in order to tell him her troubles . . . and to drink a preliminary cocktail, and to recline, just as Cluny was doing, on that wide divan. . . . The memory was so unwelcome that Mr. Ames recognized, with a thrill of pleasure, one of the first symptoms of a genuine affair: the desire to obliterate the past. He could afford to wait — at any rate until the party was over, and Cluny was staying behind to help him clear up. To avoid temptation Mr. Ames therefore thrust himself away from the cushions, and Cluny too started erect in the belief that it was time for another sip. She leant forward to take her glass, their shoulders touched; and at that instant a step sounded in the scullery. Some one had come in through the open back-door, some one was on the threshold of the studio; and remembering the Drake woman's horrible habit of giving him surprises Mr. Ames forced himself to look round with a pallid smile.

But it wasn't the Drake after all. There, with a brow like thunder, stood Mr. Porritt.

## IV

Cluny, who was really fond of her uncle, jumped up with every sign of pleasure. Mr. Ames rose too, but more slowly. He later made a very good tale of it, but at the time the situation was hardly humorous at all. Mr. Porritt looked curiously formidable.

"Uncle Arn!" cried Cluny. "Have you come to see the sink?"

Mr. Porritt did not reply. Instead he advanced, took the

glass out of her hand, smelt it, and threw the contents onto the floor.

"I say!" protested Mr. Ames. (He was a man noted for his presence of mind, his quick wit, his *savoir faire;* such was the aspect of the plumber that for the moment all three deserted him, and this feeble ejaculation was all he could find.) "I say! What's wrong?"

"That is," replied Mr. Porritt grimly. "Giving a young girl strong drink. Cluny Brown, come here."

Cluny obediently approached a step nearer. The scent of sweet geranium hit him like a wave.

"How did he get you here?" demanded Mr. Porritt.

"He rang up because his sink was stopped."

"Which is no business of yours, as you well know."

"I thought I could fix a sink. And I did. You take a look," said Cluny, rather proudly. "Besides, he offered ten bob."

"Ten bob! And you swallowed it?"

With the mistaken idea of establishing Mr. Ames's bona fides, Cluny at once produced the note. Luckily Mr. Porritt did not look at it and see it was a pound, but took it too from her hand and cast it down. He was working up to the crucial question.

"Has he done anything to you that I ought to know?"

"No, I don't think so," said Cluny.

This answer, so highly unsatisfactory to both her uncle and the now writhing Mr. Ames, was simply an attempt at the exact truth: Cluny herself thought there was nothing, but what her uncle would think was a different matter.

"Then get your coat," said Mr. Porritt thickly.

Cluny looked at Mr. Ames, and the latter, with as much nonchalance as he could muster, went into the bedroom to fetch it. As he opened the door he could feel the plumber's inimical gaze boring into his back, piercing him, alighting (with furiously unjust suspicion) upon the double bed. Unjust now, at least; for the last few minutes had most thoroughly purged Mr. Ames of every indecorous thought.

"Uncle Arn," said Cluny.

"Well?"

"Before we go, wouldn't you like to see the bathroom?"

Mr. Porritt had never in his life raised his hand to a woman, but he nearly raised it then. And Cluny knew it. Only Mr. Ames's return saved them both. Cluny seized and dragged on her coat, Mr. Porritt automatically picked up his tool-bag, and they marched together out of the studio, both furious, both spoiling for a row, taking no more notice of Mr. Ames than if he had been — a tiddlywink.


# V

The row broke as soon as they got outside, raged all down Carlyle Walk, and reached its height on the Embankment. What chiefly infuriated Cluny was that she was six-and-sixpence down, the change from the pound note; and this attitude in turn exacerbated the fury of Mr. Porritt. He was more deeply shaken than Cluny realized; and her obtuseness driving him from his natural decorum of speech, he proclaimed in so many words his belief that Cluny had narrowly escaped being seduced, and the further belief that she had been asking for it. At that Cluny stood stockstill on the Embankment and turned first scarlet and then so white that her uncle thought she was about to faint. She did indeed feel qualmish, but that was because the cocktails, on nothing but orange juice, were at last taking effect. What she chiefly felt was an overpowering, hopeless sense of rage at the stupidity of the universe as represented by Mr. Porritt. It was so great as to be almost impersonal: it was the generous rage of ignorant youth; and Cluny had to steady herself against the parapet as it swept over her.

"All right, you didn't," retracted Mr. Porritt. "I believe you. But as for him —"

"He isn't!" cried Cluny. "You only just saw him, and I was there hours!"

"And it don't take hours to fix a sink!" shouted Mr. Porritt.

"I had to have a wash, didn't I? I nearly had a bath, too —"

"You nearly *what?*"

"Had a bath. He said I could. It was lovely."

"If I'd known that —" roared Mr. Porritt; and paused, because people were beginning to look at them. But his blood boiled. He had by this time entirely forgotten what Mr. Ames really looked like; he saw instead a huge bloated figure of wicked luxury. Cluny saw a kind little elderly gent; the midway truth eluded them both. But on the balance Mr. Porritt had acted on the safer hypothesis. "If I hadn't come!" he muttered continually, as they got into motion again; and the thought appalled him. It was by mere chance that he had left the Trumpers hours before his usual time; by mere chance that he had glanced at the order-book and seen the entry in Cluny's fist. After that of course he was bound to go after, to see that she didn't make a mess of things; but if he hadn't —

"Can't we take a 'bus?" asked Cluny suddenly.

She looked awful, all eyes and nose; once again in Mr. Porritt's breast every other emotion gave place to sheer astonishment. What did they see in her? What could any one see in her? Floss, he recollected, used to stand up for the lass, saying she wasn't as plain as people made out; but that was Floss all over. Kind. And Cluny had been fond of her; it was only since Floss went that Cluny had got so out of hand. "She's beyond me," thought Mr. Porritt unhappily. He'd stood up for Cluny against the Trumpers, but in his heart he knew they were right: the girl had to be taught her place.

As they reached the 'bus stop, Mr. Porritt came to a decision. He turned to Cluny and bent on her a long, solemn look.

"One thing this has settled," said Mr. Porritt. "Into service you go."

# Chapter 3

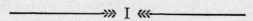

NOTHING could be easier, in that year 1938, than for a girl to go into good service. The stately homes of England gaped for her. Cluny Brown, moreover, possessed special advantages: height, plainness (but combined with a clear skin) and a perfectly blank expression. This last attribute was not permanent, but the lady at the registry office did not know, and she saw in Cluny the very type of that prized, that fast-disappearing genus, the Tall Parlour-maid. Addie Trumper too knew what was what; she had been in good service herself, and with footmen practically extinct felt there was no table in the land too high for Cluny to aspire to. Addie Trumper was in her glory — her advice taken, the whole affair put under her management. She sat beside Cluny in the registry office like an exhibitor of prize livestock.

"We must remember," said Miss Postgate repressively, "that your niece is completely inexperienced."

"So's most, these days," retorted Addie.

The two women measured each other: Miss Postgate, head and owner of a famous establishment, who when she died was to leave the sum of twenty-two thousand pounds, and Addie Trumper from Portobello Road.

"That is quite true," conceded Miss Postgate. "Now I have here a place in Devonshire — "

Cluny Brown made no remark at all. After two days of unremitting and stormy protest she had acknowledged defeat; but she was still bewildered by it. That her Uncle Arn no longer wanted her was incredible; and indeed Mr. Porritt, hard-pressed, admitted that he would be sorry to see her go. ("In a way," he added hastily.) Who, demanded Cluny, would answer the telephone for him? Mr. Porritt, remembering what had happened when she answered it on Sunday, said no doubt he would manage. And who would mend his socks? Addie Trumper would. Addie was also finding a respectable woman to come and do for him, and he could take his dinner whenever he liked in Portobello Road. Addie Trumper, thought Cluny, was properly getting her claws in; and she turned on Addie such a look of plain hatred that it was a good thing Miss Postgate didn't see.

"Two other maids," Miss Postgate was saying, "under an excellent housekeeper — a small establishment of the best sort. I know her personally. And as she knows me personally, that would solve the question of references. Friars Carmel is of course right in the country — "

"All the better," put in Mrs. Trumper.

" — but the wages are good. And if you wish your niece to get a thorough training, she couldn't do better than under Mrs. Maile. I will write at once." Miss Postgate gathered some papers together to show that the interview was at an end, and turned to Cluny with a pleasant smile. "I won't say I hope to see you again, Miss Brown, because I don't. I hope you'll go to Devonshire and stay there many, many years . . ."

"There now!" cried Mrs. Trumper. "Cluny, say thank you!"

Cluny moistened her lips. She had spoken only once before, to give her age, and Miss Postgate had been favourably impressed both by her deep voice and her subsequent silence.

"Have you ever read *Uncle Tom's Cabin?*" asked Cluny distinctly.

"No, I don't think I have," said Miss Postgate, surprised.

"You ought," said Cluny.

## II

With dreadful smoothness the negotiations proceeded. Miss Postgate wrote to Mrs. Maile; Mrs. Maile, presumably after consultation with her employer, Lady Carmel, promptly replied, enclosing the money for a single third-class fare; Addie Trumper descended on Mr. Porritt's to superintend the washing, mending and packing of all Cluny's clothes. Uniform was provided; lucky girl, cried Mrs. Trumper vivaciously, not to have to find her own aprons! Cluny said nothing. During these last days she hardly opened her mouth, and Mr. Porritt was almost as silent. In the evening, when Addie at last took herself off, silence fell like an extinguisher on the once cheerful dwelling in String Street. Each had said his say, at almost too much length, and Mr. Porritt at least was determined not to begin again. But on Cluny's last evening — exactly eight days after her excursion into studio life — he came in with a small oblong packet and laid it silently before her: it contained three old photographs, of himself, and Floss, and Cluny's mother, arranged side by side in an English-gilt frame.

"Oh, Uncle Arn!" cried Cluny.

"Thought you ought to have 'em," said Mr. Porritt gruffly. "Couldn't find one of your Dad."

"You're as good as!" cried Cluny passionately. "Oh, Uncle Arn, why have I got to go?"

"It's better," said Mr. Porritt.

Cluny looked into his square, puggy, resolute face and saw

that nothing on earth would move him. Go she must, into good service in Devonshire. It was her fate. That was what fate had up its sleeve for her. The old questions — Cluny had been aware of them too — were finally answered. *Who do you think you are, Cluny Brown?* Answer: A Tall Parlour-maid.

"Uncle Arn!" beseeched Cluny. "If I don't like it, can I come back?"

"No," said Mr. Porritt. "Not if you just don't like it."

"Well, if I don't get enough to eat? If they knock me about?" persisted Cluny desperately.

"They won't," said Mr. Porritt. "If they do, send me a line."

Cluny gazed wildly round the room as though it were a Black Maria bearing her to prison. The sight of her personal possessions still strewn about — bits of sewing, her collection of calendars, a book that had to go back to the twopenny library — mocked her with their false air of homeliness; when she looked at the spun-glass bird on top of the clock — preserved from the last Christmas-tree she and Aunt Floss had dressed together — Cluny's eyes filled with tears. But it was no good; no tears would soften her uncle, now slowly filling his pipe, hardening his heart with the thought that it was all for the best. Cluny picked up the frame of photographs and carefully rewrapped it.

"It was nice of you to get this for me, anyway. I'll think of you ever so often."

"You keep your mind on your work," said her stern counsellor.

Cluny sighed deeply, and coming round behind his chair bent over and kissed him on the cheek.

"Good night, Uncle Arn. You won't have me to-morrow."

"That's a good lass," said Mr. Porritt.

## III

Cluny Brown went upstairs and laboriously, as though gloom were a physical and hampering element, got herself ready for bed. For the first time in her life she sat down to brush her hair: achieved two strokes, and let the brush fall. She could feel gloom rising in the room like water in a cistern; and the homely simile, so suggestive of past happiness, made Cluny feel worse than ever. For the world of plumbing had rejected her. No more would she make out bills for seeing to geyser, or receive by phone exciting intimations of flooded cellar-steps, or dispatch her uncle like a fire-engine to scenes of disaster; no more, in the cosy evenings, would she welcome him back and hear how he had found a mouse in the waste. It was all over; all gone. "Why do young girls leave home?" thought Cluny bitterly. "Because they're thrown out."

This angry squib, however, usefully changed the current of her thoughts. What was her uncle's complaint? Simply — for this was all it boiled down to — that she didn't know her place. Cluny couldn't see it. Taking her two outstanding crimes, she couldn't see why her place should not include the Ritz, if she could afford to pay for her tea there, or Mr. Ames's party, if he cared to invite her. (That loss still rankled; it was like a door slammed in her face.) And if two such trifles could irritate Mr. Porritt to the point of throwing her out, life with him looked like being one long dog fight. (It never entered Cluny's head that she might mend her ways.) Good service in Devonshire, on the other hand, offered at least an enlarged horizon, and enlargement of experience generally was what Cluny unconsciously sought. She had been seeking it when she went to the Ritz, and when she drank Mr. Ames's cocktail, and when — her mind jumped back — she had bought a half-crown puppy in Praed Street. Every one of these essays had led to trouble, especially the puppy, which Mr. Porritt made her give to the milkman. Trouble, in fact, seemed to be her lot; but if more trouble awaited her in Devonshire, at least it would be a new sort.

As a result of these meditations Cluny got into bed in a much more cheerful frame of mind. She wasn't resigned, for she was never that, but she felt a certain expectancy. At least something was happening to her, and all her life that was the one thing Cluny Brown consistently desired. Not to be ignored by fate, even at the price of a bludgeoning; not to be mewed up, even from the storm; not peace, in short, but plenty.

# Chapter 4

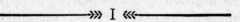

In the garden room at Friars Carmel, on the previous Saturday, Lady Carmel was trying to do the flowers. Like a good many Englishwomen of her age and station, she found in this task her one æsthetic outlet, and required no other. Her flower-pieces in the Dutch style were deservedly famous.

"Please, dear!" she murmured. "Your ash, on the prunus!"

The person addressed was her son Andrew, recently down from Cambridge, more recently returned from a continental tour, who now sat on the end of the flower table impatiently smoking. He threw down his cigarette and ground it out with his heel.

"Mother, will you please listen to me? Because what I'm telling you is fairly important."

"I am listening. You've invited a friend for a long stay, and I'm sure that will be very nice."

"He's not a friend. He's an extraordinarily distinguished Polish man of letters."

"That makes it all the nicer, dear. We'll have the Vicar to dine. He nearly went to Poland only two years ago. I'm not being stupid," added Lady Carmel hastily, "for though he didn't go in the end he read a lot about it first, in guide-books. Tell me your friend's name again, dear."

"Adam Belinski." Andrew fetched a deep breath. "He has

just come from Germany. He escaped with his life. We don't want the Vicar to dine, in fact we want as few people as possible to know he's here."

Lady Carmel smiled indulgently. Dear Andrew, she thought, what a boy he still was with his plots and mysteries! And in other ways so grown up, always worrying about politics and the Government! "Dear Andrew!" she said aloud.

Andrew slipped off the table and began to walk rapidly up and down.

"I can't make you realize it, can I?" he said bitterly.

"Realize what, darling?"

"What Europe's like. What everything's like outside this— this God's pocket." He stared through the open door at the smoothly dropping lawn, at the wooded boundary, the protective hills rising beyond. "We're sitting on the edge of a landslide, and I've seen some of the cracks."

Lady Carmel looked troubled. It was the thing to do, just then, at any mention of Europe, and indeed there had been moments, with Andrew still abroad, when she felt very troubled indeed. But now the expression was purely automatic, like looking reverent in church. Picking up a bough of rhododendron she tried its effect in a white crackle jar, and at once her brow cleared.

"For God's *sake*," said Andrew loudly, "leave those things alone!"

Shocked into full attention, Lady Carmel let the branch drop and turning to her son was shocked again by his bitter face. The rebuke died on her lips, she laid her hand gently on his sleeve to make him stand still.

"What is it, my darling?"

"But I've been telling you!"

"About your friend? Poor man, if he's had trouble that's

all the more reason we should be nice to him. Surely, dear, you can trust us for that."

Looking down into her pale, very clear blue eyes, Andrew felt suddenly calmed. There at least was something unchanging, impregnable: the hospitality of his mother's house.

"I know, darling. I'm sorry I was rude. But I do want you to realize that having him here would be a — a responsibility."

"One is always responsible for one's guests, dear boy."

"A dangerous responsibility. I've spoken to Dad, and he doesn't mind, but I don't think he takes it seriously. Please listen, Mother: we don't know whether the Nazis are still after him or not. We don't think they are, but they may be. If you'd rather not take the risk, it's perfectly natural, and you've only got to say so."

In all this fantastic, and to her ears quite incredible, rigmarole, Lady Carmel perceived only one point of importance.

"But you have invited him."

"Yes, darling; and he wouldn't accept because I hadn't asked you first."

"He sounds a very nice man. And as there are no Nazis round here, I see no reason for putting him off. It would be extremely rude."

"Can I go back to London with your invitation?"

"Certainly, dear. Or I'll write a note and put it in the post."

But Andrew, who was in a mood to make rapid journeys as often as possible, said he would go himself; and kissing his mother with sincere affection, left her to finish her flowers in peace. He felt he had done everything possible; and since no words could have expressed his chagrin had her consent been refused, was not inclined to do more. Striding across the lawn, however, making for the stables, he passed a little ornamental pond alive with ducks. They were splashing and diving, sending up showers of water, and the bright drops rolled like quicksilver off their smooth impervious backs. Andrew had not much sense of humour; but he looked at those ducks and grinned.

## II

Lady Carmel carried the big staircase bouquet carefully across the hall, mounted to the half-landing, and deposited her burden in its appointed spot. This was a broad window-sill, and with the light falling from behind the flowers there had to be strong deep colours and important shapes. Irises, peonies, foxgloves were all perfect in their season; but nothing, thought Lady Carmel, quite equalled rhododendrons; and they seemed to her so startlingly splendid that she called out to whoever was moving about above, to come down and see.

It happened to be Mrs. Maile, emerging from the linen cupboard — and a good thing too, thought the housekeeper, who strongly disapproved her ladyship's habit of calling maids from their work to look at flowers.

"There, Maile! Did you ever see anything so perfectly beautiful?"

"No, my lady," replied Mrs. Maile politely. She was not insensitive to flowers: a centrepiece of pink carnations, in properly polished silver, gave her great pleasure.

"Everything's done except the library table," continued Lady Carmel, "and for that I've still to cut; if any one wants me, I shall be out of doors. Oh, Maile!"

"Yes, my lady?"

"We're expecting a friend of Mr. Andrew's, a foreign gentleman, I think he's coming in a day or two, to pay us a long visit. He's been very ill" — into this reasonable fiction

had Lady Carmel instinctively translated the fantastic truth
— "and needs a rest. Do you think the east room?"

"The east is very quiet, my lady. And it gets the morning
sun."

"Then we'll make it the east. He can have the dressing-room
for a study, because I believe he's some kind of a Professor."

"Yes, my lady. And I've heard from Postgate's, my lady: the
new young woman will be here on Tuesday."

"Splendid," said Lady Carmel.


## III

Mrs. Maile continued on her way to the housekeeper's room,
where eleven-o'clock tea had just been brought in for herself
and Mr. Syrett. The butler was there already, reading his personal copy of the *Times,* which he courteously set aside as his
colleague entered. He was a short man with an unusually
large head and so fine a crop of thick silver hair that bets
were frequently laid, among the lesser fry of the kitchen, as
to whether or not it was a wig. But no one ever found out.

"Any news, Mr. Syrett?" asked Mrs. Maile ritually.

"Nothing of importance," replied Mr. Syrett. "Things seem
to be pretty well settling down again."

"I'm glad to hear it. Her ladyship has just told me we're to
expect a friend of Mr. Andrew's for a long stay. A foreign
Professor."

The butler's expression at once became extremely reserved.
He distrusted all friends of Mr. Andrew's, never having recovered from a Long Vacation made hideous by a Cambridge
film society. It was his private belief, which he would have
died rather than admit, that the heir of Friars Carmel was
not equal to his fine position.

"That's better than actors," consoled Mrs. Maile.

"Foreign," said Mr. Syrett darkly.

"Foreigners may be quite distinguished persons," retorted Mrs. Maile — who never forgot that she was the senior, in that household, by some three years.

"If connected with the Diplomatic, yes."

"Which he well may be. For when Mr. Andrew went abroad he took letters to the very best circles; and a person Mr. Andrew met at one of our Embassies is quite good enough for you and me. A quiet gentleman too — recovering from an operation — he's not likely to give trouble. Will I ever forget," said Mrs. Maile pointedly, "the goings-on of that young woman!"

This was a shrewd hit; for the advent, a year previously, of the Honourable Elizabeth Cream, now known as "that young woman," had been greeted by Mr. Syrett with the most reckless enthusiasm — prophecies of an Announcement, even plans for a Celebration. Alas for his hopes: Miss Cream's visit coincided with a week of superb weather. At the drop of a hat she stripped and sun-bathed — or rather, a hat was the only thing she didn't drop . . . Mr. Syrett tacitly withdrew his objections to the Professor by changing the subject.

"Have Postgate's been able to help you, Mrs. Maile?"

The housekeeper relaxed into her habitual calm.

"They are sending *some one,* for which I suppose I should be thankful. Twenty, and untrained. However, as I remarked in my reply: better no training than bad."


# IV

Before going to tidy for lunch Lady Carmel put her head into her husband's study and found him writing. As his physical powers declined, making hunting impossible, Sir Henry had taken to the pen; all over the world the friends of his youth began to receive very long, very dull letters from him. To Rhodesia, Tanganyika, Singapore; Australia, India, New Zealand and the Bermudas — Sir Henry's epistles went forth; for he never considered it worth while to write to any one nearer at hand. So the letters took a long time to get there, and the replies even longer to get back, and all the news was out of date; and this gave his correspondence a peculiar timeless quality which was very soothing.

"Harry, dear," said Lady Carmel, "did Andrew speak to you about his friend?"

"The gangster chap? Yes, he did," said Sir Henry.

"Dear, he isn't a gangster. I'm sure of that. You've got it mixed."

"Difficult to make head or tail of," admitted her husband. "Andrew says he's a gentleman, and I trust the boy's judgement. Something about the stables, too, so I hope he cares for horses. Do you know who he is?"

"Yes, dear, I do," replied Lady Carmel. "And you must pay attention, because for some reason Andrew feels very strongly about it. He is a Polish Professor who got into trouble with the Nazis. Andrew thinks they may still be trying to do him a mischief, but of course that's quite ridiculous, and what *I* think, dear, is that the Professor said he wanted a really quiet holiday, which is very natural, and Andrew imagined the rest. He always was romantic."

"Poor fellow," said Sir Henry — referring to the Professor. He had devoted his life to blood sports, and had one of the kindest hearts in the world.

## V

Thus layer by layer, without any conscious effort, the oyster that was Friars Carmel smoothed and overlaid its grain of sand, producing, like a pearl, a distinguished Professor, met at a British Embassy, recovering from an operation, and fond of horses.

No such process, naturally, was applied to the new parlour-maid.

# Chapter 5

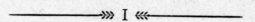

**I**

Cluny Brown arrived at Friars Carmel in a Rolls-Royce. This was not the original plan; she should have been collected, along with a parcel from Harrod's, by the gardener with the station wagon; but at the last moment it was discovered that the gardener had gone off to look at a mower, and the car was out with Lady Carmel. Mrs. Maile thereupon telephoned the stationmaster, who reported Colonel Duff-Graham on the platform; and Colonel Duff-Graham expressed great willingness to drop anything for Friars Carmel. He did not quite bargain for a parlour-maid — he himself was meeting a Golden Labrador, a nervous traveller who would require all his attention; but as things turned out the Labrador had already been met by Cluny, who, wandering about the train, discovered the glorious creature in the guard's van and spent the rest of the journey with him. They jumped out together, both very glad to stretch their long legs, and the Colonel hurried towards Roderick with the stationmaster at his heels. The stationmaster knew Cluny at once, because she was the only person on the platform he didn't know already.

"Miss C. Brown," he stated.

Cluny admitted her identity, and the situation was rapidly explained. They went out to the Rolls; Cluny of course should have sat in front, but Roderick tried to climb over to her with such persistence that after half a mile the Colonel stopped the car and took her in behind. The Labrador at once cast himself over her knees like a beautiful rug.

"He's taken a fancy to you," said the Colonel.

"I talked to him all the way down," explained Cluny.

"Did you, by Jove? That was uncommon kind," said the Colonel warmly. "He's a nervous beast."

"He's lovely."

Taking a quick look, the Colonel decided that this was more than could be said for herself: a homelier young woman he'd never seen. Not that it mattered, in a parlour-maid; and at any rate she didn't look vulgar. With great kindness he began to point out objects of local interest, good views, and barns that needed repairs.

"How far is it to Friars Carmel?" asked Cluny.

"Matter of six miles. Five to the village, six to the house."

"Are there any dogs there?"

"No, there aren't," said the Colonel, rather disapprovingly. "Sir Henry's old terrier had to be put down last year, and he won't have another. Very natural, of course. You got a dog?"

Cluny shook her head.

"My uncle won't let me. He says London's no place."

"Sensible man. Ought to be a law against it."

"Could I keep a dog at Friars Carmel?"

"I don't see why —" began the Colonel; and paused. For the last few minutes he had quite forgotten he was talking to a parlour-maid, but now he remembered. Well, of course she couldn't keep a dog; parlour-maids didn't. "I doubt it," said the Colonel hastily.

Cluny said nothing; but she turned her black eyes upon him in a most mournful look. What a look it was! At once bright and liquid, tragic and brave, innocent and deep.

Colonel Duff-Graham was quite startled. It was indeed no more than the look of any young woman feeling thoroughly sorry for herself, but the Colonel was not in the habit of observing young women at close quarters. (He had indeed a daughter, of whom he was properly fond, but he took her for granted.) And under the influence of Cluny's gaze a strangely unorthodox notion — his first in years — suddenly struck him: what was the use of treating servants well, giving 'em good food and all that, if you wouldn't let 'em keep a dog? He felt really disturbed.

"Tell you what," he said kindly, "on your afternoon off, you come over to my place, and you can take Roddy for a run."

At once Cluny's brow cleared, her eyes sparkled, she radiated happiness.

"That's a date!" she cried joyfully.

The chauffeur heard them, and was so scandalized that when they reached Friars Carmel he ignored his master's order to drive up to the house and stopped firmly at the lodge. Cluny embraced Roderick, shook hands with the Colonel, and got out with her bags. For some moments she stood there waving; she waved till the car was quite out of sight; then with a suitcase in either hand she turned and walked slowly through the gates, up the drive, into good service.

## II

"Take off your hat, my dear," said Mrs. Maile.

Cluny, standing rather white-faced in the housekeeper's room, did so. Her pony tail of hair at once sprang out and up, giving both Mrs. Maile and Mr. Syrett a surprise. (The latter was present purely by accident; as a rule he interviewed only men-servants. But there had been no men-servants at Friars Carmel for a very long time.)

"We must do something about *that*," said Mrs. Maile. "However, I understand this is your first place?"

"Yes," said Cluny.

"Say, 'Yes, ma'am.' I see we must begin at the beginning," said Mrs. Maile. "You say 'ma'am' to me, 'sir' to Mr. Syrett here, and should you be spoken to by her ladyship, 'my lady.'"

"And his lordship 'my lord,'" added Cluny, looking intelligent.

"Sir," corrected Mrs. Maile patiently. "Sir Henry is not a peer, he is a baronet — though of far older creation than many. If you have to speak to *him,* which is unlikely, you say 'sir.' Now Hilda will give you some tea, and when you have put your things away, come back to me."

Cluny got herself out of the room, leaving Mrs. Maile and Mr. Syrett to exchange commiserating looks.

"At least she's tall," said the housekeeper at last.

"Looks to me like a young ostrich," said Mr. Syrett.

"And clean. I knew I could rely on Postgate's for that."

"You always make the best of things, Mrs. Maile."

The housekeeper acknowledged this compliment with a melancholy bend of the head. She could remember the days when Friars Carmel employed six indoor maids, all hand-picked; her mind roved back over the long succession of Gracies, Florries, Bessies, ear-marked almost from birth for service at Friars, graduating in the proper, established order from Tweeny to First Parlour-maid. And Mrs. Maile sighed. If Cluny felt bewildered, so did she.

"Out of place," she said gravely. "Times change, Mr. Syrett, and we must change with them; but that's what I can't help saying to myself: in a house like this, she is out of place. However, I will take her in hand. And at least, with that appearance, we needn't expect Hilda's trouble."

"Certainly not," said Mr. Syrett.

## III

*Dear Uncle Arn,*

*This is a very large house to keep clean, looking at it from outside you would say it was hopeless, but Mrs. Maile says not. There are twenty-seven rooms, Queen Elizabeth slept in one of them but I have to share. The other girl is called Hilda. She had a baby last year but Mrs. M. overlooked it. You tell that to Aunt Addie. We wear brown in the mornings, black in the afternoon, get up at 6.30, do the stairs, do the hall, Hilda does the breakfast room, cook gets breakfast, we have ours, do the morning-room, do the beds, do the drawing-room, Lady C. does the flowers. I have seen her once, Mrs. M. took me in and said this is Brown, the new maid. Lady C. said she hoped you'll work hard and be happy Brown, then Mrs. M. took me out. Is there any way you can tell a wig by just looking at it? This may mean a bob. I also clean brass, darn sheets, no waiting at table so far. Mrs. M. says in a house like this there ought to be a linen-maid, but where can you get them, girls to-day have no sense.*

*Your affectionate neice,*

CLUNY BROWN

*P.S. If you want me, I will come back at once.*

# Chapter 6

THE CIRCUMSTANCES of Andrew Carmel's acquaintance with Mr. Belinski agreed at no point with the picture drawn by Mrs. Maile. For they hadn't met at any Embassy; they had met at a party in Hampstead, to which Andrew was taken by Betty Cream, in company with a Cambridge friend, John Frewen. It was the usual rather untidy affair, semi-artistic, semi-literary, and they were all getting a bit bored when John came back from the bar with an astonished expression.

"Do you know who's here? Adam Belinski."

"What, European literature?" exclaimed Andrew.

"Never heard of him," said Betty, who was quite uneducated.

"Darling, he's *the* man," Andrew informed her. "But I thought they'd jugged him."

"No. They just beat him up," said John grimly. "He was lecturing at Bonn, and said something the *Herrenvolk* didn't like. I saw him last year in Warsaw and I recognized him straight away. He's over there by the piano."

They all three stared. The celebrity was standing in a peculiar position, cramped between the keyboard and the wall, as though he had retreated till he could retreat no farther. He was a man in his early thirties, compactly built, with light blue eyes in a square face.

"He doesn't look very pleased with life," remarked Andrew.

"He probably isn't."

"If you ask me," said Betty suddenly, "he looks utterly miserable."

It was as though the force of their concentration plucked at his sleeve. He turned, for an instant met their three pairs of eyes, and at once turned away again.

"Come and talk to him," said Betty. "Ask him what he's doing here. I believe he loathes it."

Too lovely ever to have known diffidence, she marched across the room with the young men at her heels. Belinski watched them come towards him — watched even Betty come towards him — without a flicker of interest.

"We know who you are," said Betty, unabashed, "but you don't know us. I'm Elizabeth Cream, and these are Andrew Carmel and John Frewen."

"We are your great admirers," said John, in German.

Belinski gave them a grave bow.

"We are very glad to see you here," said Andrew, in French.

He bowed again.

"And we wondered whether you were enjoying this," said Betty, speaking her native tongue, "because as a matter of fact, we aren't."

The Pole appeared to turn this simple remark very carefully in his mind. Carefully, in excellent English, he answered it.

"It is some time since I have been to a party, I feel a little bewildered. But I find it charming."

But Betty was unsnubbable. Her bad manners at least gave her ease.

"Oh, you can't!" she protested. "You needn't be polite with us, it's not our party. How did you get here?"

For the first time his face relaxed.

"It is indeed quite strange. I came to enquire after a friend who lived here, but who it appears has gone away. So I was brought in to the party. Why? I do not know."

"I do," said Betty. "Sylvia's always short of men. But there's no reason why we should stay if we don't want to. As a matter of fact, we're just going to eat somewhere. Will you come too?" She kicked John lightly on the ankle.

"We should be extraordinarily honoured, sir," said John Frewen. "That is, if it wouldn't bore you."

Belinski turned his serious glance upon Andrew. It was strange: he spoke English so well, he obviously understood perfectly; yet seemed not to comprehend what he heard. He wanted everything — rechecked.

"Nothing would give us greater pleasure," said Andrew formally, "than your company."

"Now?"

"Yes, of course now," said Betty, "before we get caught up. Go and fetch your coats."

They had a moment together, the three of them, while Belinski punctiliously sought out his hostess. Betty Cream was in the highest spirits, but Andrew and John looked rather solemn. They realized, as she did not, their guest's importance.

"I don't know how you had the nerve," said Andrew. "He's one of the most distinguished men in Europe."

"He looked so lost," said Betty absently. "Where shall we take him?"

"Claridge's," suggested John.

"Too stuffy. Let's go to Soho, to the Moulin Bleu."

"We ought to go to the Club," said Andrew. "Damn it, we ought to be giving him a Dinner!"

"The Club's out because of Betty. I still think Claridge's."

At that moment Belinski reappeared. Betty at once took him into their confidence.

"Would you rather go somewhere where it's good food but a bit like the grave, or somewhere queer but rather amusing?"

"I am in your hands," said Mr. Belinski.

## II

They went of course to Soho; and minute by minute, all through the prolonged meal, the atmosphere grew queerer. There was no means of getting Belinski to talk, except by direct questioning; and his answers revealed a state of affairs startling in the extreme. To take his itinerary: from Bonn, where the trouble started, he had been going back to Berlin; political events, he said simply, made this unwise; so he went in the opposite direction, to Paris. There he found himself with the name of a trouble-maker: the Polish authorities discouraged his return to Warsaw, the French police took a marked interest in him. He sold a couple of jewelled Orders and came on to London, hoping to find his American publisher, who had unfortunately left a week earlier. On this publisher Belinski still pinned his hopes, for there had been some talk of his going to the States himself; apart from this he was apparently without any plan whatever. In the meantime, from day to day, he lived as in a vacuum. He had a room in Paddington, and spent most of his time in public libraries. He had made himself known to no one, and did not look to be sought out. His melancholy voice gave these facts not reluctantly, but as though they were uninteresting commonplaces which must be rather boring to hear.

"But, good God!" exclaimed John at last. "There must be people, places, simply asking for you. Cambridge, for instance, any of the universities. I mean, you're famous. You'd be an — an ornament to them. I don't understand."

"Well, I've had enough of it," said Mr. Belinski.

They were more surprised than ever. Their young eyes widened with astonishment as Adam Belinski addressed himself to his zabaglione. Enough of it? Enough of being a trouble-maker? Enough of being the centre of rows, secret enquiries, international complications? Such an attitude was explicable to them on only one ground, that of physical ill health. He couldn't have recovered from his beating-up. . . .

"You want a good rest," said Betty encouragingly.

"I want to do some work," corrected Mr. Belinski. "I am an artist, not a political figure. That is the trouble in Poland: there are not enough distinguished Poles to go round; every one must do double duty. Look at Paderewski — the greatest musician in the world, we had to make him President as well. If you win a motor race, you are made Secretary to the Board of Trade. I have a success with my writings, so I must become a lecturer. Thank heaven they did not give me the Police Force. So I get into a fight, and soon I can do no work at all." He flung out his hand; for the first time they noticed that the wrist was crooked, as though it had been broken and badly set. "I do not wish to be anything but what I am, and that is my determination. Also, it appears that I bring trouble. Even if I would lecture again, I would not go to one of your universities, and perhaps bring trouble there."

"In fact," said Betty, with great interest, "you're hot."

But Belinski's knowledge of English evidently did not extend to American colloquialisms. He looked blank.

"She means," translated Andrew, "she quite understands — we all understand — why you have to lie low. But it's pretty damnable."

He looked across at John Frewen, and at that moment, in the minds of both, the great plan was born. It hardly needed communicating; in a few words, under Betty's chatter, everything of importance was practically decided. "Horsham?" murmured John — referring to his home. "Better my place in Devon. Right off the map," murmured Andrew. JOHN: What about your people? ANDREW: All right, I think. Ask him now? JOHN: No, later. To-morrow. Show we've slept on it. . . .

But when it came to the point they were both afraid that once they parted Belinski might disappear again before they could save him; so while John took Betty home Andrew walked with Mr. Belinski to Paddington, on the plea — for his company was at first refused — of having to meet a train. With complete gravity the Pole in turn insisted on accompanying Andrew into the station, but the latter, who had thitherto been unable to get their conversation off an abstract plane, was long past feeling foolish. The opportunity was nearly gone, and he was determined not to miss it.

"Mr. Belinski," said Andrew.

"Yes? Cannot you find the train?"

Andrew discovered that he had been staring up at the indicator, and flushed.

"Mr. Belinski, would you care to come and stay with my people in Devonshire?"

"I beg your pardon?"

"At my home in the country. Very quiet, and all that. You could certainly work there, because there's nothing else to do."

Belinski regarded him with amusement.

"Is it another party? This time for the week-end?"

"Oh, no," said Andrew, "I thought you might stay a few years."

Just then they were jostled by a porter (actually Cluny's

Uncle Trumper) who also wished to look at the indicator. Andrew stepped one way, Belinski the other; and during the moment of separation the latter's mind must have worked with great speed, for when he joined Andrew again he looked no longer astonished, but simply pleased.

"My dear young friend," he said warmly, "I cannot say how much I appreciate such generosity. It is magnificent!"

"Oh, rot," said Andrew. "When will you come?"

"But of course, I cannot accept," said Mr. Belinski hastily.

Andrew immediately asked why not. Mr. Belinski hesitated. He had what he considered a perfectly adequate reason, but he did not think it would appear adequate to his new young friend. He therefore selected another.

"I am not a suitable guest."

"Nonsense," said Andrew cheerfully. "I've taken home much rummer chaps than you." The adjective slipped out before he could retrieve it, but Belinski did not seem offended. He stood looking at Andrew warily, but with something like affection.

"Please do not press me, because I feel so discourteous to refuse. For example, your parents do not know me. What you suggest is most generous, but also quite impossible."

"I don't see why," argued Andrew stubbornly. "You'd find it fearfully boring — "

"It is not to be thought of," said Mr. Belinski.

Without another word he turned and walked rapidly out of the station. But Andrew hared after him, and followed him home, and once they knew the address he and John Frewen were able to dog Mr. Belinski's path, and argue with him in relays; and Andrew (as has been seen) went down to Devonshire to get his parents' approval, and came back with a written invitation from Lady Carmel; and at the end of another two weeks Mr. Belinski (other factors influencing him as well) suddenly gave way, and bent once more to his erratic fate.

### III

"We'll go down in my car," said John Frewen. "Can Betty come too?"

Andrew looked thoroughly horrified.

"I'll say she can't. Last time she upset the whole house. I'm not taking home any more disturbing influences," said Andrew righteously.

# Chapter 7

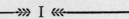

ONE PERSON at least welcomed this fortnight's interval: Mrs. Maile felt she really couldn't do with visitors until she got her staff into some sort of shape. It was no easy matter. Friars Carmel, like many another once lavish household, was still strong on the administrative side, but weak on the executive. The rôles of butler, housekeeper, cook, were all filled; but Cluny and Hilda, like a stage army, had to march round and round — now housemaids, now parlour-maids, now kitchen-maids, laundry-maids, linen-maids or tweenies. This made them very hard to discipline, for though Mrs. Maile could easily keep in her head what each of six girls ought to be do-ing at any given hour, two girls doing six jobs confused her sadly. When she found Hilda upstairs at noon, or Cluny peel-ing potatoes at tea-time, she had to go away and think things out before going back to rebuke them; by which time Cluny was probably in the pantry and Hilda in the wash-house. What particularly upset Mrs. Maile was that Cluny at least evi-dently took this as the normal state of affairs in a well-con-ducted household. She was very good-natured. But Mrs. Maile would almost have preferred a complaining expert who knew what was what.

The two girls themselves got on very well. Cluny at once took the lead, bossed Hilda a good deal, and in return told her all about London and taught her many useful and amusing phrases. (The first time Hilda replied "Oh yeah?" to Mr. Syrett was a happy moment.) Their common bedroom was large, and they divided its conveniences meticulously, the only advantage retained by Hilda being an art-silk bedspread bought out of her own money. As a counter to this Cluny had her three photographs in their gold frame, which she stood in the centre of the mantelpiece. Hilda had no photographs as yet, because Gary was too young to take.

Gary was her infant son, and a source of great pride to her; she wagered that when his Dad came back and saw'n him'd wed she for sure — though whether her'd wed he was another story: him'd have to mend his wild ways, said Hilda sternly, afore her went to church with'n. Hilda's seduction by a seafarer, in fact, gave her the only consequence she was capable of, and she naturally leant on it. Cluny listened with great interest, and nearly invented an infant of her own; but Mr. Porritt's eye, even in a photograph, restrained her. Hilda thus kept an incontestible point of superiority, which usefully checked Cluny's instinct to domineer.

But all this was more trouble for Mrs. Maile. Before Cluny arrived the housekeeper had instructed Hilda to suppress, on pain of instant dismissal, all mention of young Gary; and she imagined herself obeyed. Then arose the question of Cluny's afternoon off — two till seven on Wednesdays. (Other maids had had till nine-thirty, but this was a special arrangement, made through Miss Postgate and Aunt Addie Trumper, on account of Cluny's youth and inexperience.) From two till seven, what was the girl to do? Her natural occupation, a visit to Hilda's home in the village, was barred by the presence there of Hilda's illegitimate offspring. Cluny missed her first Wednesday because she arrived on a Tuesday, but even in nine days Mrs. Maile had not discovered an answer. The problem really bothered her. In fact, only one thing bothered Mrs. Maile more, and that was Cluny's solution of it.

In answer to a tentative enquiry, Cluny said she was going to the Colonel's.

"The Colonel's?" repeated Mrs. Maile blankly.

"Colonel Duff-Graham's. To see Roderick," explained Cluny.

Mrs. Maile's eyebrows rose. Had Cluny said to see Mabel, or Annie, she would still have been surprised — for how on earth had the girl made contact with them? — but approving; both Mabel and Annie were steady enough to be suitable friends. But Roderick sounded suspiciously like a chauffeur.

"*Roderick*, my dear?"

"He's a Golden Labrador," said Cluny. "He was in the train. The Colonel said I could come and take him out."

"Well!" said Mrs. Maile. Whether this made things better or worse she really did not know. She had never heard of such a thing; it was an evidence of social enterprise quite beyond her. And what was the Colonel thinking of? She had made it quite clear over the telephone who Cluny was, and the stationmaster repeated every word back. . . .

"I *love* him!" added Cluny enthusiastically.

Mrs. Maile asked no more. She felt it quite possible that if she asked who, Cluny might reply not "Roderick," but "The Colonel" and the idea was altogether too unnerving to pursue.

In her distress of mind the housekeeper mentioned this incident to Mr. Syrett, who immediately disposed of it on the hypothesis that Cluny had been telling lies. But Mrs. Maile remained uneasy. She remembered some of Mr. Andrew's sayings — reported by Syrett himself — about cracks in civilization, the breaking-up of society, world revolution, the decay of the West; and for the first time, their meaning struck home.

## II

So the uneasy fortnight passed; Andrew, John, and Mr. Belinski arrived. The first person to see them was Sir Henry, who happened to be looking out of the window as the car drew up; he watched the three young men get out, and at once nipped down to his wife's drawing-room to warn her that the Professor hadn't come. "Feller's too young," proclaimed Sir Henry. "Andrew's thought better of it and brought some other chap." He was firmly reiterating this statement as Andrew brought Belinski in.

"Mother — " said Andrew clearly — casting his other parent a glance of filial rebuke — "this is Mr. Belinski."

Lady Carmel intercepted the look, threw Sir Henry a frown on her own account, and swam benevolently to meet them.

"How nice!" she exclaimed. "My son has told me so much about you, Professor; we are so glad you could come. My husband, Professor — and now, Professor, let me give you some tea."

Belinski sat. Thus far he had not uttered a word, so emphatic a welcome having stopped his mouth; he could hardly shout them down. But now his chair was placed close by Lady Carmel's, and her mild eyes encouraged him.

"I cannot express," he said gravely, "how grateful I am for your kindness. It is something that does not often happen. If your son has indeed spoken of me, you will understand all I do not say."

"How well you speak English," observed Lady Carmel.

"It is the universal tongue."

"Ha!" exclaimed Sir Henry, much pleased. "That's what I say. As a young man my dear parents sent me on a tour round the world. I left speaking English and I came back speaking English, and I never spoke a word of anything else the whole time. Didn't need to."

"And did you enjoy your travels, sir?"

"No," said Sir Henry.

"Harry, dear!" Lady Carmel signalled to Andrew to give his father several scones. "The Professor will think you quite stupid. You know you enjoyed them."

"I didn't," said Sir Henry stoutly. "I went to Rome and I saw the Pope, I went to St. Petersburg, and saw the Czar, and when I got home I took a good look at the first London bobby and I thanked my stars. If a man's got a home, he should stick to it."

For a moment this extraordinarily unfortunate remark seemed to Andrew to lie visible, like a broken bowl, in the middle of the floor. Then his mother tidied it up.

"Now I," she said blandly, "am a natural cosmopolitan. If one never gets out of one's own country one becomes quite pot-bound. Personally I should like to spend nine months of the year abroad."

This thumping lie drew upon her the eyes of all three: Andrew's sending a message of love, Belinski's bright with comprehension, Sir Henry's simply aghast.

"Allie — !" he protested. "Do you really — "

"Have some cake, dear," said Lady Carmel meaningly. "Andrew, where is John? Professor, are you fond of gardens? I shall show you mine till you think me a great bore. Ah, here is John: get your tea, dear, you must be famished. And now, Professor, tell me: who is Einstein?"

Under this firm handling the rest of the meal passed off

very well, and as soon as it was over Lady Carmel made good her threat and took Belinski off to the garden.

### III

Mrs. Maile, presiding over a rather superior spread in the housekeeper's room, waited impatiently for Mr. Syrett to come back and report.

"Well, Mr. Syrett?"

The butler put off his front-hall manner and sat down.

"Pretty punctual, for once," he announced. "I had just carried in the tray, and her ladyship's kettle was on the boil. Mr. Andrew looks well, though somewhat more distracted than usual, and Mr. John of course lingered in the garage messing about with his car."

"And the Professor?"

The butler considered. He was about to pronounce the judgement of below-stairs — no light responsibility.

"Young," he said at last. "Younger than one would expect, or indeed consider suitable. But quite gentlemanly."

Mrs. Maile nodded, to show she understood this fine distinction.

"I shall try him on the Richebourg '26," continued Mr. Syrett.

"It's always champagne on Mr. Andrew's first night back."

"Mr. Andrew has been coming and going at such a rate that I have decided to count him back for good. When will Brown be ready to help wait?"

Mrs. Maile reflected.

"If you like to risk it, she might try to-night. Though with two guests, it does seem chancy."

"At least she can reach to set a plate," said Mr. Syrett, "without biting Sir Henry's ear, as is Hilda's practice. In fact, she has as good a reach as I've ever seen. Try her."

Which seemed to show that Cluny, as a Tall Parlour-maid, was at last finding her place.

## IV

Walking between the box edges of the pixey-garden, Lady Carmel continued to handle the situation presented by Mr. Belinski with marked success. She told him simply and carefully all the things she thought he should, but probably did not, know, and refused to hear a word in return. After two or three attempts Mr. Belinski (henceforward the Professor) gave up, even admitting a certain good sense in Lady Carmel's attitude; having successfully palmed off on herself a perfectly satisfactory Professor, what did she want with the scarred and uneasy figure of truth? It made no difference in her reception of him whether Mr. Belinski had been the victim of appendicitis or of mob violence; but it made a great difference to Lady Carmel, who was mildly interested in the first, but could not bear to contemplate the second.

"Have you a dinner-jacket?" asked Lady Carmel.

The Professor shook his head.

"I am so sorry. I have only this suit and one other. And four shirts." (He found he didn't mind telling her this in the least.)

"Then Andrew, who has two, shall lend you one; you're much the same build. That is because," explained Lady Carmel, "my husband always dresses for dinner, but if he saw you didn't, he wouldn't, and that would worry him, because he likes me to dress, always. I'm being so frank because we hope you'll stay with us some time, and to have poor Harry worrying for months would be too bad. You don't mind?"

"I do not think I would mind anything said by you."

"That's a great compliment. You mustn't mind anything my husband says either. Though I'm so fond of travel myself," explained Lady Carmel, "he is not; and he's so used to England as home, he quite forgets other countries are home too. It must be very sad to be away; but let us hope, only temporarily." (By this oblique reference Lady Carmel covered the entire European situation, and felt she had said quite enough.) "So you must borrow anything you want from Andrew, Professor, and there are several thousand books in the library; my husband sleeps there in the afternoon, but otherwise it is very little used. Syrett will valet you — "

"Dear Lady Carmel, I was never valeted in my life."

"Well, do you mind letting Syrett, so as not to hurt his feelings? I don't suppose he'll do much, in fact Andrew says he just eats his head off, but he wouldn't like to be told not to. I'm being so perfectly frank, Professor, because I never forget how once as a girl I completely disorganized a French household by coming downstairs to breakfast. When I found out by accident, after nearly three months, I was so mortified that I've never liked France since. It's the other countries I want to travel in," said Lady Carmel hastily.

## V

As Andrew and John Frewen were returning from the stables, whither they had gone to inspect certain arrangements made there by Andrew, they were crossed by Cluny Brown, travelling at great speed.

"Who's that?" asked John.

"New maid," said Andrew indifferently.

"Looks to me like an anarchist," said John.

Cluny's appearance was indeed rather wild, for she had pulled off her cap and released her pony tail when she ran out to get a breath of air. But her determined expression (like her need for a breather) was purely professional: her coming début at the dinner table was weighing on her more than she would own. The ousted Hilda, on the other hand, was even then singing "Jeepers-Creepers" in the larder. A girl entirely without ambition, she had hailed their change of functions with frank delight. (And she was good-hearted as well: the reason she was in the larder was because she was getting Cluny a snack to fortify her for the coming ordeal.) Cluny was not exactly ambitious — at any rate so far as parlour-maiding was concerned — but she had a great desire to startle Mr. Syrett. She was keyed up like a prima donna, and far too preoccupied to notice either of the young men.

"Sit down a minute, my dear," said Mrs. Maile kindly, as Cluny came loping back into domestic territory, "and then get Hilda to help you fasten your hair."

"Shall I cut it off?" suggested Cluny desperately.

"Certainly not; for when it grows a little longer, you will be able to have a proper bun."

Hilda at that moment placed a sandwich before her. Cluny took a large semi-circular bite and chewed and chewed.

"Do nothing until Mr. Syrett tells you," continued Mrs. Maile, "and you can't go wrong. When he says 'Plates,' either take the used ones or set fresh, as the case may be; when he says 'Vegetables,' or 'Sauce,' hand vegetables, or sauce."

"And mind you don't go breathin'," exhorted Hilda.

"Nonsense, of course she can breathe," said Mrs. Maile liberally. "The trouble with you, Hilda, is that you breathe into persons' ears."

"Mother says my lungs be like bellowses," agreed Hilda proudly.

"Suppose I get hiccups?" muttered Cluny.

Mrs. Maile looked at the pair of them and repressed a sigh. She was not poetically inclined, but the names of Bessie, Gracie, Flora, did at that moment chime in her mind like three sweet symphonies.

"Hilda, go and help Cook," she ordered sharply. "Brown, go upstairs and tidy; you will not get hiccups. If you both thought more of your duties and less of yourselves, we should all get on a great deal better."

No mention has so far been made of Cook because she was merely a temporary. She was obliging Lady Carmel for six months while her own employer was in the Argentine, and had therefore no roots at Friars Carmel. In her own kitchen her personality was a rather interesting one, unusually sardonic, as she herself was unusually thin, and expressing itself in savouries and sharp sauces. So she turned out steamed puddings for Sir Henry efficiently, but without enthusiasm. She did all that was required of her, and kept herself to herself. This left in the servants' hall what might be described as a cook-shaped space, and removed a good deal of the wholesome pressure to which Hilda and Cluny would normally have been subject.

# VI

Sir Henry and Lady Carmel kept early hours; for them a pleasant evening ended at ten-thirty, and Andrew, who wished his protégé to make a good impression, remarked at twenty-five past that they had all had a long day. Mr. Belinski at once rose and kissed Lady Carmel's hand; after so mild a programme — a game of auction bridge, a little talk on gardening — he did indeed look curiously exhausted. Andrew took him up to his room in the east corridor, where Belinski immediately sat down on the bed. (A predecessor of Cluny's once divided all guests into two classes: those who sat on the beds, and those who sat in the chairs provided.)

"Everything you want?" asked Andrew.

Belinski looked at the bedside table with its lamp, its carafe, its silver biscuit-box, its two books, one of them in German. A lower shelf held cigarettes, matches, ash-tray. He looked at the primroses on the bureau. The warmth of a hot-water bottle communicating itself, he shifted a little and looked at the small mound it made through the bed-clothes. Then he looked at Andrew.

"It is unbelievable," said Mr. Belinski.

"What is?"

"All of it. That I should be here — in this house — with your parents — is like a dream."

"Particularly my parents," suggested Andrew.

Belinski nodded seriously.

"I had forgotten that such people were. No, that is wrong: I never knew of such people. They are good like saints."

"Do you mean — not of this world?"

"Of a far better."

"Like a dream." Andrew grinned. "You're dreaming them, and they're dreaming you."

"They can never have had such a dream before. Tell me: why does your mother call me Professor?"

"Well," said Andrew, "she's got it into her head that that's what you are. I mean, she's not in the least dense — "

"Certainly not. She is rationalizing her dream."

"You don't mind?"

"On the contrary, if she wishes, I will be a Rector. But —
but I am still perplexed. I ask myself, Why am I a Professor?
Why am I here? You and your friends, why should you in-
volve yourselves? Why?"

Andrew walked across to the window and looked out at the
moonshiny night. Very far away an owl hooted; then silence
again, dropping like dew.

"Well, at Cambridge they thought rather a lot of you."

"Then I am to be respected, yes. Cheered, after a discourse
— if you happen to agree with my opinions. But you and your
friends — I may tell you, I do not agree — believe me to be
in some sort of danger. I saw that young man who drove the
car put a pistol in his pocket! If there are such risks, why
should you take them?"

"Well, we think you're a valuable sort of man."

"And that is sufficient?"

Andrew hesitated. Then he turned round from the window,
and all his father came out in him as he answered.

"If you must know — there's also the sporting interest of
the thing. . . ."

The effect of this admission was not such as he expected.
Adam Belinski leaped up from the bed with a beaming smile.

"That is such a pleasure to me," he said warmly, "you do
not know!"

## VII

There were several things Andrew did not yet know about
Mr. Belinski; for even left-wing authorities on European
literature have their human side, and Andrew, being young,
expected people (and especially celebrities) to be all of a
piece. He would have been much surprised, and even rather
shocked, to know the true reason of both Mr. Belinski's

melancholia and his reluctance to leave London; but the fact
was that besides being interested in prose, Mr. Belinski was
also interested in women.

He was particularly sensitive to certain attributes in them.
These included length from hip to knee, ability to interpret
Chopin, very dark eyes, very light eyes, impregnable virtue,
insatiable temperament, and a trustful disposition; and a
week before the party in Hampstead he had met a young
lady who combined no less than three of them. She was tall,
dark and virtuous; the married daughter of his landlady. When
John Frewen espied him behind the piano, such was the vision
that filled Belinski's thoughts: lovely and cruel Maria Dillon.
No wonder he looked wretched. And when Andrew followed
and argued with him — hopeless yet ever hoping, repulsed
yet enchanted, in the first throes of a new passion — how could
Belinski tear himself away? He couldn't. But at last he was
given notice; and so allowed himself to be carried off into
Devonshire under armed guard.

And Adam Belinski had also a conscience, though an erratic
one. The precautions taken by young Andrew had touched
him: he felt he had pulled a double bluff, assuring the boy
there was no danger, yet allowing him to believe in it. Now
Andrew's confession had put all to rights; he too, in a sense,
had deceived Belinski: he was not all pure altruism, he was
enjoying himself like hell; and so they were quits.

Mr. Belinski lay between the smooth, cool, lavender-scented
sheets and thought of Maria Dillon. He found her image curiously hard to fix: it was overlaid by too many other impres-
sions, of the great house, of the candle-lit dinner table, of
Lady Carmel and Sir Henry. This was no unusual phenomenon
with him: ardent in pursuit, he was also rather easily distracted. Besides, he was in Devonshire, and Maria in London.

(As Hortense was in Paris, and Sonia in Warsaw, and another girl in Budapest.) "Good-bye, Maria!" thought Mr. Belinski sadly; luxuriated a moment in this fresh loss, and so fell into a sound sleep.

## VIII

*Dear Uncle Arn,*

*I waited at table to-night for the first time. Two guests, a friend of Mr. Andrews and the Professor, and Mr. Syrett said I might have been worse. The only thing I did really bad was offering mayonaze again with the trifle, thinking custard. The Professor took some before Mr. Syrett saw but ate it up, we think perhaps being a foreigner he wouldn't notice. But he speaks English like you or I. Her ladyship wore grey velvet though not low-necked, all the others in evening clothes just like the films. This is the brightest spot so far in my hard life. I hope you are quite well and not missing me too badly. It would be funny if after all these years you did not miss me at all. What I think is if you miss people why not say so.*

*Your affectionate neice,*

CLUNY BROWN

# Chapter 8

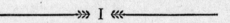

## I

THE BEAUTIES of a Devonshire spring — exquisite in detail, splendid in broad effect — are too well known to require description. Natives, from old habit, keep their heads pretty well; they do not (as might be expected) unanimously down tools and give themselves up to admiration; but both Cluny and the Professor were powerfully affected. The latter's sensibility made Lady Carmel like him all the more; she felt that a Devonshire spring was just the sort of thing a foreigner ought to see, and she determined that he should see it thoroughly. They took packets of sandwiches and tramped for miles, leaving Andrew and Sir Henry, who was no pedestrian, to face each other over the lunch table. The meal was usually a silent one, for Andrew, like many another young man of his generation, was extremely fond of his father but had nothing to say to him.

"I'm glad your mother's got some one to walk with," observed Sir Henry. "I don't like her going alone."

Andrew nodded, but without conviction. Lady Carmel, known to and revered by every man, woman and child within a radius of ten miles, could scarcely come to harm. She occasionally overtired herself, and then stopped the first vehicle going her way and asked for a lift. Once she came home in a char-à-banc, once sitting serenely on the front seat of a lorry. In a quiet way Lady Carmel was one of the pioneers of hitch-hiking in Great Britain.

"You didn't go with 'em?" added Sir Henry.

"Letters," mumbled Andrew, avoiding his parent's eye. On him too the season was having its effect — and so conventional a one that he instinctively repudiated it. But the Tennysonian jingle, like all platitudes, could not be denied: in the spring a young man's fancy lightly turns to thoughts of love. So Andrew's thoughts had turned, though not lightly — so seriously, in fact, that he could not endure to contemplate a bank of primroses except in company with the beloved. This was all the more annoying to him because he had only just decided that far from being in love with Betty Cream, he rather disliked her, and she had therefore no business to pop out as it were from under the first violet. This horrid image produced a certain amount of revulsion, but not much.

"Pity the Duff-Graham girl's away," said Sir Henry suddenly.

"Why?" asked Andrew.

"Well, she'd be company for you," said Sir Henry; and then, remembering several warnings of his wife's, began to talk about trout.

## II

Mr. Belinski's reactions to the spring met with every encouragement; not so Cluny Brown's. What was an asset in the guest became a liability in the parlour-maid: for only by scamping her work could Cluny spend enough time out of doors, and every day she scamped a bit more. She left hot-water bottles in the beds, and omitted to refill the carafes. She substituted Kia-Ora for Mr. Andrew's orange juice.

With real ingenuity, she dropped the key of the linen cupboard somewhere in the orchard, and had to spend a whole afternoon looking for it. Above all, she picked things. Every time she ran out she came back with her hands full — of catkins, violets, primroses, daffodils. Born and bred in London, she could not get over the fact that these were all there free. (Pussy-willow that sold for a shilling in Piccadilly and sixpence even in Paddington.) In the room she shared with Hilda every available surface was soon covered with chipped vases and old jam-jars, filled with these spoils. She brought moss into the kitchen, also a thrush's egg, fallen from the nest, which she tried to hatch in a tea-cosy. Later she tried to blow it. This thorough-going attempt to cram a whole country-childhood into the space of a few weeks was very much in Cluny's character; it was not however in Mrs. Maile's character to allow it.

Mrs. Maile put up with a great deal, almost any parlour-maid being better than none; but after Cluny played truant for two hours, simply to look at lambs, the housekeeper decided that the time had come to give her a thorough dressing-down. This was something Mrs. Maile did particularly well: generations of Bessies had been reduced to tears in an average of five minutes, and to penitence in an average of ten. Mrs. Maile rather grimly allotted Cluny a quarter of an hour, and there is little doubt that Cluny too would have succumbed, but for one unforeseeable accident. "Who do you think you are?" demanded Mrs. Maile coldly; and this question, awaking such familiar echoes, effectually distracted Cluny's thoughts. The rest of the scolding was lost on her: she was far away, back in String Street with Mr. Porritt. Passionately she wondered how he was managing without her; whether Aunt Addie darned his socks properly; whether the respectable woman gave him his favourite liver and bacon on a Saturday night. It was quite wonderful how little his letters managed to communicate: "*All well, everything much the same,*" wrote Mr. Porritt — with such regularity that Cluny sometimes wondered why he didn't send a post card with just "*Ditto*" on it . . .

"Well?" repeated Mrs. Maile impatiently. "Have you anything to say for yourself?"

"I do wish Uncle Arn was here!" sighed Cluny.

The housekeeper's face relaxed. She had, as it happened, actually been speaking of Mr. Porritt, drawing a most harrowing picture of his emotions on learning of Cluny's wickedness: she thought perhaps Cluny wished he were there so that she might promise him to do better.

"And why do you say that, my dear?" asked Mrs. Maile helpfully.

"I'd like him to see the lambs," sighed Cluny.

Like Mr. Ames a month earlier, Mrs. Maile felt baffled. For it wasn't even impertinence; it was something far more elusive and — and unnatural. The housekeeper was so put out that she actually waited for Cluny to resume the conversation, on the chance that her next remark might prove more answerable.

"I'm sorry, I didn't hear what you were saying. Have you sacked me?" asked Cluny hopefully.

Mrs. Maile would have given a month's wages to be able to answer, "Yes, I have."

### III

It was on one of her legitimate excursions, however, on a Wednesday afternoon, that Cluny, having upset Mrs. Maile, upset Andrew Carmel. Andrew was tramping the lanes at a steady four miles an hour, trying not to observe the beauties of nature: he was out purely for exercise. As he had hoped, exercise drugged his mind; he achieved an almost complete unawareness of his surroundings — until suddenly, at a point where Colonel Duff-Graham's boundary marched with the road, there leapt through a gate a golden dog followed by a tall dark girl in a mackintosh.

A mackintosh, especially in the country, has peculiar properties. It blends people into the landscape, making them look as if they belonged there. Worn with heavy shoes and a battered hat, or no hat at all, it is for several months of the year the uniform of the country gentlewoman. A dog goes with it. Andrew therefore did not recognize Cluny for at least five seconds, or four seconds after he had recognized Roderick.

"Hello," he said. "Where are you going?"

"It's my afternoon off," said Cluny.

"You've got the Colonel's Roddy."

"I've just fetched him. Isn't he beautiful?"

"Grand," agreed Andrew.

Cluny grinned, twisting her hand in the animal's collar.

"It's all right, the Colonel knows. And Mrs. Maile knows. I'm let."

"Well, I didn't think you were stealing him," said Andrew.

"I take him out every week, and he's mine for the afternoon. He's going to have puppies — I mean his wife is." All at once Cluny's friendly look changed; she stared at Andrew inimically. "Mr. Syrett," she stated, "says you're ever so worried about Europe."

This sudden change of subject took Andrew aback.

"How on earth does he know that?"

"There's nothing much goes on he doesn't know," said

Cluny darkly. "I suppose he hears you talking. He says you think it's just awful."

"So it is."

"Well, *here*," said Cluny, "I'm not allowed to keep a dog." She turned and made rapidly off, Roderick following.

Andrew was so struck by this encounter that as soon as he got home he went straight to his mother in the garden room and asked if there were any reason why the maids shouldn't keep dogs.

"They don't, dear," said Lady Carmel. "Have you had a nice walk?"

"Grand," said Andrew. "And I know they don't, but is there any reason why they shouldn't?"

Lady Carmel carefully filled a jar with water.

"There's no place for them," she explained. "Chauffeurs sometimes keep dogs, but then there's the garage. Coachmen used to keep dogs. Housekeepers have cats — and I'm sure I wish Mrs. Maile would, because Syrett has seen a mouse. Have you seen a mouse, darling?"

Andrew picked up an iris and began to bite the stalk.

"Cluny Brown wants a dog, and from something she said I believe the Colonel would give her one of Roderick's puppies. Should you mind?"

"Of course not. Don't eat that, dear, it may be poisonous. But Mrs. Maile would. She doesn't like dogs *or* cats."

"My dear Mother, you give orders here, not Mrs. Maile."

"Perhaps I do," admitted Lady Carmel — though not as though she were very sure of it. "All the same, Mrs. Maile has been with us thirty years, and puppies do so chew things. When did Brown tell you all this?"

"I met her out with Roddy. The Colonel lets her take him on her afternoon off."

"And did you go a walk with her?" murmured Lady Carmel absently.

"No, darling. She bolted. I do wish you'd reason with Mailey."

Lady Carmel stepped back to look at her finished jar. All through the conversation her clever hands had moved quietly and deftly, leading their own sensible life, and now they had something to show for themselves.

"I once," she said thoughtfully, "many years ago, knew of a butler who hunted."

"Good for him," said Andrew.

"No, dear, it wasn't good for him. He broke his neck trying to follow a young man in the Hussars over a bull-finch."

Lady Carmel sounded quite upset — though whether over the long-ago fate of the hunting butler, or the dogless state of her new parlour-maid, Andrew could not be sure. At any rate, she was upset.

## IV

When not going on walks with Lady Carmel the Professor spent a good deal of time in the stables. On the morning after his arrival, as soon as they had seen John start like a rocket back for London, Andrew led the way through the pleasant yard and up a steep outside stair to a small hayloft. It was a hayloft no longer: under the freshly-cleaned window stood a table, before it a chair; there were also a book-shelf, a waste-paper-basket and a camp-bed.

"The oil-stove's coming to-morrow," explained Andrew.

Mr. Belinski gazed thoughtfully round. It didn't look quite like a study, nor yet quite like a prison: what it most strongly suggested was a hide-out. Reading his young companion's mind with great accuracy, Belinski saw himself leaning from that window pulling up provisions on the end of a string.

"My very dear friend," he said gently, "I assure you this is not necessary."

Andrew looked unnaturally stupid.

"I thought you might like to work here sometimes. I know my mother says no one uses the library, but that doesn't mean she isn't in and out half the morning doing flowers."

"But that is not what you had in mind when you arranged me this little room. You thought, this is where he will hide, when they come after him!"

Andrew flushed.

"All right, I'm a well-meaning ass. Wash it out."

He looked so crest-fallen, however, that Belinski said he would certainly use the loft to work in, so long as Andrew did not sit outside with a shot-gun on his knee; and on these terms the loft was a success. As time went on Belinski used it more and more, until he spent a great part of the day there — engaged, it was believed, on a new book. He never actually said so, but that was the general impression, work on a new book being considered a suitable occupation for him; and a great comfort it was to Lady Carmel to know in the first place where he was, and in the second, what he was doing there. Within the house Belinski found another occupation, that of bringing up to date the library catalogue. This had not been properly kept since the days of Sir Henry's father; Sir Henry was no bookman, but on his accession, with filial piety, he lodged an order in Exeter for new works to the tune of fifty pounds a year. They had been accumulating ever since — all good solid stuff, biography, travel, memoirs — in complete disorder, so that the Professor's offer to sort them was a perfect godsend.

"I like the feller," said Sir Henry. "Wherever Andrew picked him up, I like him." He came up behind his wife (they had both just finished dressing for dinner) and stared at her through the glass. "Allie," said Sir Henry, "doesn't it strike you there's something wrong?"

"Wrong with what, dear?"

"With all these places abroad. Here's the Professor, as nice a young feller as you could wish to meet, clever and all that as well, and Andrew tells me he can't go home because of some political dog fight. There's something wrong somewhere."

"Andrew," said Lady Carmel, adjusting a diamond star, "says everything's wrong, all over Europe. He says we ought never to have supported Franco. Dear, who was Franco?"

"Spanish feller," said Sir Henry. "Did Andrew say that?"

Lady Carmel nodded through the glass.

"He says we're going to have another war. . . . Harry."

In the glass, their old eyes met. They were an old couple to have so young a son; Lady Carmel, over thirty at his birth, had now reached the point where her appearance was stabilized for the next twenty years. Sir Henry was seventy. He could remember the Zulu wars, and the Boer War, and the Great War; and they had hardly affected him. In 1914 he had offered his services, and been told to grow wheat. But if another war came, it would take Andrew. He looked at his wife through the mirror and gave her the only advice he knew.

"No use thinking of it till it comes," said Sir Henry.

"I try not to, dear."

"But I tell you one thing," said Sir Henry stoutly. "I

remember in '14 there was a fuss about the Colonel's governess, poor creature, because she was German. If it should happen again, which God forbid, I won't have the Professor hounded."

## V

So the grain of sand was received into the oyster, and the oyster got to work. Within a few weeks the Professor's writing had become as much an accepted feature of life at Friars Carmel as her ladyship's flowers: Mrs. Maile and Mr. Syrett referred to it with respect, feeling it did the house credit; even Ernest Beer the groom, after watching the Professor's comings and goings with deep suspicion, admitted him to be a wonderful hard toiler.

In point of fact, Mr. Belinski was not yet actually toiling at all. He was preparing to toil. Every day he spread out a quantity of paper, saw that his pen was filled, and then settled down to read a book. Or to draw elaborate pictures of castles. Or simply to sit, staring out at the sky, promising himself that when such a cloud had passed, or such a shadow touched the sill, he would take up his pen and begin. This state of affairs was as familiar as it was odious to him, but so far as he knew he could do nothing about it. He had to wait until his hand moved of its own accord and the words began to come out of the pen. In the meantime, any distraction was welcome, and he was very pleased, one afternoon about three o'clock, to see Cluny Brown walk slowly across the yard.

Cluny had discovered the stables soon after her arrival, and been chased out by Ernest Beer, who nursed a secret resentment against all the indoor staff, thinking that if he'd been Sir Henry he'd have sacked the lot and bought horses. For there was only one horse left, the old hunter Golden Boy. The names above half a dozen empty stalls — GALGA and COQUETTE, NUTMEG, LADY MAB, DANDY and BROWN PETER — were but sad reminders of a better day, upon which Ernest Beer liked to brood undisturbed. On this occasion, however, Cluny had seen him stumping off to the village, and the coast was clear.

Believing herself to be alone, therefore, she was considerably startled when Mr. Belinski addressed her. He was leaning out of his window, his body in shadow, his head projecting like a gargoyle and in Cluny's opinion just about as ugly.

"Hi!" said Mr. Belinski. "What is your name?"

"Cluny Brown," said Cluny.

"Come up and see my room, Cluny Brown."

But Cluny stood where she was at the bottom of the steps, gazing up at him. In her black stuff dress, still lacking apron and collar, she looked curiously timeless; she might have been any girl in any century — or all the young girls who in all centuries have stood, looking up, at the sound of a man's voice. She summed them, as a figure in a ballet sums religion, or knighthood, or fear, or love.

"Come up, you black cat," said Adam Belinski.

Cluny shook her head.

"Why not? Are you afraid of me?"

"Ought I to be?" asked Cluny interestedly.

"That depends on what you consider the object of existence. What is your object of existence?"

Cluny considered; for this was a subject on which every one else seemed to have so much more definite opinions than she did herself. Mrs. Maile and Aunt Addie Trumper and Mr. Porritt, for instance, were all unanimous: in their view the object of her existence was to become a well-trained parlour-maid. Mr. Ames thought she ought to go to parties. A gentleman in a 'bus had once advised her to become a model. But Cluny herself was still uncertain.

"I want something to happen," she said vaguely. "I want things happening all the time. . . ."

"Then make them happen. Why not?"

"You don't know my Uncle Arn," said Cluny sombrely. "The minute *any*thing happens, he stops it. I dare say it's on account of being a plumber. The way he goes on, I might be a burst pipe."

Mr. Belinski, who was finding this conversation interesting but obscure, said he would like to make Uncle Arn's acquaintance.

"You can't," said Cluny regretfully. "He's in London. I'm from London too, I don't really belong here." She sighed. "As a matter of fact, I didn't seem to belong there either. I don't seem to belong anywhere."

"Like me," said Mr. Belinski. "The situation has its advantages." He met Cluny's surprised look and nodded. "For instance, if one belongs nowhere, if one is not already rooted, one has choice. One can regard the countries of the world as a man regards a house-agent's list. That is not quite true for me, because there are several countries where I should be very uncomfortable indeed. But for you, I imagine, the whole universe is to let."

Cluny listened to him as she had once, at a church concert, listened to a poem about people who ate lotus (which she imagined as some sort of melon). She couldn't make head or tail of it, but it sounded lovely. Now she had the same, to her very rare, feeling of mental excitement, the sensation of being on the verge of a great discovery.

"Say that again," she ordered sharply. "That last bit."

"For you, I imagine, the whole universe is to let," repeated Mr. Belinski obligingly. "Now come up here."

But Cluny was no longer interested in Mr. Belinski, only in his words. She wanted to take that magic phrase away with her and examine it carefully, by herself. Without even another upward look she just said, "No, thanks," and walked off.

# Chapter 9

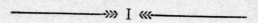

### I

AT THE moment Cluny's universe was the smallest she had ever known.

This fact, when she came to contemplate it, surprised her, for she had not been aware of any narrowing of interest. In a world containing and contained by no more than Friars Carmel and its demesne, the ten minutes' run to the Duff-Grahams' and a couple of square miles explored with Roddy, Cluny had lived as usual at full stretch. Her Devonshire world might be small, but it was new — and also full of house work. Her life was a good deal busier than had been her life in London, and certainly less lonely. And — again when she came to consider it — was her Paddington patch in town really larger than her Friars Carmel patch in the country? Had she not, like most Londoners, lived as much in a village as any born villager? "I didn't get about enough," thought Cluny, mourning her lost opportunities. . . .

Yet she had tried. She had got to the Ritz. She had got as far as Chelsea — put her nose, so to speak, to a couple of doors — and each time been pulled back by Uncle Arn, or Aunt Addie, people who knew what was best for her, only their idea of the best was being shut up in a box — in a series of smaller and smaller boxes until you were safe at last in the smallest box of all, with a nice tombstone on top. Cluny of course exaggerated; but meditating on Mr. Belinski's words she did most bitterly regret the life she and Mr. Porritt might have, but hadn't led. Well-off as he was, Mr. Porritt could have gone anywhere. He could have taken her, Cluny, anywhere. "He could have bought an opera-hat," thought Cluny Brown.

Preyed upon by such wild imaginings, Cluny's reason did not exactly totter, but she passed a day or two in a very surly frame of mind, her resentment on the point of crystallizing into a grievance, her temper in danger of being spoiled by Mr. Porritt's cloth caps. But a fortunate circumstance supervened: Mrs. Maile developed a cough which caught her in the chest, and this had the effect of enlarging Cluny's universe to take in the village of Friars Carmel, in which, though it lay only a mile off, she had thitherto never set foot. ("Just shows you!" thought Cluny obscurely.) There is always something stimulating about being dispatched post-haste to a chemist's, especially on an early-closing day — it was Thursday — when the chemist has to be summoned from his private life. "Ring the bell," directed Mrs. Maile, "and tell Mr. Wilson you're from me"; armed with which countersign Cluny set off at top speed, and feeling almost as important as a plumber.

## II

It was a mixed sort of afternoon, now bright, now dull, with a wind blowing down the valley. This meant rain, but Cluny wore her mackintosh simply because it was the only outdoor garment she possessed apart from her best black coat. It was the first time she had been to the village, but as Mrs. Maile said, she couldn't possibly miss it, since it lay across the main road to Carmel. To the main road Cluny therefore kept, but with a speculative eye to the lanes which ran up

on her right and down on her left: one of the former particularly attracted her, it was so deep and narrow, like a
gorge between cliffs of red earth. She determined to come
back and explore it with Roddy. A little farther on a runnel
of water no thicker than her wrist fell out of the hedge into
a rough stone basin: a good place to give Roddy a drink.
(Cluny would have had a drink herself, for the sheer romance of it, but she still mistrusted all water that didn't come
out of a tap.) At every step almost there was something to
look at, something to come back to; and with an unusual flight
of her town-bred imagination Cluny suddenly thought that if
she came back this time next year, everything would be more
interesting still, because she would remember *this* walk, and
all the changes that had come between. She had a glimmering,
in fact, of the true pleasure of country life, which is not to
be enjoyed merely at a summer week-end; the word con-
tinuity was not in her vocabulary, but she groped for it;
and in her shaken-up frame of mind these new ideas struck
home with extraordinary force. Because if there was space,
there was also depth: you could unroll all the countries of
the world, thin as maps, or dig down among the roots of your
own patch. "Or dig down for a grave," thought Cluny. She
was thinking almost too much, she was getting muddled;
but swift motion in the open air saved her from the worst
consequences. After half a mile Cluny stopped thinking altogether and simply enjoyed her walk at her normal level of
consciousness — which (when taking outdoor exercise) was
about the same as Roddy's.

The village of Friars Carmel is large enough to give the
name of Lesser Friars to an outlying hamlet, and to support
three public houses — the Lion, the Artichoke, and the Load
of Hay; it is also far enough (five miles) from Carmel to

need half a dozen shops of its own. All these, when Cluny passed outside, had their shutters up, but she at once identified the chemist's by the three coloured jars appearing in the top part of the window. Above them a very neat fascia displayed the name of T. WILSON in black letters on a white ground; the blind drawn behind the door repeated it in white on red. It was by far the sprucest shop in Friars Carmel.

Cluny rang the bell and waited, though with fading hopes: it was inconceivable to her that any one should voluntarily spend such an afternoon indoors. But this was what the whole population seemed to be doing: not a soul was in sight. The street was deserted, and so still that Cluny distinctly smelt her own mackintosh.

The sun went in and came out again. Cluny was just about to ring for the second time when the door was opened by a tall, youngish–middle-aged man who stood looking at her through horn-rimmed glasses.

"I'm sorry to trouble you," said Cluny politely. "Are you the chemist?"

He nodded.

"I've come for Mrs. Maile's cough medicine. She's sorry to trouble you on a Thursday, but it's taking her in the chest."

"Come in," said Mr. Wilson.

He stepped back and Cluny followed him into the shop. She could see at once that it was very high-class. There were glass counters on each side, running up to a glass door at the back, curtained on the inside: the familiar names of PEAR'S, POND'S, VINOLIA, ODORONO and COTY met the eye on every hand. There was an upright weighing-machine, and one with a basket, for infants. A boxed-off corner accommodated various scientific-looking appliances on a white enamel shelf.

CLUNY BROWN 85

"What a lovely shop!" exclaimed Cluny impulsively.

"I try to keep up-to-date," said Mr. Wilson.

He spoke with a certain sternness, as though implying that other people didn't. He had a very faint Scots accent.

"It's just like London," went on Cluny — giving the Cockney's compliment.

"There'll be finer shops there by far."

"Well, of course they're bigger. Some of them have libraries."

"I consider libraries no part of a chemist's business," said Mr. Wilson.

But he looked pleased. After a moment or two, while he was putting up Mrs. Maile's bottle, and Cluny stood about examining things, he observed thoughtfully: —

"So you come from London? That's a long way to be from home."

"Oh, it wasn't home really," said Cluny; and paused, for the truth was much too complex for any such simple expression. In one sense London, Paddington, was of course her home; she had lived there for eighteen years, and on the whole been quite happy; it was her home as much as anywhere. But it wasn't home inevitably; it hadn't the power that draws a grown person back to the scene of even an unhappy childhood. It made no claim on her. To Mr. Wilson, waiting with an earnest expression, Cluny added hastily, "I hadn't any mother or father, not since I was a baby."

"That's a terrible thing," said Mr. Wilson.

Cluny now felt she had been disloyal to Mr. Porritt, and though she loved sympathy, her conscience made her stand up for him.

"But Uncle Arn — and Aunt Floss — brought me up and everything. Uncle Arn would have kept me, he only sent me here because he thought good service might do me good."

"I'm glad you had some one to think for you," said the chemist.

Every word he spoke made Cluny feel more like an orphan. (Usually she did not feel like an orphan at all.) But his sympathetic interest was very agreeable, and she instinctively played up to it by looking sad. Cluny could look sad very easily, she had only to drop long dark lashes on a colourless cheek. Appropriately enough, a first spatter of rain just then struck against the windows; the shop grew dark, and away towards Carmel thunder rolled.

"You can't go back in this," said Mr. Wilson.

"I don't mind," said Cluny bravely. "Mrs. Maile's waiting . . ."

But they neither of them took this objection very seriously. The chemist, after a moment's reflection, came from behind the counter and threw open the door at the back of the shop. It was a very manly, no-nonsense gesture; and Cluny (still an orphan) submissively followed him through into a small cosy room.

Cluny liked this room at once. It reminded her of the Porritt kitchen, though it was not a kitchen but a parlour, and much neater and brighter than anything in String Street: the likeness lay chiefly in its unlikeness to the rooms at Friars Carmel. A dark red wall-paper was enlivened by many coloured pictures of gardens, ladies, children and pet animals; the round table was covered by a red cloth, on which stood a large brass lamp; the curtains were bright green. In the midst of all sat a very old lady whose white shawl made her quite restful to look at.

"Mother," said Mr. Wilson loudly, "here's a young lady to see you."

Mrs. Wilson slightly turned her head; she looked at Cluny without much change of expression, nor did she say anything; but out from under the shawl fumbled a little brown old hand like a rabbit's paw, and poked towards the chair on the opposite side of the hearth. Cluny obediently sat down on it. Mr. Wilson meanwhile lit the lamp. Its light made the room seem smaller and brighter, and the sky outside darker.

"I've got your place," said Cluny.

"I'll sit here," said the chemist, pulling out one of the four straight chairs that stood round the table.

He seemed to have run out of conversation, but the silence was not embarrassing, even when broken by a light snore from the old lady. This, in fact, by giving them a good reason not to talk, eased the whole situation. Mr. Wilson reached to the book shelf and pulled out a large illustrated volume of British Poets, for Cluny, and a *Blackwood's Magazine* for himself, and they settled down as for a quiet afternoon. But Cluny needed no steel engravings to keep her happy: it was so extraordinary to be sitting there at all, with these two perfect strangers, that the sensation was enough in itself. She felt like a doll that has been picked up and put into a doll's house: the doll at once looks completely at home, as though it had been there always. Cluny thought that if any one suddenly came in, he would take her for a relation. . . .

This peculiar situation lasted about fifteen minutes. Then the sky began to clear; a watery beam of sun mingled with the light from the lamp, making it look like a lamp that has been on all night. (Making Cluny feel as though she and Mr. Wilson had been sitting up all night.) He at once turned it out, glanced at the window, and gave Cluny an affirmatory nod. She put her book on the table and followed him back to the shop.

"You'll be all right now."

"Thank you for letting me stay," said Cluny, blinking.

"Mother's taken a liking to you," said Mr. Wilson. "I can see that."

Cluny wondered how he could tell. Several years before she had made quite a friend of an old man who took a tortoise into Kensington Gardens; and he told her he was never sure whether the tortoise enjoyed these outings or not, whether it didn't after all think, "Damn this grass." However, Cluny supposed that from long experience Mr. Wilson could detect in his mother shades of expression, intimations of pleasure, unapparent to any one else.

"She likes to see a young lady who doesn't put stuff on her face," said Mr. Wilson. "If I may say so, so do I."

"Well, it wouldn't do any good," said Cluny frankly. "I've tried it, but I look worse."

"They all look worse," said the chemist. "Only they haven't the sense to know it." He did up the bottle very neatly, with white paper, thin pink string, and a blob of sealing-wax. "When you're passing this way again, perhaps on your afternoon off, I hope you'll look in on us."

"Thank you very much indeed," said Cluny.


## III

This minute adventure pleased her so much that she thought about it all the way home. How different now was her mood from that in which she set out! A door had opened in Friars Carmel, a door of the most fascinating possibilities; for in retrospect the chemist's shop and the room behind appeared not only attractive, but mysterious. Who kept them so bright and clean? Who looked after Mrs. Wilson? (Not for one moment did Cluny visualize a Mrs. Wilson Junior.) Did Mr. Wilson spend all his spare time reading *Blackwood's* while his mother slept? And what was he doing there at all, keeping up-to-date in a place like Friars Carmel? "He can't be dodging the Police," reflected Cluny, "he isn't that sort. I dare say he's had some dreadful tragedy."

This heartening thought carried her along at a good pace, and having been delayed already she honourably refrained from stopping to pick things. But she had to pause just once, at the lane she had already named "The Gorge." Rills and rivulets of rain-water were still running down its sides; against the dark red earth the newly washed ivy-trails stood out darker still, yet brighter too, like greenish jet. Every detail of stem, leaf, pebble, raindrop, showed brilliant and precise. Cluny stared and stared. She advanced just a step, and felt the ring of stone under her heel. The lane was paved in the centre for a width of about two feet. So it was used (or had been); it went somewhere. A beautiful smell of warm wet earth puffed out to meet her. A little farther on, where a sapling grew out of the bank, crinkled primrose leaves invited. Cluny took another long step forward, and as she did so something in her mackintosh pocket banged against her knee.

It was Mrs. Maile's cough cure. Cluny took it out and looked at it. So neatly wrapped, in its white paper and pink string, it seemed to retain something of Mr. Wilson's personality. It did not exactly rebuke, but it reminded. Cluny returned the bottle to her pocket and set her face towards home.

# Chapter 10

————— ≫ I ≪ —————

Now ANDREW's original plan had been to stay down at Friars Carmel as it were on guard; and when it became apparent that there was nothing to guard against, he naturally grew restless. He decided to go up to London and see John.

"You don't mind, Mother?" he said. "I mean, you and the Professor get on perfectly well without me?"

"Of course we do," said Lady Carmel. "Really, dear, it's quite strange to me that you make all this fuss about the one friend who's no trouble at all." (She had not really answered the question, but Andrew did not notice.) "Give my love to John, and I hope you'll have a gay time. I don't suppose there'll be very many dances yet — "

"I shouldn't go to them if there were," said Andrew, rather sternly.

Lady Carmel sighed. She had taken great pains to keep up her London relations, so that Andrew should have nice houses open to him; but Andrew seemed to scorn nice houses as he scorned deb dances and garden-parties. He was too clever for them. Which was very odd, thought Lady Carmel, since for the exactly opposite reason his father hadn't liked parties either. He said all the girls were too clever for *him*. Sir Henry had been to precisely two dances in his life: at the first he met his future wife, at the second he proposed to her, and after that he cried off. But at least he had realized what dances were *for.* . . .

"Andrew," said Lady Carmel suddenly, "do you ever think of getting married?"

"No," said Andrew at once.

"We'd be very pleased. . . ."

He grinned at her.

"Yes, darling, if I married some one suitable. Like the Duff-Graham girl. Holy mackerel!"

"What a nice expression," said Lady Carmel. "But I wasn't thinking of Cynthia. In fact, I don't think Cynthia would do at all. I think she'd bore you. Isn't there some one else?"

"No," said Andrew.

His mother looked at him thoughtfully.

"Now, that's where we're so different," she said. "You talk about war, dear, as though it were inevitable; and you think me rather foolish because I still hope we may have peace. But if you really think like that, you should marry immediately."

"Even if there's no one I'm in love with?"

"That's not altogether the point — though of course your wife must be some one you are fond of, and respect. But this property has been in the family for three hundred years; you should at least get an heir," said Lady Carmel.

Andrew considered her with attention.

"Is that how you really feel?"

"Yes, my dear, it is."

His next words had a dreadful relevance.

"Do you remember Betty Cream?"

Lady Carmel instinctively closed her eyes, but bravely re-opened them.

"Certainly I do. I think she's the most beautiful girl I've ever seen, and so does your father. Would she make you happy?"

"I shouldn't imagine so," said Andrew. "But as you say, that's not the point. Not that she'd have me, of course."

He looked at his mother, expecting to see her bristle; but Lady Carmel gazed blandly back.

"Then dear, we'd better start a few house-parties; and I shall expect you home before the end of the month."

Before he left Andrew performed a last duty towards his guest which involved him in an interview with Cluny Brown. He had no difficulty in finding her, because she was singing — in the housemaid's pantry on the first floor — and her deep resonant tones, particularly when echoed back from beneath a draining-board, were very audible. Cluny was so absorbed in work and song that for a moment Andrew stood unperceived in the doorway; stood and stared, for the last time he had consciously seen her had been out of doors, striding along in her mackintosh as though she owned half Devonshire. Now she didn't look like the same person: her brown stuff frock, inherited from a predecessor, had been cleaned but not altered: it was much too short in both skirt and sleeves, and the waist only vaguely approximated her own. The stiff white cap had slipped forward over her nose, and her pony tail of hair, escaping from its pins, stuck out behind. But her manners remained easy.

"Hello," she said pleasantly. "Want to wash?"

"No, thanks," said Andrew. "Are you the one who hoovers the east corridor?"

Cluny at once looked defensive.

"Yes, I am," she said. "I'm Cluny Brown. And I'm being as quiet as I can."

"Well, I'm sorry, but it still makes a row. It wakes the Professor every morning. Can't you muffle it?"

"No," said Cluny. "It's the way it works — like Hilda breathing."

"Oh, damn," said Andrew.

He looked so put out that Cluny felt sorry for him. She cogitated.

"There's one way," she said at length. "I could just not *do* the corridor. . . ."

"Won't that get you into a row?"

"I'm always in rows," said Cluny, reassuringly. "One more won't make any odds. You needn't know anything."

Andrew regarded her with more interest.

"That's very decent of you. But why are you always in rows?"

"Mrs. Maile's training me," explained Cluny, without rancour.

"If she bullyrags, I'll speak to my mother."

Cluny had been only six weeks at Friars Carmel, but that was long enough to have taught her the unwisdom of such a course; she thought it nice of Mr. Andrew to suggest it, but also rather simple. However, the incident as a whole amused her, and as soon as she had finished upstairs she went off to discuss it with Hilda in the laundry. Hilda was ironing; her own things and Cluny's were finished, because she always did them first, while she was fresh; now she was engaged on a night-dress of Lady Carmel's. Cluny cast an eye over it, half-expecting to see a coronet or two, but no, it was perfectly plain, and rather like those still laid away in Aunt Floss's bureau. Sir Henry wore nightshirts, and Andrew blue poplin pyjamas.

"Hilda," said Cluny, "I've been talking to Mr. Andrew."

"Get along!" said Hilda admiringly.

"He's upset about the hoover in the East, on account of the Professor. What's the matter with the Professor? Is he ill? He doesn't look ill."

"He's had an operation. I shouldn't wonder if it was for gall-stones," said Hilda. "See how I've done your knickers."

She had done them beautifully, pleats from the waist and the frill all goffered. She had become very attached to Cluny, and this was her way of showing it. Admiring the result, Cluny suddenly remembered an oft-repeated injunction of her late aunt's: always have your underclothes nice, in case you get run over by a 'bus. But there seemed little danger of such an accident at Friars Carmel — even on the main road.

## II

This road, with its implication of going to the chemist's, now occupied a large place in Cluny's thoughts; for she had lost no time in extracting from Hilda and Mrs. Maile the history of the Wilsons, and it turned out to be even as tragic as she had guessed.

The facts were these. Mrs. Wilson had been born at Friars Carmel; while in service at Exeter she married a Scottish gardener, who took her to the Midlands; on his death she settled in Nottingham with her son Titus, whose brilliant career (scholarship after scholarship) there culminated in his own chemist's shop. Titus Wilson was a flourishing and a lucky man; successful in love as in all else, he became affianced to a beautiful Miss Drury. They waited for two years, methodically and happily preparing their future home; for both were prudent; and a week before the wedding Miss

Drury was injured in a traffic accident, survived four days in great pain, and died.

Titus Wilson's subsequent conduct revealed a strength of emotion unsuspected even by his mother. He was a broken man. He still ran his business efficiently, because efficiency was in his blood and bones, but ambition seemed to have died. One day about six months later he asked his mother whether she would not like to return to Devon. This had been a long-cherished wish of Mrs. Wilson's, and she said that she would. Titus did the thing thoroughly by taking her back to Friars Carmel. He deliberately buried himself. But the sale of the Nottingham business had left him sufficient capital to make a good start; besides giving Friars Carmel a better chemist's than it had ever dreamed of, he gradually acquired the custom of all the big houses round about. It was easier to send to Wilson's than to write to the Stores; where his predecessor sold corn-plasters to the servants, Titus Wilson was soon selling expensive soap to their employers. Doctors and farmers found him equally reliable in the matter of a prescription or a fertilizer; a shed behind the shop developed into a sort of agricultural branch. Almost in spite of himself, Mr. Wilson prospered. In six years he made no friends and few acquaintances, but Friars Carmel became rather proud of him.

"For sad as it all was," said Mrs. Maile sententiously, "we are very fortunate to have such a good chemist so close at hand. He is very much better than the man at Carmel."

Cluny listened to this tragic story and pitied Mr. Wilson with all her heart. She also felt very flattered by the notice he had taken of herself.

"I suppose he's hated women ever since?" she suggested hopefully.

"Certainly not. He simply pays no attention to them."

"Us be just so many images," put in Hilda, with a certain resentment. "Old Sourface, I call'n."

"He is an excellent son to his mother, and a very superior man," pronounced Mrs. Maile, "and that is quite enough about Mr. Wilson."

If she were speaking to Cluny, she might just as well have spoken to a bloodhound on the trail.

# Chapter 11

————— ≫ I ≪ —————

WHEN in London Andrew shared with John Frewen a bachelor apartment in Bloomsbury consisting of one room. It was quite large, it was about as big as the smaller box room at Friars Carmel, and chiefly remarkable for its store of old newspapers. These (a great nuisance to the landlady) were roughly filed in old cardboard boxes, or elsewhere as space permitted — six months' *Evening Standards* under John's mattress, the *New Statesman* under Andrew's — or stacked on the floor, or simply left about. When asked why they kept them all, John and Andrew replied, rather aloofly, "For collation." It was extremely interesting to see how the same item was treated in, say, the *Times* and the *News Chronicle*. ("But not a *life* interest?" said Betty innocently.) They made notes of the most striking examples, and had an idea of some day publishing their findings to prove whatever the findings proved; and as these notes too were roughly filed, or simply left about, the general effect was one of great intellectual activity. Sometimes the co-editors Box-and-Coxed it, often they were there together, and when Andrew arrived from Devonshire he found his friend already in possession. John, however, appeared surprised to see Andrew, and at once asked where was Mr. Belinski.

"At Friars, of course," said Andrew. "Working on a new book."

"You mean you've left him there?"

"Of course," said Andrew, rather impatiently. "He's perfectly all right. It was a sound scheme to get him down, but we overdid the deadly peril."

"You'll look well if you get back and find him kidnapped," said John gloomily.

He seemed to be in a gloomy mood, but since they made it a point of honour never to question each other, Andrew ignored it and went out to tea with a man who kept a left-wing bookshop. Apart from his editorial work, Andrew sometimes thought of keeping a left-wing bookshop himself, as he also thought of going into publishing proper, or making films, and a great deal of his time in London was spent eating meals, preferably on an expense account, with friends already engaged in one or other of these vocations. He returned about six and went out again, leaving John still lounging by the fire; returned finally at midnight to find his friend in precisely the same position. But this time there was a difference in his clothes. During the interval he had changed from flannels to tails. A white carnation was dying in his buttonhole. Andrew thought this strange.

"Been out?" he asked casually.

John nodded.

"Good show?"

"I haven't been to a show," said John.

Andrew poured himself a glass of beer. They didn't question each other — but he sat down on the table and waited, in case John was working up to get something off his chest. It flashed through his mind that perhaps his friend had joined the Oxford Group.

"I have just," said John Frewen, "asked Betty to marry me."

## II

Andrew put down his glass with great care, taking pains to set it in the exact middle of the table-centre.

"That was a bold act," he said. "Is she going to?"

"Don't be a damned fool. Would I be here if she were?"

"Depends how it took you," said Andrew, suddenly feeling quite bright and conversational. "You might have come back to brood on it a bit. Or you might want to give me the big news. Or—"

"Shut up," said John Frewen.

The bluntness of a friend in pain is never hurtful. Andrew poured out a second glass of beer and silently proffered it.

"You might say something," complained John.

"My dear chap, what can I say? I'm beastly sorry, if that's any use."

"It isn't. You've no idea how ghastly I feel. It's like the moment before a car smash, only going on and on. You can't imagine it."

Andrew detected a first spark of spiritual pride, which he made haste to fan.

"I can see you've taken an awful knock. What did she say?"

"Nothing much. I can't remember her exact words. Something like, 'What a fool idea, darling'—darling!—and then I asked if I could get her a taxi, and she said no, thanks, she thought she'd join up with the Mallinsons. They were at the next table, butting in all the time. The last thing I saw of her," said John bitterly, "she was doing the Lambeth Walk. Oi."

Andrew felt extraordinarily sympathetic.

"She's got the worst manners of any girl I know," he said.

"That's exactly what I think. I mean, it's not as though I were an absolute outsider. . . ."

"She ought to have felt extremely bucked. The trouble is, every one's made such an absurd fuss of her since she was about ten years old that now she's simply unbearable."

This abuse of the beloved made them both feel pleasantly judicious and detached. John Frewen was able to take a swallow of beer.

"I'll tell you what I've often thought," went on Andrew. "Betty's just the sort of girl to have a marvellous time for years and years, and then never get married at all."

"Perhaps she doesn't want to get married."

"She mayn't now, but she will. What's she to do? She hasn't any brains, she can't start a career. She'll turn into one of those haggish females who get up parties for charity balls."

For a moment they both contemplated this picture with grim satisfaction. But it didn't convince. With the best will in the world, neither could foresee any future for the Honourable Elizabeth Cream that was not brilliant, enviable, and undeserved.

Andrew's situation was now extremely trying. He had come up to London in two minds — he might propose to Betty or he might not; John Frewen's essay decided him, perhaps illogically, that he would; and having once come to this decision he was in a fever of impatience. He desired to propose to Betty immediately. Against this was the feeling that she might be in a refusing mood, and a natural reluctance to appear to be taking his place in a queue. The wench thought quite enough of herself already; to have two proposals on two consecutive days would set her up beyond bearing. (Andrew was often surprised at the clear-sightedness with which he saw Betty's faults.) However, he took the preliminary step of telephoning her, and was shaken to learn that she hadn't a free five minutes for the next week. She was rehearsing for a Pageant of Fair Women. "Good God!" exclaimed Andrew disgustedly; and only just brought himself to ask her to dinner when the beastly thing was over.

## III

Like most young and therefore self-centred persons, Andrew rarely gave a thought to scenes he had left behind, and this was especially the case when that scene was Friars Carmel. He did not wonder what was happening there without him, because he could not imagine anything happening at all. In a way this belief was justified: the life of the old house ran deep and slow, Andrew's presence was the sun on its waters, and when it was withdrawn the surface took on a uniform tint: dullness rocked like a halcyon on its tranquil bosom. Without Andrew all interests, and all conversation, suddenly narrowed, until often at table there was no conversation at all; the telephone ceased to ring, and lights were out by eleven o'clock.

But the dullness wasn't dull to Lady Carmel, waiting for her son to come back, busy with all sorts of maternal plans, and Sir Henry had just got hold of the address of a very old friend in Zanzibar. As for the Professor, his reputation for quietness was by now so well established that neither Sir Henry nor Lady Carmel ever doubted his perfect satisfaction. He missed Andrew, of course, as was only suitable, and Lady Carmel made a special effort to take tea with him every day, even if it meant coming in early from her rock-garden, or her duck pond, or her greenhouse, and Sir Henry taught him piquet. They thoroughly approved of him; and Andrew, could he have witnessed these mild amenities, would have approved also, and with an equal confidence in the general content.

In point of fact Mr. Belinski rapidly became so desperate as to throw a copy of *Gulliver's Travels* from the stable window and hit Cluny Brown on the head.

"Hi!" called Cluny, naturally indignant. "What d'you think you're doing?"

Mr. Belinski did not even apologize. Cluny promptly picked up the book and shied it back. This relieved her feelings, and as she was not really hurt annoyance rapidly gave place to curiosity. On closer inspection she saw that the Professor was seriously put out.

"What's biting you?" asked Cluny kindly.

"I have the wind up," stated Adam Belinski.

Cluny looked at him uncertainly. Though his English was so good, he did sometimes make mistakes, and for a moment she wondered whether the distress were physical. But he suddenly stretched himself with great vigour, not at all like a man in pain.

"Do you mean you're frightened of something?" asked Cluny incredulously.

"Of everything," said Mr. Belinski. "I am afraid to the marrow of my bones, and *of* the marrow of my bones, which I feel gradually turning to a white soup. I feel my brain turning to sweetbreads. I am losing my virility. If you were to boil me down as I stand, you would get a cup of chicken-broth. You observe how all my metaphors come from the table. That is another symptom. I am always eating. If you have not noticed the change in me, you must be blind."

"Well, you haven't got any fatter," said Cluny. "Mrs. Maile was remarking on it."

He looked at her with dislike.

"You are probably one of the stupidest girls in the world, which with a face like that is little short of dishonest. If you cannot understand me, at least do not make idiotic remarks. I talk to you because I have no alternative, as I would to a black cat."

"Now I'll say something," retorted Cluny. "If I was a cat, I wouldn't listen."

Mr. Belinski took no notice of this whatever. He put his hands on the window-sill and leaned out, as though addressing a mob; and in spite of her veiled threat Cluny obligingly sat down on the steps in a mob of one.

"What you are now privileged to hear," said Mr. Belinski loudly, "is a statement of the soul. You do not talk about your souls in this country, but to Poles they are important. Here I am, then, and my soul with me. Instead of bread and black coffee we consume the *vol-au-vents* of Mrs. Maile. We sleep between fine sheets, and our clothes are brushed by Mr. Syrett. Do not mistake me: we have no contempt for luxury: luxury is a fine thing. But it should not be daily. We pray, give us this day our daily bread — not our daily *caneton à la presse*. Luxury should be the *détente* after work, the riot after abstinence, one should not become used to it."

"You're wrong about one thing," interrupted Cluny. "It isn't Mrs. Maile who does the cooking, it's Cook."

"Be quiet."

"You may as well get it straight."

"Be quiet! There is also," continued Mr. Belinski, "the luxury of being always with the well-bred, with people who give way, who consider one's pride, are delicate, till one no longer has need of one's weapons and throws them away. Till one begins to think, where else shall I find people so kind, so gentle? Where else shall I find this luxury I am used to? And then, if one is lucky, one gets the wind up. Cluny Brown, I am getting used to being here."

There was a long silence. Cluny, who had listened with great attention, nodded her head.

"That's just how I feel about being a parlour-maid."

"You are quite impossible," said Mr. Belinski.

"But it *is* the same," persisted Cluny. "Mrs. Maile's been here thirty years, not that I suppose she wanted anything else, she hankers a bit after Torquay, but that's just talk. But look at me. I didn't want to go into service. I stood up to Uncle Arn and everything. And now it doesn't seem so bad. I'm getting used to it."

"You don't matter," said Belinski gloomily.

"I matter to me."

"That is not the point. I matter because of my work, and I am not working. It is like living with a wolf. I ask you, what am I to do?"

Cluny heaved a sigh. She knew he wasn't asking her really, he was asking Fate, the universe, his own Polish soul; but she did her best. And at least she was practical.

"If you're stuck for your fare, I can lend you a quid."

Belinski looked at her, threw back his head, and uttered a melodramatic crow of laughter, like a man laughing in the face of the ironic gods. Then he looked at Cluny again, and said hastily: —

"I will not take it now, but if I need it, I will ask."

## IV

Cluny's contribution to this debate was not entirely ingenuous. "I'm getting used to it," said she; in truth she was not so much getting used to service as ignoring it. Her domestic duties simply formed the background to a variety of interesting preoccupations, of which Mr. Belinski was not even the chief. (For instance, the above-reported tête-à-tête, which to many a well-bred, personable young woman would have been an event of the first water, to be brooded upon, kept secret, perhaps entered in a diary, registered with Cluny Brown as a passing chat.) The focus of her mind was the tragic chemist; she thought of Mr. Wilson all the more because she could not see him, whereas she saw Mr. Belinski every day — made his bed, sorted his linen, watched him eat his dinner. Titus Wilson had the attraction of the inaccessible; and to Cluny's intense chagrin, looked like keeping it.

Because the next step in their acquaintance should obviously have been a chance encounter in the lanes: Miss Brown surprised, Mr. Wilson deferential; request from Mr. Wilson to accompany Miss Brown on her walk, and at the end of it an appointment for the week after. But these moves, as well-known and respectable in domestic circles as the Ruy Lopez opening at chess, were made impossible by the circumstance that Cluny's afternoon off, Wednesday, and Mr. Wilson's early closing, Thursday, did not coincide.

There is nothing so intractable as a calendar.

Still, shops are open to all. What need to wait on chance? Disguised as a customer, Cluny could revisit her glimpse of the moon without any loss of dignity, and indeed did so on the Wednesday following. But she took Roddy with her, and dogs were not allowed in. There was a drinking-bowl for them by the step, punctiliously filled with clean water, but not even the Colonel's Roddy might cross the threshold. Cluny had to tie him up outside, and his offended howls almost drowned her request for toothpaste. No conversation was possible, and Cluny got out of the shop as fast as she could and made for open country without — literally — a word to throw to a dog.

But it was Roddy, after all, who set matters in train again. Actually upon a Thursday, the generous animal came lolloping over to Friars Carmel on his own initiative, waving his beautiful tail, leaping up at Hilda and Cluny, and knocking down a jar of preserved plums which the former happened to have in her hand. The two girls looked at each other in dismay.

"Talk o' bulls in china shops!" cried Hilda. "Cluny Brown, now you be for it!"

"He's got to go back," said Cluny desperately, "or they'll never let me have him again. Roddy, go home!"

Roddy waved his tail and bounded towards the pantry. Cluny caught his collar just in time.

"I'll have to take him back," she said. "Mailey and Syrett won't be down for an hour. I'll run all the way."

"What about Cook's plums? They be out of the store-room, and Mailey's got the key."

Cluny thought rapidly. They had the kitchen to themselves, all three seniors being engaged, as was usual at that hour, in taking their rests.

"There's a jar on our window-sill with moss in it. Wash it out and put the plums in that. The floor's quite clean. If there's not enough juice, use the pineapple left over from our dinner. If the lid won't fit, say you opened it ready."

This masterly plan filled Hilda with admiration, and she at once rushed upstairs. Cluny, still grabbing Roddy's collar with one hand, removed her apron with the other and rushed out. They ran all the way to the Hall — across fields, over banks, through hedges, into the stables, where Cluny hustled Roddy inside his pen, secured the gate, embraced him over it,

and left him. Halfway back her wind not unnaturally failed;
she had to sit down a minute on the crosspiece of a stile,
and while she was sitting there Mr. Wilson came along the
lane.

## V

"Good afternoon," said Mr. Wilson, enquiringly. He seemed
to know it wasn't her day off.

"Good afternoon," panted Cluny. "I've been on an errand."
This was better than saying she'd been illicitly returning the
Colonel's Labrador, but it put her, as she at once realized,
under the suspicion of loitering. It was strange how Mr.
Wilson's presence seemed to act like a magnifying-glass on
the least unevenness of conduct. "I ran," added Cluny.

"You appear to be out of breath," said Mr. Wilson.

He approached the stile. He wore a raincoat and a soft cap,
both of excellent quality, and beautifully polished black boots.
Cluny felt very conscious of her own dishevelment.

"It's pretty round here, isn't it?" she said nervously.

"A very beautiful countryside. It must be a great pleasure
to you when you go walking."

"I go a walk every Wednesday afternoon."

So far their conversation had followed the conventional
path, presenting no difficulty to either. Now they were pulled
up, they had to make a détour.

"We close on Thursday," said the chemist.

"Yes, I know," said Cluny.

"Otherwise we might have chanced to meet."

"It's nice to have some one to walk with."

"Though I am not," continued Mr. Wilson, "a very gay
companion for a young lady like yourself."

Cluny hesitated. It was impossible to contradict him, and

equally impossible to explain that in this lack of gaiety — or rather in the cause of it — lay his chief charm. She said, rather uncertainly: —

"I hate people who pretend to be gay when they aren't."

"There I agree with you. But natural cheerfulness is a very good thing," insisted Mr. Wilson.

"You can't be cheerful when you've nothing to be cheerful about. I mean, the Lord loves a cheerful giver, and all that, but if a thing's just taken, you haven't a chance. I mean," plunged Cluny, "when Aunt Floss died, Uncle Arn never pretended to be merry and bright, and no one thought the worse of him. . . ."

She kept her eyes on the distance as she spoke, but without looking at him she could feel his sudden rigidity. He stood so still, for so long, that she wished with all her heart she had held her tongue.

"You'll have been hearing about me in the village?" said Mr. Wilson at last.

"No, not in the village," said Cluny quickly. "From Mrs. Maile. I'm sorry if — if you didn't want to be talked about."

"A man's private affairs are naturally not a subject for discussion."

"I'm sorry," said Cluny again. She was indeed; she drooped with sorrow. The chemist, glancing down at her, said more kindly: —

"I doubt you meant no harm."

This slight encouragement somewhat revived her. Swiftly, before the subject was closed for ever, Cluny said: —

"I do think you were wonderful, leaving everything and coming to live here just because your mother wanted to."

"It was a matter of indifference to me where I lived. I was naturally glad to gratify her wish."

Cluny stole a long look at him. He had relaxed again, he was leaning easily against the stile; behind the formality of his speech she now suddenly divined, not strain, but a steady, imperturbable secureness. If you give up enough, what remains is safe. . . .

"You're all right now, aren't you?" asked Cluny impulsively.

Mr. Wilson nodded. Silence fell between them. Half an hour must have passed since Cluny fled out of the kitchen, Hilda was waiting for her, but she could not tear herself away. Still less could she have put into words the feeling that held her at the stile; as though, a traveller, she had stumbled upon the frontier of a new land, wherein all was safe, ordered, and indestructible, and which she greatly desired to explore. . . .

"Blest," said Mr. Wilson — so suddenly that Cluny was quite startled, especially as he paused a moment before going on, measuring out the lines in a deep, solemn voice: —

> "Blest, who can unconcernedly find
> Hours, days, and years slide soft away
> In health of body, peace of mind,
> Quiet by day."

When he had finished, when Cluny's ear could no longer hold the last vibration of the last word, she drew a long breath.

"That's beautiful," she said softly.

Mr. Wilson stood up, away from the stile. He was smiling, though sternly, though not at her.

"It took a deal o' learning," said Mr. Wilson, and walked on down the lane.

## VI

When the heir is absent, the great house drowses: such is the law, for great houses and the heirs to them, all the world over. But neither Cluny, nor Mr. Wilson, nor Adam Belinski owed any real allegiance to Friars Carmel, and things went on happening to them whether Andrew was there, or not.

# Chapter 12

------ »»» I «««  ------

ANDREW in London was distressed to find himself thinking at least as much about Betty Cream as about the European situation. She was incomparably the less important subject, but she had somehow got into his mind and wandered about there like a child in a laboratory. He also blamed John Frewen, who had abandoned himself to chagrin, refused to discuss Czechoslovakia, and (against all their principles) required constant sympathy. Andrew was reduced to the banality of telling him to take it like a man, to which John replied that he was taking it like a man, and not like a sexless intellectual. All in all they were not very comfortable together, in eight days they did not collate a single paragraph, and Andrew also suffered from a slight feeling of treachery with regard to his own intentions. This did not prevent him from profiting by his friend's experience: from internal evidence he gathered that John had taken Betty to Claridge's, a place where her attention had always many claims on it: Andrew took her to the Moulin Bleu. John had peacocked forth in tails; Andrew wore his usual tweed jacket. He did not exactly intend to treat Betty rough, but he wasn't going to make too much fuss of her. "No glamour," thought Andrew sternly; and as a consequence behaved with such unnatural boorishness that Betty at once guessed what was in the wind.

"Darling," said Andrew, as they finished their coffee, "would you like to marry me next month?"

"No, thank you," said Betty. "What a fool idea, darling."

"It's my mother's, actually," explained Andrew, "and when you look at it, it's rather sound. I say, 'There's going to be a war.' She says, 'All right, get an heir.' Their generation at least has its feet on the ground."

"Well, I don't belong to it," said Betty. "If there's going to be war, I shall be belligerent."

"Driving Generals round in cars," said Andrew sardonically.

"Better me than an able-bodied male. What about you?"

Andrew hesitated. He had a private idea that in the event of war he would do something rather special, he did not know exactly what, but his fluent French and German and his knowledge of Europe put him, he felt, in a special class. If he didn't quite see himself hanging round the Reichstag in a false beard, no more did he see himself on the barrack-square. There was something about Betty's clear and inquisitive gaze, however, that prevented his explaining this, and in the end he merely shrugged his shoulders and got the bill.

"Let's go somewhere and dance," said Betty.

Not without satisfaction, Andrew indicated his jacket.

"We can't. Wrong clothes."

"Oh, don't be so hide-bound," said Betty sharply. "You're just like John, all you can think of is Claridge's." (The injustice of this remark annoyed Andrew very much.) "We can go to Covent Garden, or Hammersmith, and at least there'll be room to move."

She stood up. Andrew held her coat, and as she slipped into it let his hands rest a moment on her shoulders; and this brief contact had the effect of making him forget all her worthless qualities.

"And if there isn't a war?" he asked.

"You won't be in such a hurry to reproduce your kind."

"The offer still stands."

Betty turned to look at him, brushing his chin with her golden topknot.

"Andrew," she said, "do you notice that out of all our crowd, we're the only ones who talk about war? John does too, sometimes, but no one else. Why is it?"

"I don't know. Unless we've got more sense."

"Then I wish we hadn't. It's rather blighting."

She walked quickly towards the door, too quickly, for she had to stand there waiting while Andrew got his change, and he annoyed her by being so slow. She couldn't see herself as he did, in the moment when she turned and set her heels together and lifted her impatient chin. Her full, tightly waisted coat was crimson, opening on the primrose of a dress that frothed into ruffles at the neck, and out of the deep and pale colours her golden head rose brighter than a Lent-lily. Against the drabness of the little restaurant, she startled: not Andrew alone was held at gaze. But Betty was used to being stared at, and in fact liked it. She decided to give the waiters a treat, and bent on each in turn — young Mario, grizzled Pierre, the aged Bertrand — her most angelic smile.

"I love this place," she said clearly, blessing them. "We'll come again. . . ."

But as soon as they got outside she ceased being an angel and baited Andrew so unmercifully that he heard the midnight chimes alone, as he tramped round and round round and round, round and round Bloomsbury Square.

## II

The next day was Sunday. This made little difference to Andrew and John Frewen, who were not church-goers: they had breakfast at the usual time, which was in any case late, read all the papers, and by lunchtime had usually slight headaches from sitting over a gas-fire. If Sunday, in Blooms-bury, had any character at all, it was that of being the most characterless day of the week. At Friars Carmel, on the other hand, it meant sausages and kidneys at nine instead of bacon and eggs at half past eight, and the car round for church at a quarter to eleven, and the Vicar to midday dinner, and an afternoon of peculiar stillness — in fact, every moment of the day, until Sir Henry at last pulled down the weights of the grandfather clock, was as strongly impregnated with Sunday-ishness as Lady Carmel's linen cupboard with lavender. Friars Carmel kept up its standards — in every respect save one, and for that one backsliding Mrs. Maile honestly and remorse-fully took the blame.

Every week, as Mrs. Maile took her place in church, she in-stinctively glanced at the pew behind. The purpose of this glance had once been to review the maids' Sunday hats: not a new flower, not a turned ribbon, but caught and trembled under her eye; now it rested on empty air. Once five heads at least had been bent to her inspection; now she couldn't get even Hilda and Cluny to church. They had every excuse, they had too much to do — but Mrs. Maile felt that were she still in her prime, she would have got them there somehow . . .

Another point troubled her. They had too much to do, but were they doing it? Mrs. Maile was as reluctant to turn her back on them as a lion-tamer upon a cage of lions. When she thought of Cluny and Hilda at large in the empty house (for she put no confidence in Cook, and little in Syrett) it was all she could do to keep her mind on the service. Not that the housekeeper suspected them of prying — certainly not of pilfering: they were good honest girls. Required to put her suspicion into words, Mrs. Maile would have said that she feared they might be playing billiards. This really imaginative piece of deduction, from what she knew of Cluny's character and influence, surprised even Mrs. Maile. It could not but distract her; and they were often at the Second Lesson before she got her thoughts under control.

As a matter of fact, Hilda's and Cluny's favourite employment during this unguarded hour was the comparatively innocent one of laying traps for Mr. Syrett to find out if he really wore a wig. (Their ruses were too numerous to detail, and all failures. They never, though they often planned to, applied the crucial test of a lighted match.) They never went into the billiard room, and until the day after Andrew's rejection by Miss Cream Cluny had never been into the library. On that Sunday morning, for the first time, she set her ear to the door just as the Vicar gave out his text; softly opened it, as Lady Carmel put away her spectacles; as Sir Henry (reverently) closed his eyes, she slipped in. A Sabbath calm enveloped the great room; secure in the virtue of others, Cluny embarked on her quest.

It was no easy one. Gazing on the thousands and thousands of books — they looked to her like millions and millions — Cluny felt her heart sink. She had none of the library user's technique: to find four lines, in all that, struck her simply as looking for a needle in a haystack. However, she stepped to the nearest shelf and pulled out the first volume that came to hand: *A Sportsman in the Levant*. It was solid prose. So were the next four. But the sixth (*My Garden in Spain*) cheated:

it had verses at the head of each chapter. Cluny read one or two of them in an unhopeful sort of way, moved down the shelves and found herself up to the neck in Shakspere, Byron, Milton, Browning — poetry every word of it, pages and pages, books and books, the glory of English literature tight-packed and appalling. Some spirits indeed might have soared; might at a verse, a line, have taken fire and lived from that moment in a changed universe; but not Cluny's. Her spirit, omnivorous of experience, had no use for experience at second hand, even were that hand Shakspere's. Only the living voice could catch her attention long enough to inflame it. If she pulled out book after book, opened and quickly shut them, it was simply with a gambler's irrational hope; and she had just flung herself down in the very attitude of the penniless rake — legs out-stretched, hands thrust deep in her apron pockets — when Mr. Belinski quietly entered the room.

He looked at her in surprise. Cluny, without moving, gazed morosely back.

"What the hell are you doing?" enquired Mr. Belinski.

Whacked as she was, Cluny just managed to counter.

"Why aren't you at church?"

"Because I am a wicked man. If you are contemplating suicide, they will be back in about fifteen minutes."

Cluny wearily pulled herself out of the chair and stared down at the heap of books. Then she glanced at Mr. Belinski, who quickly and accurately read her mind.

"No, they will not think it is I," he said firmly. "If necessary I shall deny it. What were you looking for?"

"A piece of poetry."

"Any piece?"

"No, of course not. A piece I heard."

Mr. Belinski looked at the catholic array at her feet and lifted his eyebrows.

"I see you have a long task. You don't know the author?"

"Not unless —" Cluny was suddenly struck by a new thought — "not unless Mr. Wilson made it up himself. And I don't think he did, because he said he'd learnt it. It began 'Blest.'"

"Blest pair of sirens," suggested Mr. Belinski.

Cluny shook her head.

"No. Something about hours days and years slip something by."

Mr. Belinski reflected a moment, and to Cluny's amazement and admiration repeated the whole stanza.

"However did you know?" she marvelled.

"It is the second and less quoted verse of a very famous poem," said Mr. Belinski.

> "Thus let me live unseen, unknown,
> Thus unlamented let me die;
> Steal from the world, and not a stone
> Tell where I lie.

"The man who wrote it would do anything to make himself conspicuous."

Cluny did not quite take this in. To her a piece of poetry was something that existed in a vacuum.

"Would you write it down for me?" she asked. "I want to learn it."

Mr. Belinski obligingly went to a table and did so. Cluny followed, like a child following a Punch and Judy, to watch over his shoulder and admire again as the neat lines ran out of his pen. For the first time he had really impressed her.

"I do think you're clever!" she said sincerely.

"I am, very clever," replied Mr. Belinski, without looking up. "Who is Mr. Wilson?"

"He's the chemist."

"If he is endeavouring to form your mind with this sort of stuff, he must be a great fool."

"He isn't!" cried Cluny indignantly.

"Do you mean he isn't trying to form your mind, or he isn't a fool?"

"Neither. And it isn't stuff, you said yourself it was famous. I think it's beautiful."

"If you had a smattering of education you would realize that perfection of form can give validity to any sentiment, however preposterous. 'Steal from the world' my foot," said Mr. Belinski colloquially.

But Cluny, without paying much attention, took the finished copy and folded it very carefully and put it in her apron pocket. Mr. Belinski watched her with a peculiar expression.

"Don't you want to know who wrote it?"

"Is he alive?"

"No, he's been dead about two centuries."

"Oh," said Cluny, at once losing interest. "Well, thank you very much."

"If there's anything else I can do for you, let me know."

"Then you might just put those books back," said Cluny. "I ought to be cleaning the bath."

# Chapter 13

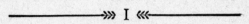

## I

THE RODDY episode taught Hilda and Cluny a useful lesson: that between three and four in the afternoon it was quite easy for one or other of them to slip out on their private affairs, and no one the wiser. Hilda ran out to see Gary: her mother's cottage was on the hither side of the village, which made things easy for her, but if Cluny wanted to go (for instance) to the chemist's, she had to run all the way, and arrived looking as though she had come for an antidote to poison. If there were any one in the shop Cluny looked through the door, paused as though she had left her purse behind (or as though the poison must by now have worked, and there was no hope) and made off again. These proceedings, in so small a village, could not fail to attract attention, and Mrs. Maile received several unexpected enquiries as to the state of health at Friars Carmel; but before she caught up with their origin Cluny had for once found Mr. Wilson disengaged. She entered, and asked for cough drops.

"Is it for yourself?" asked Mr. Wilson.

"No, for Hilda," said Cluny. This was more or less true; Hilda had no cough, but she liked anything to chew or suck. Mr. Wilson selected a moderately priced brand (sixpence) and wrapped the package with his usual care. He was very much the chemist; so different from the Mr. Wilson of the lane that Cluny had to take a firm grip on her resolution. She did so.

"Will there be anything else?" asked Mr. Wilson.

"Yes," said Cluny. "Listen": and standing with her hands behind her back she repeated from beginning to end the whole of Mr. Alexander Pope's verses on the subject of Solitude.

"Well, well!" said Mr. Wilson. He was obviously more moved than his features, so long set in lines of endurance only, were able to express. They worked to a smile. "And where did you find it?" he asked.

"In the library. At least, I didn't find it myself." said Cluny honestly, "I asked the Professor."

"And then you got it by heart?"

"Yes," said Cluny.

He did not ask her why; the reason was obvious, she had done it to please him. And Cluny could have done nothing in the world to please Mr. Wilson more. She brought him, as she might have brought a bunch of flowers, an intellectual achievement; and the fact that he guessed it to be about her first filled Mr. Wilson with a pedagogue's delight.

"You've got it perfect," he said solemnly, "and it's no an easy piece. You've a good brain in that shaggy head."

Cluny blushed furiously. It was a moment of exquisite embarrassment to both of them, and fortunately a moment was no longer than it lasted. The shop door opened, in came a customer, and Cluny fled.

On the way back, however, she stopped to buy herself two snoods, one black, one scarlet, with bows to tie on top. With her usual generosity she gave the black snood to Hilda (as well as the cough drops) and Hilda was so pleased with it that the next afternoon she ran off to the village on her own account to change it for a scarlet one like Cluny's. Thus adorned they appeared in the servants' hall after dinner, and were met by universal reprobation. Mr. Syrett said they looked like ponies at a Show, Mrs. Maile said she had never seen such a thing, and even Cook came out of her habitual silence with a reference to Christmas crackers.

"But they're to keep us tidy!" protested Cluny.

"Your caps keep you tidy," retorted Mrs. Maile.

Mr. Syrett, gazing critically at Hilda, observed that on second thought she looked not so much like a pony as like a plum-pudding with holly on top. Hilda, always easily swayed, at once struck her colours; but Cluny sat defiant, with cheeks flaming scarlet as her bow.

"Cluny Brown, go upstairs and put your cap on," ordered Mrs. Maile.

Cluny set her lips together. She did not quite dare to say, "I won't," but her expression said it for her.

"She'd better go upstairs and stay there," said Mr. Syrett.

Cluny instantly rose. It was ten o'clock, a face-saving circumstance welcome to all parties.

"Good night, all," said Cluny.

She cast an urgent glance at Hilda, but Hilda had just got hold of *Home Chat,* and until she had read the correspondence there was no shifting her. She bent her snoodless noddle over the page, pretending not to see or hear. Cluny stalked out — taking by error not the door to the back way, but that to the main hall. Dignity forbade her to return, and after a moment's hesitation she proceeded defiantly up the broad shallow treads of the great staircase. She hoped she wouldn't meet any one, but didn't much care if she did; and this was lucky, for there on the landing stood Mr. Belinski.

He was standing motionless, as though he had been watching her come up, and Cluny (in a mood to anticipate criticism) prepared to meet some comment on her illicit presence. His first words, however, were unexpected.

"Surely it is the male bird," remarked Mr. Belinski, "who changes plumage?"

Cluny stopped short and glared at him.

"What d'you mean by that?" she snapped.

"In the spring, in the season of courtship, the male bird produces finer feathers, in order to attract the hen. Have you never seen a pigeon?"

"Are you referring to anything to do with me?" asked Cluny coldly.

"I refer to your very becoming headdress. You should wear it all the year round. How is Mr. Wilson?" asked this odious man.

"Quite well, thank you."

"I hope he appreciated your poetic *tour de force*."

"I don't know what a *tour de force* is."

"Any unusual enterprise, frequently undertaken with the object of arousing admiration, or love. But if he just wants to make you recite, he might as well buy a parrot."

Cluny pushed past him — she had to, for he would not move — and swept along the corridor with an air of icy disdain. Or such was her intention; but when she reached her room, and looked at herself in the glass, and saw her flushed face and eyes big with tears, misgiving overcame her. She thought she looked just like a jugged hare.

"Who do you think you are?" demanded Cluny of her reflection; and pulled off her bright adornment and threw it on the floor.

But before getting into bed she picked it up again. It hadn't been bought, after all, for the benefit of Mrs. Maile, or

Syrett, or the Professor. Burrowing her head into the pillow, Cluny summoned up a kinder face than any of theirs — a face lined and resolute, sober, inapt to smile, but neither mocking nor severe.

## II

Fortunate Cluny, to have such a face to turn to in distress! Fortunate Cluny, in the volatility of her spirits! She was never down for long. Had she been drowning, she would have come up not three times, but nine. (Like the black cat Mr. Belinski once called her.) Andrew in London, with a greater trouble to bear, was also far less resilient. If he stayed in town a week longer it was without enjoyment, and chiefly for the purpose of showing Betty Cream how little her refusal had affected him.

He did this by ringing her up and asking her to lunch or dinner at very short notice, and then ringing off again almost before she had time to explain a previous engagement — or even time to accept. On the one occasion when Betty rang up him, he perversely assumed she wanted John Frewen, who without the least pride grabbed the receiver and the consequent privilege of escorting Betty to a movie. Andrew met them after it (as though by chance) and they all had supper together. If the company of two rejected suitors had any effect on Betty, she did not show it; practically every young man she went out with had proposed to her at one time or another, and she never let it make any difference. (This attitude, sometimes known as having your cake and eating it, occasionally drew unkind comment from young women.) Betty tucked into creamed haddock and contributed her usual carefree observations with the greatest friendliness; John

Frewen basked in her mere presence; but Andrew was so struck by the hollowness of life in general, that the next day he went home.

Leaving his bags at the station, he walked the six miles to Friars Carmel. His spirits were now low but calm, for he had come to a decision: he had decided to put Betty finally out of his mind. She was incurably frivolous, and incurably shallow; without setting up to be anything special himself, Andrew could not but see that she was unworthy of him. The only wonder was that he had ever given her a serious thought. "I suppose every man makes a fool of himself once," reflected Andrew — perhaps optimistically; and at least he had had the excuse of extreme youth. When he first saw Betty, at a May Week Ball, he had been no more than twenty: one ages a great deal between twenty and twenty-three. Moreover, she had been wearing a white frock, and Betty in white was an admitted knock-out. The second time, on the river, she wore a floppy sort of hat, which undeniably suited her. His infatuation had been perfectly natural, and the fact that it had lasted three years was a tribute rather to his own character than to hers. He had thought seriously of her, in fact, because his was a serious mind.

Serious and calm, therefore, drained of all passion, Andrew reached Friars Carmel and met his mother in the hall. Lady Carmel was carrying a large china swan, which she had just unearthed from the back of a cupboard, and which she proposed to fill with wild cherry, if it did not leak. She set it down in order to embrace her son, and as Andrew glanced at it over her shoulder a wry notion struck him: that there, aptly materialized, was his own emotional lot. For some moments he did not hear a word his mother said: he was too overwhelmed by what was practically a portent. The hard white

china mimicking soft plumage, the rigid pinions that would
never answer to a breeze, the hollow body and moveless eye
— the whole a mere simulacrum of something lovely and alive:
such would his own life be. Andrew suddenly saw himself,
a very old man without a heart, doddering around like a character in one of Chekhov's plays. Or possibly Ibsen's.

"Andrew!" repeated Lady Carmel. "Did you have a nice
time?"

"Splendid," said Andrew.

"How is John?"

"John's splendid."

"I suppose you didn't see Cynthia Duff-Graham?"

"Is she in town?"

"Well, she was, dear, but only for two days, on her way to
visit in Kent. So the Colonel's all alone, but I shall ask him
to lunch anyway, and then he'll ask us back. That's two
things," said Lady Carmel. "If the weather warms we might
have a picnic —"

"Darling," said Andrew, "what on earth are you talking
about?"

"About the week after next, dear. There didn't seem time
to get up a proper house-party, but I've asked Elizabeth
Cream."

Andrew sat down on the chest beside the swan. He felt
as though he had received a sudden blow, below the belt. The
monstrous news shattered at a stroke all his hardly won peace
of mind. (The china swan in smithereens.) It upset all his
calculations. And then another thought, or blow, struck him:
when had the invitation been sent?

"Mother, when did you ask her?"

"Soon after you'd left, dear."

Andrew made a hasty calculation. Between his arrival in

London and the night of his proposing just a week had elapsed. It was possible, it was probable, that Betty had even then received the invitation. What was not probable, knowing her habits, was that she had even yet replied to it. But he had to know.

"I don't suppose you've heard from her?"

"Yes, dear, I have — though only just." Lady Carmel smiled indulgently. "I heard from her yesterday."

"Do you mean she's *coming?*"

"But that's what I'm telling you, dear! She's coming next Friday week!"

Andrew was dumbfounded. The facts, it seemed, were beyond dispute; they were only incredible. Only the night before he had bidden Betty farewell — not formally, of course, not sentimentally, but in so many words. "I'm going back to Friars," he had told her, "I don't suppose I'll be seeing you for some time." And Betty had smiled. She hadn't actually said anything, he remembered, in either agreement or denial — which didn't alter the deceitfulness of her conduct. The deceitfulness of it! To stand there smiling, letting him say good-bye to her, when all the time she knew that within a couple of weeks they would be under the same roof! What the devil was the meaning of it? Or was there no meaning at all, beyond sheer mischief-making and an innate love of devious ways? Considering Betty's character as a whole, Andrew decided that this was probably the correct answer.

His eye lighted upon the swan; but it no longer reminded him of his own hollow life. It reminded him of Leda, who had fallen for a bird, of Helen, who had brought down the towers of Troy. He thought that Betty belonged to the same race.

"I'm sorry, Mother," he said aloud, "but I'm afraid I shan't be here."

"You won't be here!" Lady Carmel stared at him. "But, my dear boy —"

"I've got to go up to town again. I've a lot to do."

For a moment Lady Carmel paused; then, as once before, made her unanswerable point.

"But I have invited her."

"My being in town needn't stop her coming."

"It would look extremely rude," said Lady Carmel firmly. "She is invited as your friend. I know you are very worried about the fate of the country, Andrew — but that is no reason for losing your manners."

Andrew looked at the china swan, and wished he could wring its neck.

# Chapter 14

WHENEVER ANDREW returned to Friars Carmel, after however brief an absence, he had always to struggle against a rather disturbing sensation. He could describe it only as Lord-of-the-Manorishness. Convinced that he felt more at home in Bloomsbury; frequently upsetting his mother by saying the whole place ought to be turned into a guest-house for miners — Andrew nevertheless felt a strong desire that Friars Carmel should remain exactly as it was. (He disliked even the most trifling changes: once when Lady Carmel altered the arrangement of the drawing-room, Andrew walked round it all evening like an uneasy dog, refusing to settle; until Lady Carmel intuitively decided that she liked the old arrangement best.) The simple explanation, that he had a lot of his father in him, disturbed Andrew even more: much as he respected many of Sir Henry's qualities, Andrew could not but realize that in the modern world Sir Henry was as much a survival as the platypus — and that in fact only inherited property (Friars Carmel) enabled him to survive at all. Here Andrew did his father an injustice: simple, willing and conscientious, Sir Henry would have made a happy carpenter; but it was quite true that he had gone through life without ever realizing the narrowness of his pleasant path. Andrew realized it very clearly; he saw, for himself, that path narrow into nothingness; and if the day of the squire were over — what was he, Andrew, doing with Lord-of-the-Manorish feelings?

They were a sort of moral appendix. He was suffering from a moral appendicitis.

He was also suffering from unrequited love, and a growing conviction that the object of it was coming to Friars Carmel from purely sadistic motives.

Andrew, in short, was in a mood where he had to discuss himself with some one, and the obvious person was the Professor. (He did not know it, but it was as Lord of the Manor that he had brought Belinski to Friars Carmel: as his grandfather had domiciled a stray Nihilist, and his great-grandfather a French prisoner.) The morning after his return he wandered off to the stables to see whether Belinski was working, and found him in the yard watching Sir Henry mount Golden Boy.

Sir Henry's promenades on horseback were now few and far between, partly because he resented his diminished powers, partly because he felt it so deuced hard to leave Ernest Beer behind. (The last time hounds met in the neighbourhood it was said that the two old men had gone out to look at them ride-and-tie, and no one who knew Sir Henry disbelieved the story.) He had to mount now from a block, the groom standing watchful at the horse's head; Sir Henry heaved up his stiff bulk and came down in the saddle light as a lad.

"Sorry I can't mount ye," he said to Belinski. "You should ha' been here ten years ago."

Ernest Beer muttered something under his breath and went to open the yard gate. Sir Henry gathered up his reins. They folded like ribbons; every inch of leather, saddle, girths, head harness, gleamed from years of rubbing; on Golden Boy's quarters light rippled like watered silk.

"You're in good trim, sir," said Andrew.

Sir Henry grunted, and took Golden Boy through the gate and turned him into the lane without a break in the smooth rhythm of his pace. The two young men followed and ranged alongside; they had no difficulty in keeping up.

"I don't like leaving old Ernest," complained Sir Henry, as the gate shut behind him. "One time we were out together four days a week. What d'you think of *that,* Professor?"

He flicked up with his whip towards a great barn, now empty since he had ceased to farm in the slump after 1918. Belinski looked at it seriously.

"It is magnificent. I have never seen a thatched roof on so large a building."

"Wheat-straw," said Sir Henry proudly. "Grew it myself, sold the grain. That's the sort of thing this lad ought to be occupying himself with."

For some reason Andrew remembered Cluny's complaint about not being allowed a dog.

"It is altogether admirable," said Belinski.

Sir Henry considered this remark showed uncommon sense for a foreigner, but as his wife was training him not to give such thoughts utterance, he merely grunted again and slightly increased his pace. He did not really want company. In a few minutes Andrew and Belinski found themselves left behind; they halted, and watched Sir Henry ride off with very similar expressions.

"Old English," said the Professor suddenly. "I know that is very banal, but I cannot help it. It is what comes into my mind every time I see your father."

"Nothing would please him better," said Andrew. There was a rather long pause. "Do you think I ought to imitate him?"

"Could you?"

"No," said Andrew honestly. "He's good. I don't believe he's ever had a mean thought, or told a lie, or taken advantage of any one, in all his life. On the other hand, his life's been pretty easy. He's had literally everything he wanted. But now he'd like me to come home and live down here and take over, and he's a bit puzzled and worried because I don't."

They were standing by the entrance to a field, where the green verge broadened into a small bay of worn turf, that under the hedge on either side grew long and thick, mixed with primrose clumps and a few late-flowering violets. Belinski sat down on the grass like a tripper and hooked his hands round his knees.

"It is very nice here," he said amiably.

"That grass is probably damp. The point is, my father's idea of taking over is . . . getting back. He still thinks that hunting four days a week is a sufficient occupation. Possibly he thinks I could take in the home farm again. And if you tell him all that finished a hundred years ago, he can't believe it, because he's always managed to keep a hundred years out of date himself."

Belinski sighed. The soft air was as usual making him feel sleepy; he did not want to talk sense. But Andrew continued to stand over him, with a stern impatient face, until he pulled himself together.

"I think that if you stayed here long, you would find that sort of life very agreeable. After all, it is your national ideal — since you do not care for women."

"I don't see the connection," said Andrew, disconcerted.

"But surely it is obvious? I have so often thought how in all English art the place of women is taken by landscape. Your poetry is full of it, you are a nation of landscape painters. In other countries a man spends his fortune on a mistress; here you marry a fortune to save your estates. *En revanche,* the ladies have their flower-gardens. You yourself have travelled abroad, you take an interest in politics and so on, you feel yourself one of the new restless generation; but you are fighting against the landscape all the time."

There was enough truth in this to make it difficult for Andrew to reply. He said, rather pedantically: —

"What about the industrial revolution?"

"Oh, that!" Belinski shrugged. "That was real life, that was business. But when a business-man has made money, what does he do with it? He buys a place in the country. That is what you all want. You cannot escape it. Your green grass is as strong as the creepers of a jungle, with the additional advantage that you are able to play games on it. Or lie on it . . ."

As though in demonstration, Belinski unclasped his hands and let himself drop back. Andrew looked at his crooked wrist, outflung on the green, and said abruptly: —

"You of all people — you of all people can't advise me to bury my head in the past. In the grass, if you like. You know what's coming."

"You mean the war?"

"Yes."

Belinski sighed again.

"I remember being taken to see the new Post Office at Gdynia. It is a nice Post Office, but they wanted me to write in all the European papers about it. I mean, if you are a Pole, you are expected to be violently nationalist. I am not. I am a sort of *lusus naturæ.* Like all artists. I don't think about the war because it would stop me working. But if the war is really on your mind, join your Air Force." Belinski yawned. "This air!" he said. "It is like milk!"

For a moment Andrew stood very still. Then he said: —

"Do you mean that?"

"That the air is like milk? Have you not noticed?"

"Do you think I should join the Air Force now?"

"But naturally. If you are serious. If you are simply brave, you will no doubt wait till war comes — that again is the national habit. But as an artist, and therefore a serious man, I should think you would be more use if you were trained."

"As a matter of fact," said Andrew stiffly, "when I was at Cambridge, I belonged to the University Air Squadron."

Belinski grinned.

"That must have been quite a rag."

"I don't understand," said Andrew, more stiffly still.

"Nor did I. I had heard of it, you see, I was interested. I met a young man who belonged to it, a rich young man a little like yourself. He said it was quite a rag."

With that Belinski rolled over on his face and apparently went to sleep. Andrew stood beside him a few moments longer, and then walked off.

## II

Sir Henry rode gently on, not thinking much, absorbed in an almost physical pleasure of recognition. Every least landmark, every turning, gate and tree, was as familiar to him as the lines on his hand, and all that he saw he loved. It was a love free from the desire to possess; much of the land over which he rode had belonged to his father, more to his grandfather; time and taxes had shorn the Carmel estates. Sir Henry for himself hardly regretted their passing; land was a great trouble, always had been; never would he forget the struggles he went through, between 1914 and 1918, with the Ministry of Agriculture. ("Ignorant fellers," thought Sir

Henry automatically.) But if Andrew wanted to take in the home farm again, it could no doubt be managed; let the lad try his hand, thought Sir Henry. Though there was nothing in Andrew's education or tastes to fit him for such a project, Sir Henry had come to think of the home farm, in connection with his son, as a sort of lure. "For he's not an idle chap like me," reflected Sir Henry simply. "He wants to be doing. . . ."

Smoothly Golden Boy carried Sir Henry on, the choice of road as much his as his master's. Whenever they passed a labourer in the fields the man would stop working, and straighten his back, and stare — the elder among them touching their caps and waiting while Sir Henry plunged into his memory for their names. They were pleased to have seen him. A farmer's wife came to her door to watch Sir Henry go by, and afterwards told her husband of it. A couple of intellectual hikers stopped him and asked the way, for the mere pleasure of conversing with such a piece of local colour. The postman saw him, and carried the news on his rounds. By the time Sir Henry turned his horse's head for home the whole neighbourhood knew that the Squire had been out, and in the Artichoke at Friars Carmel wagers were being laid as to the age of Golden Boy.

Among the most interested observers of this progress were Cluny and Mr. Wilson.

### III

They had met at the foot of the Gorge, Cluny accompanied by Roddy, who with tactful enthusiasm leapt up at the chemist, leaving large smears of mud on his raincoat. But Mr. Wilson fended him off most good-naturedly, and said he was a handsome beast.

"I take him for company," explained Cluny. She threw an apologetic glance at Roderick as she spoke—but there was something about Mr. Wilson that always made her feel orphanish.

"To-day, if you like, you can have mine," said Mr. Wilson. He spoke rather as one conferring a favour, but since Cluny also saw it in this light, no harm was done. She was only surprised.

"But you don't shut on Wednesdays?"

"I do now," said Mr. Wilson. "I have decided that it would be beneficial to the village to have one shop open on a Thursday noon."

Cluny was quite overwhelmed. For though the change might benefit Friars Carmel—and would certainly do business no harm—she did not believe that this was Mr. Wilson's sole reason for making it. He had made it in order to be free to come for walks with herself. (To walk out with her, in fact.) It was the greatest compliment she had ever received, and she turned upon the chemist such grateful, such fervent and startled eyes, as to leave no doubt of her emotions.

"Puir lonely lass!" said Mr. Wilson—almost affectionately; and then, as though afraid of going too fast, as indeed he was, for one of his temperament, quickly remarked that there was a fine prospect from the brow of the lane. Cluny willingly fell into step beside him, and with Roddy ranging ahead they began to mount the Gorge. As once before, Cluny's heels rang on paving-stones, and with a delightful sense of confidence she asked Mr. Wilson why.

He did not fail her.

"It used to be an old road for pack-horses. You'll observe it's just wide enough to take a pack, or pannier, on either side."

"What a lot you know!"

"I naturally interest myself in my surroundings. If you like, I'll lend you a book on the subject."

"Thank you very much," said Cluny.

They walked up to the crest, and it was from thence, looking down over the Carmel road, that they saw Sir Henry pass below. Like the men in the fields, like the farmer's wife, they instinctively stood to watch him.

"Now, there's a sight I like to see," said Mr. Wilson suddenly, "and yet I couldn't tell you why."

"It's Sir Henry," said Cluny. "I didn't know he went riding."

"You'll rarely see him, for he's almost given it up. Yet they say at one time it was his whole life."

"He's very fond of Lady Carmel," said Cluny, defending him.

"I've no doubt of it, for he's a good body — although a do-nothing. I've a sympathy for a man who sticks as he has to his home-soil."

Cluny hesitated.

"Mr. Wilson," she said cautiously, "have you ever thought that if you don't always live in the same place, the whole universe is to let?"

"What's that you say?" asked Mr. Wilson, with a frown.

"I mean" — instinctively Cluny toned down the flamboyance of the phrase — "if you're not quite settled, you can choose where to live."

"That is perfectly true. Where there are children, for example, it is necessary to be near a good school. But as for the whole universe, all the countries of the world — I do not see how one could form a sound judgement. Surely it would be necessary to visit them all first."

"I suppose so," admitted Cluny.

"It would be a fine project for a Methusaleh," said the

chemist, smiling at her. "The average man does better to stick where he's born."

"I suppose he does," agreed Cluny.

They agreed more and more. Not that Cluny, on this walk or on the walks that followed, ever suppressed even her flightiest fancies: only Mr. Wilson examined them all so reasonably, and with such good humour, that she always came round to his point of view. When Cluny said (for instance) she wished she were a Golden Labrador like Roddy, with no house work to do and no stockings to mend, Mr. Wilson reminded her of Roddy's indignant howls when tied up outside the shop: a collar and chain, he said, were the true fundamentals of a dog's life. When Cluny said she wished she *had* a Labrador, Mr. Wilson pointed out that so long as domestic service survived, the convenience of the employer naturally came first. Whether Cluny would have learnt these lessons so readily from any one but a tragic bachelor, is open to doubt; as it was she tasted for the first time in her life the pleasures of discipleship, and it would have been hard to say which of the two, pupil or pedagogue, enjoyed these conversations more.

"Well?" said Mrs. Maile kindly, when Cluny came in at seven o'clock. "Did you have a nice walk?"

"Yes, thank you," said Cluny. "With Mr. Wilson."

The housekeeper looked surprised.

"On a Wednesday, my dear?"

"He's changed his early closing," said Cluny calmly.

She said no more, and there was no need; the implication was enough. Cluny went upstairs with a demure yet conceited step, happy in the knowledge that Mrs. Maile could have been knocked down with a feather.

## IV

*Dear Uncle Arn,*

*The weather is still very fine, and how I wish you could see the lambs, also the primroses and other flowers, how they have the nerve to charge what they do in Paddington beats me. Mr. Wilson says it is transport. He is the chemist in Friars Carmel and very well-educated, Mrs. Maile says we are lucky to have such a chemist in a place like this. Mr. Andrew is home again, another room to do. Life here is as hard as ever, but I suppose so long as domestic service survives the convenience of the employer naturally comes first. I suppose you wouldn't like a Golden Labrador puppy. If you would, I think I can get you one for nothing, it would be company now you haven't got me. I think of you often and hope the plumbing goes O.K., not too many calls at night or when you are tired. I told Mr. Wilson I had an uncle who was a plumber, he said it was a very necessary calling. Tell Aunt Addie I am sick and tired of sending love when she never sends so much as a post card back.*

*Your affectionate neice,*

CLUNY BROWN

# Chapter 15

## I

THE AFFAIRS of both Andrew and Cluny were at this time in a very interesting state. For each events were impending that would change the course of their lives, and though Andrew far more than Cluny was still a free agent, both were momentarily held in suspense. It was not disagreeable, for they both, also, felt peculiarly important, as though Fate had put all other interests aside to concentrate on them alone. How wrong they were! Fate was indeed hovering hawklike over Friars Carmel, but when it struck it swooped not upon Andrew, not upon Cluny, but upon the Professor.

From one minute to the next, in the space of time it took to slit an envelope, the Professor became a wealthy man. He received a letter, forwarded by Maria Dillon, containing a draft for five hundred dollars on account of his American royalties. It seemed to surprise him very much.

"But didn't you expect it?" asked Andrew curiously. "I mean, wasn't it in your contract?"

"That is what I am trying to remember," said Mr. Belinski. "I am not really unbusiness-like, but my contract is in Berlin. That is where all my papers are, at the Adlon. I left them all in my large suitcase, because I was coming back after I had been to Bonn, but when I had delivered my famous lecture I naturally did not return. So I suppose my contract is still in my suitcase at the Adlon, if that is where my suitcase is." He sighed. "My American agent was there too."

"Who's he?" asked Andrew.

"Not he, she. Miss Dunnett. In America women do everything."

"Is she good?"

"Very," said Mr. Belinski regretfully. "She would not even let me kiss her. And business-like! That is why I do not worry about my contract, I am quite certain all is safe in her hands. She had beautiful hands, indeed she was beautiful altogether, very slight but well-built, with dark hair and eyes. And dressed with great *chic*. You can imagine how sorry I was to leave my American agent at the Adlon!"

Andrew could imagine it very well, and felt great sympathy for the beautiful and business-like Miss Dunnett. Making an attempt to be business-like himself, he asked who was publishing the book in England.

"No one, because there is no manuscript. The other two copies besides the one in America were in my suitcase too. But it does not matter, because my publishers here are the Oxford University Press."

"The Oxford University Press obviously want to publish anything you write," objected Andrew.

"Not this time," said Mr. Belinski firmly. "This time I am different. This time I am very, very popular. In eighty thousand words I tell you all about all European literature, also what Balzac paid for his shirts. What is important is that I can now buy some shirts for myself."

So the following morning Andrew drove him into Carmel, and helped him to open a bank account, and also drove him to an Exeter shirt maker's. Here Belinski's behaviour was rather trying: against all advice he ordered pastel-shade silks, which Andrew privately considered caddish, to be made up with very pointed collars. Then he bought a really beautiful Chelsea china figure to give to Lady Carmel, a copy of *Gulliver's Travels,* and two pairs of silk stockings. Andrew could not help cocking an eye at these last, especially when, in the car going back, Belinski arranged them like book-marks in the *Gulliver,* the feet hanging out at one end and the tops at the other.

"Ha ha!" said Mr. Belinski.

It was extraordinary what a difference a hundred pounds had made to him: or so thought Andrew, not making allowance for several other factors, such as improved health due to regular living; for Mr. Belinski, in spite of his bitter complaint to Cluny, or rather as that complaint proved, had been accumulating a new fund of vitality which needed only just such an incident to release it. He was in a mood to start a newspaper. In Poland he and his friends frequently started newspapers, which were either suppressed or died a natural death after an average life of two months: they were like tadpoles, all head and tail.

"When do you suppose your book will come out?" enquired Andrew, who really took a great interest in it.

"Oh, quite soon," replied Mr. Belinski confidently. "They have had the manuscript a long time. I dare say it is out now. Whether there will be any more money is of course a different matter. If I could sell the film rights — !"

Andrew did not see how this was possible, as one could hardly film literary criticism, and Belinski reluctantly agreed.

"But there could be a very good film about Balzac and the Countess Hanska," he pointed out. "That is quite full of sex, which literary criticism, as you say, is not." (Andrew had said nothing of the sort, but he took the point.) "And I could

write such a book most easily," went on Belinski, with growing enthusiasm. "It would also be a study of the Polish erotic
temperament. In fact, if I cannot start a newspaper, I think
that is what I will do next."

His immediate act, however, while Andrew was still putting the car away, was to seek out Cluny Brown to present
her with the copy of *Gulliver* (for the one he had hit her with)
and the two pairs of stockings (for having hurt her feelings
over her snood). He was in a mood of universal benevolence.

Cluny, on the other hand, was not. She was hanging out
washing at the time, and at first would not even notice his
approach.

"Miss Brown!" said Mr. Belinski winningly.

Cluny continued not to notice him.

"If any of my remarks have at any time offended you, I
apologize. These small gifts are a peace-offering."

"Thank you, I don't want them," said Cluny.

"But what is wrong?" Mr. Belinski examined the stockings
anxiously. "They are pure silk, and fully fashioned. Also
they are both pairs the same colour, in case one ladders."

"They're swell," said Cluny, more kindly. "I can see you've
had a lot of experience. But you can't give me stockings."

"Will you tell me why not?"

Cluny picked up a traycloth, flicked it out, and pinned it
very carefully on the line. There was a primness, almost a
priggishness, about her movements which the Professor found
both unusual and irritating.

"I suppose," he said angrily, "Mrs. Maile would object?"

"I don't know. Very likely she would. But I wasn't thinking of Mrs. Maile."

"Who are you thinking of, then?"

"If you must know," said Cluny, "and I really don't know

that it's your business, but let that pass — I'm thinking of Uncle Arn."

Considerably nettled by this treatment, Belinski made his way to the library to put the *Gulliver* on the shelf beside its duplicate, and there was lucky enough to receive a little undeserved balm from Sir Henry. Sir Henry came in (from the midst of a letter to British Guiana) to look up the name of the Derby winner of 1904, and with his ready curiosity at once demanded to know what Belinski was doing. "I am repairing a damage," explained the latter, holding up a book in each hand. "The leaves in your *Gulliver* are a little loose, since I had the misfortune to throw it out of a window."

"Out of a window, my dear fellow?"

"At a cat," said Mr. Belinski.

Sir Henry was much amused. (If Belinski had said, "At a dog," he would of course have taken a different view.) He was also impressed by the Professor's keen sense of honour, and praised it very highly. They spent a pleasant five minutes in mutual compliments, and Belinski went off in search of Lady Carmel in a more cheerful mood. With her too he fared well; she was so charmed by the Chelsea figure, as also by the little speech he made as he presented it, that she took him all around the herbaceous borders explaining what was going to come up. But the two pairs of stockings still burnt a hole in the Professor's pocket; and he formed the audacious plan of presenting them to Mrs. Maile.

After tea, therefore, when Syrett came for the tray, Belinski followed him out and through the baize door into the domestic quarters. It was the first time he had ever entered the kitchen, and he was at once struck by its size. The room itself, the immense canopied range, the huge dressers, all seemed to have been designed for a race of giants; and this lent a curious charm to the small domestic group established by the fire. It consisted of three persons, Hilda, Cluny, and Mrs. Maile herself. Hilda and Mrs. Maile each held one end of an old sheet, which they were cutting into pudding-cloths; Cluny was peeling almonds. She sat very still, because of the bowl of water in her lap; her long neck was bent above it, and even the pony tail sticking out behind could not detract from the general impression of meekness. As Mr. Syrett came in their three heads turned; for a moment, at the sight of Belinski coming in after him, their three pairs of hands stopped working. Then the housekeeper laid aside her scissors and courteously rose.

"Yes, Professor?" she said enquiringly. "Can I do anything for you?"

But Belinski still had his eyes on the two girls. The black of their dresses, the white sheet and aprons, the band of blue on the white bowl, produced a very satisfying effect; as did Hilda's tawny head and round red cheeks in contrast with Cluny's etched profile. After that first instant Cluny had bent again over her almonds — meeker than ever, and very aloof. Mr. Syrett meanwhile deposited his tray on the table, and the housekeeper spared him an annoyed glance. If gentlemen wished to come into the kitchen, it was Syrett's duty to give her warning. . . .

"Yes, Professor?" repeated Mrs. Maile.

Belinski detached his gaze from Cluny Brown and unfurled the stockings.

"I wish you to accept these, as a small token of my esteem."

Mrs. Maile stiffened. As she told Mr. Syrett afterwards, she could hardly believe her ears. Even for a foreigner, it didn't seem sensible. She looked at Belinski suspiciously.

"I'm sure it's very kind of you — "

"Not at all. It is you who have been kind to me."

" — but I hardly think," said Mrs. Maile — and paused. She really didn't know what she hardly thought, and the Professor's earnest stare was making her feel quite silly. He said firmly: —

"It is the custom, in Poland, to make gifts at Christmas time."

"So it is here," said Mrs. Maile, with more confidence. "Only it isn't Christmas."

"But last Christmas, *I* was not here," explained Mr. Belinski.

The housekeeper paused again. A woman of sense, this specious argument did not for a moment take her in, but she was increasingly aware not only of the Professor's eyes on her, but also of the eyes of Mr. Syrett and the girls. (Cluny as a matter of fact was not looking at Mrs. Maile at all, she was seizing the opportunity to eat a few almonds, but the housekeeper did not know.) If she felt silly, it was possible that she appeared silly — which was something no housekeeper could afford. At all costs the situation had to be ended; and as the quickest way of doing so Mrs. Maile took the stockings into her own hands and thanked the Professor for his gift.

She did more than that. Visited by a genuine inspiration, she thanked him in French.

"*Je vous remercie mille fois*," pronounced Mrs. Maile.

The effect was sensational — not indeed upon Belinski, who was used to servants speaking French when they didn't speak German — but upon Mr. Syrett and Hilda and Cluny Brown. They hardly saw Mr. Belinski depart, they were gazing, but now with admiration, at the accomplished housekeeper.

"Dear me," said Mr. Syrett, "dear me, Mrs. Maile, I had no idea you could parley-vous."

"I learnt French as a girl," replied Mrs. Maile modestly.

She did not add that she had learnt exactly three phrases, the other two being "*Quelle heure est-il?*" and "*Comment vous allez-vous?*"; but with the air of a Cincinnatus returning to his plough went back to the fire and took up her end of the sheet. The rest of the evening she was in an unusually good humour; in fact the whole incident had pleased her very much.

# Chapter 16

————— »» I «« —————

MR. BELINSKI's prospects continued to brighten. At Andrew's suggestion he cabled to Miss Dunnett giving his Friars Carmel address, and a day or two later received a cable back. "CONGRATULATIONS," it said, "RAVE NOTICES ANTICIPATE GOOD SALES"; and this shout of encouragement from across the Atlantic stimulated the Professor quite as much as his new wealth. He began work on his new book about Balzac and the Countess Hanska, wrote six hours a day and was often late for meals. He told Andrew that under some such simple title as *Genius and Sex,* or perhaps *Sex and Genius,* he anticipated for it even raver notices and better sales. Andrew rather dubiously agreed, at the same time throwing in a word or two on the prostitution of talent; for he felt a certain (Lord-of-the-Manorish) responsibility for whatever was written under his roof. The Professor, however, was not deterred.

"It is surely better that people should hear of Balzac, even through the medium of his amours, than that they should not hear of him at all?"

"I suppose it is," said Andrew — still dubiously. "Though not if you leave them thinking of him as a super man-about-town and nothing else."

"Even that is to the good," argued Belinski. "To know merely that such a man has lived enlarges the experience. I shall send a few, no doubt, from the Countess Hanska to the *Comédie Humaine;* but even those who stop at the Countess will know something they did not know before. And fortunately Balzac was such a vulgar fellow himself, one need have no scruples."

Andrew abandoned the argument. He disagreed; nothing could make him approve this extraordinary downhill rush of a fine critical talent; but he did at the same time acknowledge that to Adam Belinski the material he worked in was thoroughly alive. Alive and kicking. He might vulgarize Balzac, but he wouldn't mummify him. He took liberties with him as with a personal friend, whereas Andrew defended him out of academic piety.

"I would never think of behaving in the same way," added Belinski reassuringly, "to John Milton. . . ."

He sent another cable to America and received an enthusiastic reply; for half a week he worked with fury; at the end of which period Balzac, the Countess, and the whole United States were wiped from his consciousness by the arrival of Betty Cream.

## II

It will be remembered that when Betty and Mr. Belinski originally met, the latter was still emotionally in thrall to Maria Dillon: he had not really seen Betty at all. Now his heart was vacant, his eyes were open, and the consequences inevitable.

Andrew drove over to Carmel to meet her, and on the brief journey back asked her in so many words why she had come. What was sauce for the gander was sauce for the goose; he was merely imitating her own candour; and Betty as candidly replied.

"Because I like the country in spring. I like your mother and father."

"That's fine," said Andrew. "I needn't ask you not to sunbathe, because it won't be warm enough."

Betty looked genuinely apologetic.

"I'm sorry about that, darling. I was just a brat. And I'd got in with a lot of nudists."

"*Nudists?*"

"The body-beautiful crowd. Only most of their bodies weren't beautiful, they were rather shocking. I only went once, and it was actually just after I'd been here and you were all so stuffy; in fact, you drove me into a nudist camp."

"Oh, all right," said Andrew. "Forget it."

"I have. I'm not morbid." There was a slight pause; then Betty looked at him thoughtfully and said, "Why did you think I was coming?"

Andrew kept his eyes on the road.

"I had no idea, and that's why I asked. I shouldn't have thought about it at all, except for the fact that you knew in town you'd be down here, and never mentioned it."

"I forgot."

"Rubbish."

"Very well, then," said Betty, "I'll tell you. When you asked me to marry you — and it's you who've brought this up, Andrew, not me — I'd just had Lady Carmel's letter. I could hardly tell you about it then, could I? I could hardly say, 'No thank you, darling, by the way your mother's just invited me to stay.' So I didn't mention it. Then afterwards you were quite normal again, you didn't seem in the least upset, and I thought how idiotic to miss a week in Devon on account of your non-existent feelings. So I accepted. I didn't see you again till the night we had supper with John, and he *has* feelings, so I didn't mention it, again."

Like all Betty's explanations, it was highly plausible. There wasn't a hole anywhere. It was even, quite possibly, true.

"Thanks," said Andrew. "What a simple little thing you are!"

"Yes, I am."

"And you've just come down for a simple rural outing."

"Yes, I have."

"Oh, all right," said Andrew.

They had reached the lodge gates and turned up the drive. Betty added a film of powder to the rose-petal texture of her nose and adjusted her hat. It was a simple hat, of dark-blue felt with a wide drooping brim. Her suit was of dark blue tweed worn over an egg-shell blue blouse that was not exactly a shirt, but still very simple. On her left shoulder was pinned a simple bunch of geranium made of pink cotton.

Andrew looked down at her feet. She had on a pair of low-heeled brogues, and very fine woollen stockings.

"Oh, Lord!" said Andrew to himself; but whether in admiration or mockery — or even apprehension — even he could not have told.

Lady Carmel was waiting for them in the drawing-room, her welcome kind and placid as always; Belinski, who was there too, reacted more violently. He could not leap to his feet, since he was already on them, but he gave the impression of leaping. He then froze. His body in fact performed a motion very similar to that of a Guardsman's hand when brought to the salute. His gaze became glassy; and Betty's laugh relieved a slight but definite tension.

"We've met before," she said. "Don't you remember?"

"No," said Belinski. "That is, I remember you were there,

but I cannot have remembered you, or I would have thought of nothing else since."

If there was one thing Betty could do on her head, it was handle a compliment.

"You were so absorbed in the conversation," she said lightly; and turned back to Lady Carmel. "They were all talking politics," she explained, "Andrew and John and Mr. Belinski. I'm simply no good at politics at all."

But Mr. Belinski would not let this pass. Indeed, he seemed to feel her explanation as an insult.

"It was not the politics," he assured her earnestly. "No politics could have distracted me like that. If you wish to know —"

"Come and have tea, my dear," said Lady Carmel.

They sat down, all except Belinski, who after one more bedazzled glance rushed away to shave. Sir Henry came in and kissed Betty. As he told his wife afterwards, he didn't know the child very well, but she looked up at him, so he kissed her. Syrett brought in the scones, and within ten minutes the soothing ritual of country-house tea overlaid all recollection of the Professor's peculiar behaviour. There was plenty to talk about. How was John? asked Lady Carmel; and Betty said he was very well. She described the Pageant of Fair Women, in which Sir Henry took an ingenuous interest. But she had brought with her (as the good guest brings a piece of embroidery) a more fruitful topic still: her mother proposed to decorate her town house with window-boxes; there were eight windows and a porch-top; would Lady Carmel be so very kind as to give a few hints on the most suitable flowers for the different seasons? This was a commission after Lady Carmel's own heart; she accepted it with delight, happily prophesying that it would take a long time to work out, for she would begin by making lists and end by making charts. "You mustn't take *too* much trouble," said Betty anxiously. "My dear, it will be a pleasure," said Lady Carmel.

Andrew sat and listened with sardonic admiration. He had never before seen Betty in this decorous mood; on her previous visit she had behaved, as she said, like a brat, and he had not realized, in the year between, that her cavalier treatment of himself and John Frewen was no longer universal. If one ages a great deal between twenty and twenty-three, one also ages between twenty and twenty-one. Betty Cream had in fact now two sets of manners, one for her contemporaries and one for her elders; possibly in the course of time both would merge into the latter and leave her altogether polite. Andrew did get a glimmering, however, of what really accomplished politeness entailed; those window-boxes, for instance, so exquisitely suited to Lady Carmel's taste, which were obviously going to prove of such value during the coming week — had Betty "planted" them before she left town? Did her mother really desire them? Or had they been first "planted" on Lady Cream, perhaps in the guise of a kindness to some one setting up a flower shop? What complicated lives women led, reflected Andrew, if they took this business of social relations seriously; what infinite care and foresight they constantly expended! Even their physique was schooled: now, at precisely the right moment, Betty began to look a little tired; it was time for the tea-things to be cleared, and for Lady Carmel to show her her room. . . .

"That's a nice girl," said Sir Henry, as soon as Betty and his wife had withdrawn. "Pretty as a picture. I'd like to have seen her in that pageant. Did you go?"

"No," said Andrew.

"God bless my soul!" said Sir Henry.

He looked at his son uneasily. He so rarely gave Andrew advice that he did not know quite how to set about it. A most apposite memory came to his aid.

"Your mother was in a pageant once, before we were married. She was the goddess Flora and carried an Arum lily. *I* went."

"I hope it was a success, sir."

"It would have been, but for the rain. Your poor mother was soaked. But she didn't mind, because the gardens needed it. I told her — " Sir Henry smiled happily at the memory of his thirty-year-old joke — "I told her it wasn't an Arum she should have been carrying, it was an umbrella."

Andrew smiled too, and walked out of the room.

## III

As he went upstairs he heard voices on the landing above. Betty Cream, incautiously stepping out of her door to view the lie of the land, had been waylaid by Mr. Belinski.

"One moment, please!" he implored.

He had shaved too impetuously and cut his chin; Betty noted the dab of cotton-wool. She had no illusions as to the effect she had produced on him, and genuinely regretted it.

"I wish to tell you why I did not remember you."

"There's really no need," Betty assured him.

"But there is, otherwise you will think me just another of your British fish. It was because I happened to be in love. And I must have been more in love than I thought," added Mr. Belinski, with an air of surprise. "However, that is all over now, in fact it was over before I came to Friars Carmel, and you must please forgive."

"I won't give it another thought," promised Betty; at which point Andrew reached the landing. She smiled at him and disappeared into her room. Belinski looked at him without seeing him and walked off towards the east corridor. As promptly as a character in a play Cluny Brown shot out of the housemaid's pantry with a brass can.

"I've seen her!" cried Cluny.

"Seen whom?" asked Andrew, in a unencouraging tone.

"Miss Cream. I saw her just now. Isn't she a dream?"

Andrew made no reply. He still hoped that they might be embarking upon a week of simple rural pleasures, and no more; but the hope was faint.

# Chapter 17

————————— ⇒⇒⇒ I ⇐⇐⇐ —————————

WITHIN a few days Friars Carmel, for perhaps the first time in its history, boiled with passion.

The phrase was Mr. Syrett's; he uttered it only in the ear of Mrs. Maile, but it was astonishing that such a phrase should enter his mind, let alone pass his lips. "The Professor," reported Mr. Syrett (returning from the dinner table), "boiled with passion throughout the meal; and moreover is beginning to drink heavy."

For a moment Mrs. Maile looked at her colleague as though she suspected him of drinking himself. But a glance acquitted him; he was shaken, but sober.

"What do you mean, boiled?" asked Mrs. Maile.

The butler hesitated. He found it hard to put into words the impression of suppressed but growing emotion given off like a gas from the person of Mr. Belinski.

"He never took his eyes off her," he said inadequately. "Off Miss Cream."

"Then how did he eat his dinner?" riposted Mrs. Maile.

"He didn't, not to speak of. That's what I'm saying."

The housekeeper sniffed. She was in a mood to snub Mr. Syrett, because it looked as though his original wild shot (at Announcements, Celebrations and so on) was likely to hit the mark; jealous of his superior perspicacity, she snubbed him while she could.

"Miss Cream is a very attractive young lady, and naturally takes the eye. But as for *boiling with passion* — all I can say is, Mr. Syrett, I hope you will not use such language and go putting such ideas into the heads of Hilda or Cluny Brown."

The remark was superfluous as well as unjust, for the heads of Hilda and Cluny were full of such ideas already. Love at first sight is always more quickly recognized by the young, because they believe in it: they do not automatically discount its first symptoms, putting down to nerves or the weather the (often similar) derangements induced by passion. Hilda in particular was something of an expert on the subject: it had been a case of love at first sight between herself and her seafarer, who had gazed on her, she told Cluny, with just such a mortal look as the Professor laid on Miss Cream; and all that week at Loo (the seafarer was lodging with Hilda's aunt, and so was Hilda) never did he take his eyes off her. There was Gary to prove it. This experience made Hilda sentimentally inclined; Cluny, though equally interested, discovered a more ironic attitude, which she made no attempt to conceal. In these days she saw less of the Professor than usual, for he spent little time in the stables; but that was where he was when she was sent to find him, a day or two later, with a message from Lady Carmel.

Cluny loped into the yard and looked about with quite a feeling of nostalgia. It was only twice or thrice that she had stood there talking to the Professor, but each conversation had been unusual enough — meaty enough — to leave a generally pleasing memory. When she looked up and saw his head sticking out of the window, Cluny thought, "Quite like old times." Her message temporarily forgotten, she stood waiting for him to see her, and when he did grinned and flung up an arm as though to ward off a second copy of *Gulliver*.

But Mr. Belinski had evidently forgotten about it. He looked at her as if she were doing something silly. Cluny's grin faded.

"Well?" she said sardonically. "How's your Polish soul?"

"Go away," said Belinski.

But Cluny stayed where she was, in her old position at the foot of the steps.

"Mrs. Maile," she observed conversationally, "thinks you're looking worse again."

"Do you know something that annoys me very much? Your habit of dragging in at every opportunity the opinions of Mrs. Maile. I find it tiresome and vulgar."

"I can't help it," said Cluny, "she's like cheese. She gets into everything."

"Where is she now?" asked Belinski abruptly. (Whenever he said "she" he meant Betty Cream, and whenever Cluny said "she" she meant Mrs. Maile; but they understood each other perfectly.)

"Keeping her hand in on Sir Henry."

"You are idiotic to be jealous of her. She is good even to old men, because she has a golden nature."

Cluny opened her eyes.

"But I'm not jealous. I think she's a dream. Besides—" she put on an expression of extreme sedateness—"it isn't my place."

"If you have come here simply to irritate me, it is both heartless and what I should expect of you."

"Oh, no," said Cluny, "I've got a message. Sir Henry and Lady Carmel are going into Exeter in the car, and if you'd like to go too will you get your things on."

"Is *she* going?"

"You heard," said Cluny. "No."

"Then why should I?"

"Well, you might want to get some more stockings. . . ."

Belinski reached out for the nearest book, but a sudden recollection stayed his hand. It was just possible that his shirts might be ready for him. Hastily weighing one consideration against another, he decided that it was worth missing the chance of Betty's company at Friars Carmel, in order to appear before her in dove-grey crêpe de Chine.

Even Cluny could have told him that this was a mistake, but he didn't tell Cluny why he had changed his mind. He forgot about her even while she stood there in front of him. And Cluny, as soon as she turned away, forgot about Mr. Belinski. It was Wednesday afternoon, and Titus Wilson would be waiting for her at the foot of the Gorge.

## II

"So you've company at the house?" remarked Mr. Wilson. (It was the first time Cluny had seen him since Betty Cream arrived.) "I doubt you're all fine and busy."

"One person doesn't make much difference — " said Cluny — "at least, not in the way of work."

"Miss Cream was in the shop this morning. She's a very taking young lady."

Without rancour, Cluny realized that any man who had just seen Betty would naturally want to talk about her.

"Don't you think she's beautiful?" she asked.

"I would like to see her with her face washed," replied the chemist cautiously.

"Well, I have," said Cluny, "and she's just the same, or very nearly." She sighed. "It's hard to be plain all your life."

Mr. Wilson made no pretence at misunderstanding her.

"We've all got to take what the Lord sends us," he said consolingly. "Maybe you're not plain to your friends."

"I'm plain to Uncle Arn, and he's known me all my life."

"If I may make a personal remark —" said Mr. Wilson.

Cluny glowed at him.

" — you have sometimes a very intelligent look."

They hurried on, Cluny looking as intelligent as possible. She had so little personal vanity that this meagre praise made her quite overlook his interest in Miss Cream. (After all, beauty didn't last, but intelligence did. It might even improve.) She said generously: —

"I think Miss Cream's clever too. At any rate, she isn't dumb. She's got everything."

"It's early days yet," observed Mr. Wilson. "Who knows what's in store for her?"

But Cluny — like Andrew, like John Frewen — could not visualize any sombre future for Betty Cream. Was it not obvious that she had only to say the word to become young Lady Carmel? Or if Andrew were not a brilliant enough match, were there not Dukes, Marquesses, Viscounts still unwed? Let alone Hollywood, thought Cluny Brown . . .

"If I looked liked that," she said, "I'd go on the films."

"Then you'd do a very daft thing," said Mr. Wilson severely.

"I could be the funny woman in the comics." (Cluny had already reverted to her own personality; she could never be any one else for long.) "The one who keeps a boarding-house. I could be a repressed spinster."

"Now, see here," said Mr. Wilson, really shocked, "that's no fit expression for a young woman."

"I'm nearly twenty-one," said Cluny.

Out of the tail of her eye she saw him frowning, and felt

rather pleased. She had never baited Mr. Wilson before, and the fact that she was able to do so gave her a welcome sensation of power. Parrot, indeed! thought Cluny triumphantly; and wished it were the Professor, instead of Roddy, on the other side of the hedge.

"You're twenty-one and a baby," said Mr. Wilson abruptly.

"I've been through a lot in my time."

"Havers," said Mr. Wilson.

But Cluny had now distracted herself. Hollywood and the Professor forgotten, she looked back over her twenty years, and they seemed to her very long. She hadn't made the most of them; but there were still one or two memories which she thought would surprise Mr. Wilson. That beautiful bathroom, for example, which she now saw as the permanent background to Mr. Ames. It was funny — whenever she conjured up that kindly figure in its yellow pull-over, she never saw it in the scullery or studio, but always by the bath. . . .

"It's funny," meditated Cluny aloud, "how you always see a man in the same place."

"Now what exactly," asked Mr. Wilson, "do you mean by that?"

Cluny found she had meant more than she realized. The rule did not apply only to Mr. Ames, but also to Mr. Belinski, and to Titus Wilson himself.

"Well, whenever I see you, it's out in these lanes. Whenever I see the Professor, it's in the stables. I mean, I've seen you in the shop as well, and he's about all the time; but that's where you sort of belong."

The chemist's brow gradually cleared. He thought he understood what all this daft talk had been leading up to. It was true, they did always meet in the lanes, they walked for about three hours with no more refreshment than the bars of chocolate he brought in his pocket; he thought that Cluny, in a very roundabout way, was reproaching him for never taking her home to tea. He said kindly: —

"With these fine days we've had, it's a long time since you've been to the house."

"Yes, it is," agreed Cluny, rather surprised. "How's Mrs. Wilson?"

"Much the same. The first wet day, you must come back and have tea."

The effect of these words was just such as he had anticipated: Cluny, thinking of old Mrs. Wilson in her shawls, remembering the odd cosiness of that first encounter, smiled up at him; and they walked on in their usual amity, following the old pack-road, pleasantly and safely engrossed in the history of Britain's internal trade.


# III

It was fortunate that Andrew, envisaging a week of simple rural pleasures, and no more, had not done so with much conviction. Friars Carmel boiled with passion, and the week looked like being a month.

In the first place, Colonel Duff-Graham came to lunch, and invited them all back for the week after. Betty agreed to stay on for this festivity. The original date of her departure once abandoned, no other was fixed. Lady Carmel, accustomed to the month-long country visiting of her youth, began to plan picnics and excursions for the warmer weather, and Betty, who thought nothing of running across to Paris for the week-end, agreed that it would be a pity to come all the way to Devon and see nothing of the country. She settled down: took to gardening with Lady Carmel and playing piquet with

Sir Henry; and all sorts of upsetting thoughts began to cross Andrew's mind.

A more conceited young man would have jumped to the conclusion, against any evidence, that when Betty came to Friars Carmel, it was in pursuit of himself.

Andrew was not conceited, and he was trained to examine evidence. He admitted that Betty's situation, with regard to male society, was out of the usual: to break off relations with every young man who proposed to her would leave her practically without an acquaintance, and to the common loss. (Andrew also admitted that she behaved like a gentleman; never was the name of one suitor breathed to another. It was the suitors, like John Frewen, who gave themselves away.) Moreover, in the circles in which they both moved, sentiment was so rarely admitted as a spring of action that Andrew instinctively discounted it. There had also come into fashion a simple, forthright mode of behaviour the exponents of which cheerfully went ahead, doing whatever they wished to do, readily explaining their motives, paying their way, so to speak, by their frankness. To this school Betty Cream eminently belonged, and Andrew was by now intellectually convinced that she had come to Friars Carmel because she liked the country in spring, and that she was staying on because she liked Friars Carmel.

So far, so good; and his own attitude was in theory just as simple. Betty's presence was a matter of indifference to him. If it amused her to stay on being the perfect girl guest, let her; if it amused her to treat him as a favourite brother — which was what she did — O.K. by Andrew. Conversely, there was no reason in the world why, after the official week of her visit was past, he should not go up to town again and get hold of a man he knew at the Air Ministry. The only complication, and one that he had introduced himself, was the Professor.

Andrew felt an extraordinary reluctance to go to London leaving Betty and Belinski at Friars Carmel.

For Adam Belinski had abandoned himself unreservedly to his temperament. Where was now the gentle Professor whose even quietness had won the elder Carmels' hearts? He talked either much too much, or not at all; he boasted, or gloomed; he wore caddish shirts. At times he was undeniably amusing, and Betty was easily amused; his silence had a quality which some girls might have considered flattering. Andrew found him obnoxious all round.

"Doesn't it ever get monotonous?" he asked Betty one evening. They were playing billiards; Belinski, after marking for them for half an hour, had just thrown down his chalk and walked out.

"Doesn't what get monotonous?"

"Having men fall head over heels in love with you as soon as you appear. Lying down to be walked over, like Belinski. I should think you'd find it boring."

Betty thoughtfully chalked her cue.

"As a matter of fact, it isn't at all. It's very interesting. You see, I'm not intellectual, I can't cut bits out of newspapers, but I am interested in people. And when they're being in love, you do get to know them."

Andrew threw a hasty backward glance over his own recent conduct.

"That's why I keep my friends," added Betty. "I find out much sooner than most women what a man's really like, and if I think he's nice, I'm not likely to be let down later on. I expect they feel the same about me."

There was much truth in this. Among their Bloomsbury and Chelsea and Mayfair playmates, whose friendships, like their love-affairs, often had a touch-and-go quality, Betty's own relations were noticeably stable. She knew people for years. There were men with whom Andrew had been friendly at Cambridge, but with whom he had since lost contact; every now and then he met one or other of them in the company of Betty Cream. When they married Betty naturally saw less of them, but few wives did not welcome her presence at a dinner party; Betty was always dining out in places like Ealing and Wembley and Burnt Oak and Turnpike Lane . . .

"What d'you want them all for?" asked Andrew, with genuine curiosity.

"I like them. I like having friends."

"If you're not careful, you're going to spend your whole life going to see people."

Betty leaned over the table, apparently studying the position of the balls.

"No, I don't think so," she said vaguely. "I'm nearly twenty-two."

Both she and Cluny were rather conscious of their ages, and conscious of having put their first youth behind them.

# Chapter 18

————————— »» I ««—————————

THE NEXT day brought lunch at the Colonel's. It was fine and warm, so that they were able to take coffee on the terrace, the view from which served as a useful topic for those whose conversation had been exhausted at table. The good Colonel's luncheon parties were not as a rule very lively: he was a widower, and his one daughter bred Blue Beverin rabbits. At the moment she was visiting a friend in Kent who bred Angoras, and the Colonel regretted this very much, because he wanted her to meet Betty Cream. He felt that contact with Betty might do Cynthia good, might open her eyes, as it were, to something besides Blue Beverins, and he had actually sent a telegram urging her return.

"You must meet my daughter," said the Colonel earnestly, as they took their places round the coffee table. "She's coming back in a day or two."

"I'd love to," said Betty. She was quite used to this situation; mothers of attractive sons might sometimes cold-shoulder her, but with fathers of plain daughters she always made a hit. She felt really sorry for the poor girls, and had been known to accompany them to the Flower Show. The daughters either disliked her at sight or (if particularly plain) developed tiresome schoolgirl crushes; but Betty was always ready to try again, and reiterated her anxiety to meet Cynthia Duff-Graham.

"I dare say you'll make great friends," pursued the Colonel optimistically. "Won't they, Allie?"

Lady Carmel, incurably truthful, merely smiled. She could not honestly assent. But her son had fewer scruples.

"Bosom friends," agreed Andrew warmly. "Girlish confidences and all that. I'm sure Betty needs a confidante."

"Oh, but I have one," said Betty. "I'm keeping a little diary. . . ."

Lady Carmel listened to this exchange with a doubtful mind. She was troubled about Andrew and Betty, who appeared to her to be complicating a perfectly straightforward situation for no discoverable reason. She blamed Andrew the more: unaware that he had proposed already, she couldn't imagine why he didn't at once do so; she thought he was putting Betty in a very tiresome position; indeed, Lady Carmel didn't quite know whether to admire Betty's extreme self-possession, or blame her too for not giving Andrew more encouragement. So her attitude towards the pair of them had become slightly reserved; nothing would stop Sir Henry from behaving like a prospective father-in-law, but Lady Carmel herself withdrew as it were to the observation-post of simple hostess-ship. For this both Betty and Andrew were grateful: acting on completely mistaken premises, Lady Carmel was in fact behaving in the wisest possible way; but unfortunately she did not know it.

She looked at Betty reflectively: there she sat, surrounded by four men all more or less in love with her; and because she had a fair mind Lady Carmel grudged only one of them. Such beauty had its rights — to the sentimental regard of Sir Henry and the Colonel, to the exaggerated devotion of the Professor; but Andrew was different. Andrew might take harm. Lady Carmel thought of love as it had flowered so gently, so steadily, for her husband and herself, and unconsciously sighed.

For some minutes no one spoke, not even of the view. The Colonel and Sir Henry, sipping their brandy, drowsed in the sun like a couple of bumble-bees. Adam Belinski never took his eyes from Betty's face. Andrew lay back, not relaxed, but rigid. Betty smiled at her own thoughts, and Lady Carmel tried not to think at all. From an æsthetic point of view that made a remarkably satisfying group — mellow age set off by lovely youth, the exotic note introduced by Belinski, a background of proportioned grace: a conversation-piece, without conversation. The only feature lacking was a handsome dog, and even he now suddenly appeared. But he appeared in the wrong place: instead of lying at his master's feet, Roderick was lolloping along on the far side of the brook, at the bottom of the second lawn, and out of the picture altogether.

"There's Roddy," said Sir Henry. "Who's that with him?"

With a movement of surprise, Lady Carmel recognized her parlour-maid. Hatless, her pony tail flying, Cluny Brown raced after the dog and caught him just as he was about to plunge into the brook. Their mingled cries were distinctly audible.

"It's Brown," said Lady Carmel, rather quietly. Every one else was looking the same way, and Andrew and Belinski were grinning.

"That's right, she's from your place," said the Colonel. "Comes over on Wednesdays and gives Roddy a run."

The fact that it was not Wednesday, but Thursday, struck Lady Carmel rather forcibly. However, with no family lunch to serve, it was quite possible that Mrs. Maile had given the girls permission to slip out. . . .

"Moves well," said Sir Henry.

"Of course, Mrs. Maile spoke of it," said Lady Carmel. "It's very kind of you."

For some reason the Colonel felt defensive.

"Roddy's taken to her," he explained. "She looked after him in the train. Very nervous beast." He felt this put matters on a better footing, and so in fact did Lady Carmel. The nerves of a well-bred dog deserve every consideration.

"Very kind indeed," she repeated, more warmly. "And I know Brown appreciates it. She's a very sensible girl."

At this moment Roderick made a second bound at the water and brought Cluny down in the rough grass. They appeared to roll over each other. Then Cluny scrambled up, and observed the group on the terrace, and almost waved to them.

She didn't; but the uncompleted gesture was oddly definite. Across two lawns, across the brook, they saw the instinctive movement of her arm suddenly arrested; it might have been said that they saw a thought strike her. Andrew glanced quickly at his mother; Lady Carmel's look remained deliberately bland. But Belinski was on his feet.

"If one may take a stroll?" he asked politely.

"Of course!" cried the Colonel. "Go along, all of you — and leave us fogies to our slumbers."

## II

The three young people walked quickly down the slope, Andrew and Adam each thinking how he could get rid of the other. Cluny Brown, who had set them in motion, was temporarily forgotten; indeed by the time they reached the brook she and Roderick were crashing through the far spinney. But Betty's curiosity had been aroused; when any man looked away from herself, she was naturally interested.

"Andrew, wasn't that your parlour-maid?"

"Yes, darling," said Andrew. "That was our remarkable Cluny Brown, who has upset Mailey and Syrett, and even my mamma, by her passion for dogs."

"Why should she not have a dog of her own?" asked Belinski.

"Because parlour-maids don't," replied Andrew. "That's the only answer I can find. Well, now we've deserted the party, what are we going to do?"

"Let's go birds'-nesting," said Betty. "Andrew, what a time you must have had here as a boy!"

"It wasn't bad."

"By which he means," said Belinski, looking at Betty ironically, "that the beauty of his early surroundings is still the strongest influence of his life. He has the heart of a vegetable."

"Where were you brought up, Professor?"

"In a succession of flats, each one smaller than the last, in Warsaw, where my father was a school teacher. He also took resident pupils, so that I had to sleep in the eating room."

"It doesn't sound very gay."

"It was not gay, but it was interesting. There were always people talking till midnight. Sometimes they threatened to commit suicide, sometimes they discussed politics or their love-affairs. As a consequence I grew up with the heart, as the mind, of an artist. I think it has made me a very interesting man," said Belinski simply.

They had reached the edge of the spinney and there turned, looking back at the group on the terrace. The figures of Sir Henry and the Colonel did not stir, but as they watched Lady Carmel rose to her feet.

"Your mother's moving," said Betty.

"She's going to look at the greenhouses," said Andrew.
"She always does."

"And what does your father always do?" asked Belinski.

"As soon as he wakes up, he'll go and look at the stables."

"And they have been doing so for fifty years?"

"I suppose for as long as they've known the Colonel. Why
not?" asked Andrew, rather sharply.

"Why not, indeed? In fifty years' time you will no doubt
always walk up to this wood. I am happy to assist at the birth
of a tradition."

Andrew turned to Betty and asked her whether she would
like to go on through the spinney, or back to the house. Betty
chose the house. Walking back between the two men, she
began to chatter, about Cynthia who was to be her bosom
friend, about Cynthia's rabbits, about the guinea-pigs she had
kept in her youth. Just before they reached the brook, however, she broke off and said to Belinski: —

"Apologize."

He looked at her with not quite convincing astonishment.
"For what?"

"For being so clever."

"Because I made an interesting ethnological observation — "

"Apologize!"

"You are quite right," said Belinski unexpectedly. "I am in
very bad taste. Andrew, I am sorry."

"Oh, damn," said Andrew. He looked from Betty to Belinski, who were now regarding each other very amiably, for
their sudden bicker seemed to have put them on a more
intimate footing, and went on across the bridge. The other
two followed close on his heels — rather dutifully, Andrew
felt, with a propitiating docility, as though he needed humour-
ing. Betty slipped her hand through his arm, and Belinski,

on his other side, made flattering comments on English domestic architecture. Andrew did not know why he wanted to swear again, but he did.

## III

"Here come your youngsters," said the Colonel, opening his eyes. "Henry, that's a very pretty girl."

"Pretty as a picture," said Sir Henry.

Colonel Duff-Graham continued to observe the approaching trio.

"That foreign chap," he said suddenly. "Find him much trouble about the place?"

Sir Henry looked surprised.

"The Professor? Lord, no. He's writing a book."

The Colonel nodded solemnly. To him, as to his old friend, authorship put a man, if not quite outside the pale of common humanity, at least into a special class — like vegetarians. But he was pleased to have had an author at his table, especially one guaranteed by the respectable title of "Professor"; and he felt that his party had gone off unusually well.

## IV

Cluny returned to the house feeling slightly apprehensive, for her excursion had not in fact been sanctioned by Mrs. Maile: she had simply run out. It was rash to go to the Colonel's at all, when she knew the family was lunching there, and rasher still to let Roddy off his lead. However, Lady Carmel returned, and no summons followed, and by seven o'clock, when it was time to take round the water-cans, Cluny was breathing more easily.

She liked taking the cans round. Her sociable nature welcomed any personal contact, even if it consisted of no more than a shout to the Professor, who was usually in his dressing-room, or a decorous "Your hot water, my lady," to Lady Carmel; so the extra can for Miss Cream was a positive source of pleasure. "You ought to see her in her dressing-gown!" said Cluny — perhaps rashly, since she said it to Mr. Belinski; but indeed Betty Cream in a cloud of blue chiffon was a very lovely sight. She had just slipped into it, standing with one foot bare and one thrust into a cherry-coloured slipper, when Cluny entered the room that same evening.

Cluny always took a good look at Miss Cream; now, for the first time, her curiosity aroused by the events of the afternoon, Miss Cream took a good look at Cluny. She was an extremely competent judge of another woman's appearance: almost impartial, since her own looks defied competition, with standards high but catholic. But Cluny puzzled her. Beautiful eyes, a good skin — yet not the faintest chance of ever qualifying as a Lovely; tall, and height was coming in again, but either gawkily built or made to look so by her dress. Clothes would matter a lot to her, if she could achieve the unusual without collapsing into the art-and-craft. Miss Cream surveyed this conflicting evidence, threw it away, and jumped to the correct verdict that no catalogue of attributes could explain Cluny Brown's chief and rare quality: she looked like some one.

In Cluny's own circles, as has been seen, this was not an asset at all; in Miss Cream's it was cardinal. In the three years since she had come out she had seen scores and scores of nicely dressed débutantes coming out after her, none of whom looked like anything in the world but nicely dressed débutantes. Even the plain ones were not plain enough to be striking, and the pretty were all pretty in the same way. "In *my* way," thought Betty dispassionately; only in her this conventional English beauty was raised to its highest point. She perceived, for a fleeting moment, a bond of union between herself and the tall dark girl with the water-can: they were neither of them dependent on external circumstances. In her own case these were highly favourable, but they were not all-important. Her beauty was inextinguishable; and it was equally plain that neither domestic service nor its repressive uniform had been able to extinguish the peculiar quality possessed by Cluny Brown.

Betty sat down on the bed and put on her other slipper. She said:—

"I saw you out with Roddy."

Cluny beamed.

"Isn't he beautiful? We meant to go another way, but he bolted. He likes to get me in the brook."

"Does he ever?"

"Oh, yes," said Cluny. "But I soon dry off. It makes a change." She lifted the china jug from the basin and set the brass one in its place. "Shall I pour this out for you?"

"Good heavens, no," said Betty impatiently. Most intelligent persons with whom Cluny came in contact felt a vague dissatisfaction with whatever Cluny was doing: Betty now felt it absurd that she should be messing about with water-cans. (Cook had made one of her few but apt remarks on this very point: she said Cluny always looked pro tem.) This feeling was so strong that after only a moment's hesitation Betty was led to break one of the first social laws — never interfere with some one else's maids.

"Do you like this sort of job?" she asked baldly.

"No," said Cluny. "But it's good for me."

Their common youth made any further explanation unnec-

essary. It was not so long since Betty had been taking a do-
mestic-science course, because that was considered good for
her. She said energetically:—

"There must be lots of other things you could do. For instance, if you're so fond of dogs, you could be a kennel-maid."

Cluny at once looked pleased and enthusiastic, as she always
did when any one would talk to her about herself. It was
easy to attach too much importance to this expression. Betty
tucked her feet under the folds of her blue gown (like a goddess sitting in a lotus) and considered the matter with growing interest.

"I've a cousin who breeds Cockers, to begin with," she said.
"He knows absolutely every one. And there's the woman in
Mount Street where Mother got her poodle—"

"Oh, has your mother a poodle?" cried Cluny.

"Two. She over-feeds them. It's criminal."

Cluny looked aghast. She herself always went to fetch
Roddy with a pocketful of biscuit, for along with her Cockney
impulse to pick things went the Cockney impulse to give
animals things to eat. However, she was very quick in the
uptake.

"There's nothing worse," she lamented, shaking her head.
"Especially if they don't get much exercise."

"They get none, unless I'm there. You know, I believe you're
simply cut out for a kennel-maid." Betty did at that moment
see Cluny very clearly in a long white coat, leading a Cocker
spaniel up to get First Prize; and the picture looked much
more natural than Cluny in cap and apron. "If you like, I'll
write round and make enquiries. I'll write to my cousin to-
night."

It was very odd. No two people could have been less alike,

but Cluny suddenly found herself reminded by Miss Cream of Aunt Addie Trumper. She hesitated.

"What," she asked uneasily, "does a kennel-maid do?"

"All sorts of things. There's grooming and feeding and exercising, and cleaning out kennels, and worming, and you'd probably learn to strip and trim as well."

"And all just dogs?"

"Of course. If you're so fond of them —"

"I am fond of them. But I don't know that I want *just* dogs," explained Cluny.

"There'd be people as well, naturally. And you'd go to all the shows —"

"Dog shows?"

"Of course — and meet all the other dog people. My cousin loves it."

"I expect he's fonder of dogs than I am," said Cluny apologetically, "because myself I think I'd go nuts."

With a friendly smile she left the room and galloped off to fill the other cans. (Cluny's habit of galloping down the long corridors was something Mrs. Maile had not yet got her out of.) She did not give Miss Cream's proposition another thought — Cluny knew by instinct that whatever else she was, she wasn't one of the dog people — but she recognized the prompting good-nature. She felt she hadn't done Miss Cream justice, a feeling which, being proud, she very much disliked.

Cluny always left the pantry door open, in case anything should be going on outside. Now she heard Mr. Belinski speak to Sir Henry in the hall, then come upstairs, and when he reached the top she put out her head.

"Here a minute!" called Cluny.

Mr. Belinski came into the pantry. Cluny turned off the taps and faced him seriously.

"You know you're always calling me a cat? I was, a bit. About Miss Cream. And I was wrong, because she's sweet."

"She has been sweet to you?" asked Mr. Belinski jealously. "How?"

"Oh, she wants me to be a kennel-maid," said Cluny carelessly. "But that's not the point, what I mean is, you're right about her golden nature."

Belinski propped himself against the draining board and looked at her attentively.

"Is this your blessing you are giving me?"

"Oh, rats," said Cluny. "It's nothing to do with me, it's just that if I make a mistake I like to own up. She saw me with Roddy and thought maybe I'd like to be a kennel-maid, and if so she'd ask about. That's taking trouble, and shows a kind heart."

"Her heart is not kind," said Belinski sombrely. "It is without kindness or unkindness, like the heart of a flower."

But Cluny, her debt paid, had no time to listen to this sort of thing.

"Swell," said she. "You might take your can along, I've got to wait."

## V

Cluny had by this time learned to wait at table very well: her long arms worked quickly and deftly, she never so much as brushed a shoulder, she removed all plates at precisely the right moment; all she lacked was the quality of unobtrusiveness. In a way she had been far less obtrusive in her early days of fork dropping, such an accident being automatically ignored; now she was present not only in the room, but also in the consciousness of the diners. Betty Cream was still wondering why she wouldn't be a kennel-maid; Andrew could not forget her parallel between the state of Europe and the state of things below stairs; Belinski felt her benevolent eye upon his amatory progress. The elders were less affected, but it was noticeable that whereas Lady Carmel still called her Brown, Sir Henry addressed her as Cluny. Literally addressed her, for in the middle of the sweet he suddenly remembered the outstanding incident of the afternoon.

"Cluny, don't let that animal get too much for you," ordered Sir Henry.

"No, sir," said Cluny.

"You haven't the weight to stand up to him. How much do you weigh?"

"Nine-stone-two," replied Cluny. "Mostly bone."

"Well, Roddy's all of forty pound. You remember that."

"I will," said Cluny. "There was a dog on the railway —"

"Brown!" said Mr. Syrett sharply.

Cluny turned, and misread his expression.

"He only went round with a collecting box," she said reassuringly; and moved back to her place.

# Chapter 19

AND WHAT, in the meantime, of Mr. Porritt without Cluny? Truth to tell, Mr. Porritt hardly missed her at all.

The domestic offices she used to perform for him were being adequately carried out by Mrs. Trumper's respectable woman; as for the telephone, he trusted the next-door people with the key, and when they heard the bell ringing they went in and answered it, for a very small consideration. Materially Cluny's departure had made surprisingly little difference, while the withdrawal of her personality — of her essential Cluniness, so to speak — was a relief. Not every one enjoys being constantly stimulated, and though Mr. Porritt's protective mechanism was highly developed, Cluny had kept him on the hop. Without her he could settle down into a stolid, drudging, not unhappy round that got him through the days very nicely. Young Cluny had made plumbing seem exciting: well, it wasn't. It was a serious business that took it out of a man and left him glad to get home to a plain meal and no chatter. Moreover, a burden of responsibility had been lifted from his shoulders; the question of what Cluny was doing, and where, was permanently answered. "Where's your niece, Mr. Porritt?" the neighbours sometimes asked, during the first week of Cluny's absence. "She's gone into service," replied Mr. Porritt. "She's in good service, down in Devon."

One last trace, however, of Cluny's influence persisted: she was the origin of a new habit. Every Sunday Mr. Porritt set out for the Trumpers' an hour earlier, and went for a walk in Kensington Gardens. As the weather warmed he often sat down a bit and had a look at his paper (which he never now left in the 'bus). He usually established himself outside the Orangery, and on one of these occasions was suddenly, and to his great astonishment, addressed by a young man on the other end of the seat.

"How's Cluny Brown?" asked the young man.

Mr. Porritt looked at him suspiciously. To the best of his belief he had never seen the chap before.

"Your niece who had tea at the Ritz," added the young man, grinning like a Cheshire cat.

Mr. Porritt thought as fast as he could, and came to the conclusion that this must be some one Cluny had spoken to on the telephone and told a lot of her nonsense. That also made him a client, either actual or prospective. Overcoming his instinctive reserve, therefore, Mr. Porritt replied.

"She's gone into service. In Devon."

"What a damned shame!" said the young man.

Client or no client, this was quite enough for Mr. Porritt; he gave the chap an angry look and withdrew behind his paper. He would have got up, only it was his seat first and he had the better right to it. However, a lady soon came along, and the chap went off with her; and it was not until they were in motion that Mr. Porritt was struck by a puzzling thought. Cluny might have talked to the young man over the phone, and told him about the Ritz; or she might even have met him at the Ritz, and told him about her uncle; but how, in either case, had the young man identified him, Mr. Porritt, as the uncle of Cluny Brown?

Mr. Porritt looked after the pair curiously; but since the

lady wasn't the lady with whom he had conversed in February (though the man was the same young man) he gathered no clue.

As a matter of fact, it was largely over Cluny that the young man and the first lady had quarrelled. The name Cluny Brown stuck in his memory; he began to invent anecdotes about her, to build up a fictional character, whom he introduced, now and then, out of season. The lady grew bored with Cluny Brown, and presently found the young man rather boring too, and he never became her lover after all.

This was the sole contact made by Mr. Porritt with his niece's larger circle, for though Hilary Ames frequently had trouble with his sink, which was not kept properly clean, he never again rang up the String Street number. There was another man nearer at hand; it was only by hazard, that Sunday, that he had looked for "Plumbers" in the telephone book and a little further on found Mr. Porritt. The image of Cluny continued to haunt him, but so did the image of her uncle: Mr. Ames was at bottom a prudent man. He took up, however, with a tall thin dancing-teacher, rather sallow, whom no one else found particularly attractive, and by giving her a good conceit of herself so improved her style that she entered for a Rumba competition (not with Mr. Ames) and took second place.

Only once a week, on Sundays, was Cluny remembered completely. Every Sunday at dinner Mr. Trumper, or Addie, would ask, "Heard from young Cluny?" — and Mr. Porritt would say if he had, and give any trifle of news, and for a minute or two they discussed her, agreeing how wise they had all been to send her into good service. "She's fixed for life," Mrs. Trumper used to say, complacently. "You did well by her, Arn, and I hope she's grateful." Mr. Porritt made no direct reply: none of Cluny's letters, not even the later, calmer ones, exactly breathed gratitude.

"What a time you had, to be sure!" said Mrs. Trumper.

Mr. Porritt reflected.

"It's a rum thing," he said slowly, "I was bothered all right, as you well know; but looking back on it now, I couldn't rightly say what the trouble was all about. . . ."

He looked at Trumper, who shook his head. Something disturbing, something unaccountable, had put them all into a state; no more than his brother-in-law could he now lay his finger on it. Young Cluny had been spoken to in the street, she had gone gadding a bit on her own, there was some fuss about a job she took on, which Porritt never rightly explained; but all these incidents, now that Cluny's person was removed to Devonshire, had dwindled into the commonplace.

"She was a good lass," pronounced Mr. Trumper.

It was kindly said; but if that was all he could say of Cluny Brown, her memory was wearing faint indeed.

# Chapter 20

WHEN CYNTHIA DUFF-GRAHAM received her father's telegram she had been staying nearly a month with her friend who bred Angora rabbits; and the bungalow which accommodated them, though wonderfully picturesque, had not really been designed for guests. Cynthia was therefore quite willing to be summoned home, and set out next day. It may be wondered how she was able to leave her own Blue Beverins for so long a period: the answer is Girl Guides. Miss Duff-Graham ran a small troop of Guides at Friars Carmel, its members being chiefly daughters of families employable at the Hall, and it was their privilege, while she was away, to send up a fatigue-party twice a day and a report in once a week. Cynthia considered this excellent training in responsibility and kindness to animals, as no doubt it was. But the Guides were always pleased to see her come back, and so was the Colonel, who felt bound to mitigate their labours not only with milk and buns, but also by personal encouragement. He once asked whether any of them kept rabbits at home, to which they unanimously replied, "No fear."

In person Cynthia Duff-Graham was a stocky girl with a fine complexion; besides knowing all about rabbits she played a smashing good game of tennis. Her return brought the courts at Friars Carmel and the Hall into use again, and the young people played every day. Whoever partnered Cynthia won —

even Belinski, who took both hands to a back-stroke and allowed balls to bounce twice (thus diminishing their force) before returning them. Andrew played well but carelessly, and Betty had a few good shots. Fortunately Cynthia was very sweet-tempered; she ran about exhorting and instructing like a games mistress, and offered to coach them all in turn. Betty was the only one who accepted; for Cynthia had developed the anticipated crush, and her company was less wearing on the tennis-lawn than anywhere else.

"If only we had a court marked with squares!" she lamented. "I know gardeners never have time, but couldn't Andrew and the Professor manage it?"

Betty shook her head.

"The Professor's writing a book; and Andrew's lazy."

"All right, I'll do it myself."

So the next morning Cynthia turned up at nine o'clock with tapes and pegs and a folding foot-rule, also the clock-golf numbers from the Hall, and half an hour later was observed from the breakfast table crawling industriously about the lawn. Sir Henry blessed his soul and demanded to know what the girl was at; Betty told him; and Lady Carmel directed that as soon as they had finished breakfast Andrew and Belinski should go out to help. "And make her get up, dear," added Lady Carmel, privately, to Betty Cream. "I don't know what she's wearing —"

"It's a divided skirt, Lady Carmel."

"Get her to stand up all the same, dear."

But while Andrew and Belinski ungallantly dallied Cynthia found other company. Cluny Brown, hearing from Syrett of the goings-on, naturally slipped out to investigate. She appeared just as an end of tape jerked from its peg, and promptly ran to hold it down.

"Thanks awfully," called Cynthia. "How many pegs have I put in that side?"

"Six," shouted Cluny. "What are they for?"

"I'm marking the court in squares, so we can practise properly. But I'll have to wait until the grass is dryer, or the white-wash won't take." Cynthia scrambled to her feet and approached. She of course knew who Cluny was, one of the maids, and maids were a class in which Cynthia took a special interest. "You're new here, aren't you?" she asked pleasantly. "Do you come from round about?"

"From London," said Cluny.

"Dear me, that *is* a long way!"

Now, when Mr. Wilson said much the same thing Cluny felt pathetic; Miss Duff-Graham aroused in her a spirit of mondaine independence.

"Oh, I like to get around," said Cluny airily. "It's a change from Paddington."

"Paddington!" exclaimed Cynthia. "That *is* interesting. I wonder if you by any chance belonged to a girls' club there run by a friend of mine, a Miss Packett?"

"No," said Cluny. "But I've had tea at the Ritz."

But Cynthia Duff-Graham was too occupied with a new idea to take this in. Leaning against the tennis-post, swinging her foot-rule, she regarded Cluny with growing excitement.

"I'm sure it would have been just the thing for you," she said. "They did folk-dancing. I've tried to start a club here — with folk-dancing — only somehow it never got started. If I tried again, would you join?"

"I can't folk-dance."

"That doesn't matter, you're just the type," said Cynthia vigorously. Her Guides and her Clubs had developed in her a certain rough-and-ready power of judgement: less percipient than Betty Cream, she saw no discrepancy between Cluny and her occupation, accepting her as a parlour-maid as she accepted Beer as a groom; but she did recognize in her the ability to compel other parlour-maids through the mazes of Shepherds Hey. As for Cluny, she began to feel the same slight uneasiness which used to overtake her, on the outskirts of a Salvation Army crowd, when they came round with the box.

"I'm sorry, I wouldn't have time," she protested nervously.

"Don't you get an afternoon off?"

"Yes, but I need it."

Cynthia repressed a sigh. That was the perpetual trouble, even when they were just the type: they hated to give up their afternoons off, even to enjoyment. It was extraordinary — and especially in a place like Friars Carmel, where there was literally nothing to do. She made another attempt.

"If we got up a really decent team, we could enter for the County Competitions. They're great sport."

"Are they like dog-shows?" asked Cluny unexpectedly.

"Like *dog*-shows?"

"I mean, at dog-shows, you meet all the dog people, I suppose at folk-dance competitions you meet all the folk-dancers. If you'll excuse me," said Cluny courteously, "I ought to get on with the beds."

There are certain advantages about being a parlour-maid: one can always break off a conversation without impoliteness. Cluny loped back to the house, and entering by the laundry (her usual inconspicuous route) found Hilda sorting the wash. Cluny stopped and regarded her with a speculative eye.

"Ever done any folk-dancing, Hilda?"

"Get on with'ee!"

Cluny leaned up against the door-jamb and swung an imaginary foot-rule.

"You're just the type, Hilda. You could enter for the County Competitions. Miss Duff-Graham wants to groom you for stardom on your afternoon off."

## II

It was sad that Cynthia's kind thought should have been so ungratefully received, but such disappointments frequently and inexplicably came her way. Her Headmistress's final report described her as an unusually wholesome influence, well fitted to lead others; but since those happy sixth-form days Cynthia had found fewer and fewer followers. Even as a wholesome influence she was no longer a *succès fou*. Her presence at Friars Carmel squared the young people's party, enabled them, or rather drove them, to play tennis, brightened them up with innocent jokes; yet the tempers of Andrew and the Professor at least seemed suddenly to deteriorate. Betty's did not — and for a cognate reason. She had reached a point in her relations with the two men where a chaperon was very useful. Even her wit and experience were finding difficulty in keeping the amorous Professor at bay, in keeping him so to speak below boiling-point; while Andrew began to watch her necessary manœuvres with an increasingly sardonic eye. Cynthia's heartiness, by making all but the loudest conversation impossible, afforded a respite; so Betty played up to her with great schoolgirlishness, encouraged her to spend as much time as possible at Friars Carmel, and never left her side. This annoyed Andrew and Belinski equally, and they formed a temporary disgruntled alliance to boycott all outdoor sports.

"The beastly slackers!" cried Cynthia humorously.

She didn't really mind their defection, so long as she had

Betty; but now and then the recollection that Mr. Belinski wrote books, that he was a distinguished person, impelled her to pursue him with more intellectual attentions. She asked him where he got his ideas, and Mr. Belinski told her that he cribbed them, adding, in answer to her look of dismay, that all authors did the same. This confirmed Cynthia in her belief that highbrows were an unsporting lot, but did not put an end to her investigations. She asked whether he did not get a terrific kick out of seeing his writings in print, and Mr. Belinski, possibly misunderstanding the colloquialism, replied that there were many things he would like to give a terrific kick to, but books were not one of them.

"The girl's a half-wit," said Andrew, only just lowering his voice. He and Betty were at one end of the billiard table, playing, while the intellectual conversation carried on under the score-board at the other. They were, as usual, all together. A wet afternoon — it was raining steadily — merely herded them indoors.

"She's very nice really," murmured Betty.

"I suppose she's another friend you're going to keep?"

"I expect so."

Andrew glanced up. Betty had spoken in an oddly matter-of-fact tone; he saw her now look at Cynthia consideringly, as though wondering what could be done about the girl, as though it were a matter of course that she, Betty, should be concerned. It was a look such as Andrew had often seen his mother give the Colonel, particularly in the days when Cynthia was a small girl and there was trouble with governesses: a neighbourly look. . . .

"She ought never," said Betty thoughtfully, "to wear that pale blue."

There was absolutely no connection; but Andrew had a

sudden impulse to tell Betty he was going to join the Air Force. He nearly did so; only at that moment Belinski evidently said something altogether outrageous, Cynthia jumped up with a scarlet face, and all at once they were in the thick of a silly quarrel.

"I'm going home," said Cynthia loudly. "I'm sorry, Andrew, but I'm going home."

"Don't be a nitwit," said Andrew. "What's the matter?"

"The Professor's being perfectly beastly." She turned to glare at Belinski, who with an exasperated and righteous air promptly made matters worse.

"All I said was that the extreme fertility of rabbits—"

"Shut up!" cried Cynthia.

"— probably explained their attraction—"

Betty, who was still holding her billiard-cue, reached forward with it and, very lightly, rapped Belinski over the knuckles.

"Apologize to Cynthia at once."

It was a repetition of the scene by the brook, but this time no friendly, half-humorous glance passed between them. Belinski's eyes became bright and intent; he slid his hand up the cue till it met Betty's, then swiftly bent and kissed it.

"I kiss the rod!" he proclaimed, almost hilariously. "I apologize to Miss Duff-Graham! I am a rude and ignorant foreigner! Miss Duff-Graham, unless you forgive me, I commit suicide in Lady Carmel's duck pond!"

"Oh, for heaven's sake forgive him," said Andrew.

"But I'm *not* thwarted," protested Cynthia sulkily.

"Forgive him all the same," advised Betty. "It's nearly tea."

By the time Syrett arrived to confirm this, peace had been more or less restored; they went downstairs all on speaking terms, and Mr. Belinski at least in unsuitably high spirits.

### III

Such was the result of a wet afternoon for Andrew and Betty, Belinski and Cynthia Duff-Graham; to Cluny Brown the rain was kinder. For it was Wednesday, her afternoon off, and she splashed along the Carmel road happy in the prospect of tea at the Wilson home — and happier still when, at the foot of the Gorge, she saw Titus Wilson coming through the rain to meet her.

# Chapter 21

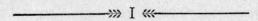

THEY TURNED and began to walk fast, the soft rain blowing in their faces, misting Mr. Wilson's spectacles so that every now and then he had to take them off and wipe them. Cluny was surprised at the difference it made: without glasses the chemist looked years younger; striding along with his shoulders back and his head up — for Mr. Wilson did not bend even to the elements — he appeared to her a brave, almost a romantic figure. Cluny herself wore her new scarlet snood, but it was concealed beneath an oilskin hood of the kind optimistically known as "pixie," but which looked more like a sponge-bag, and until this was removed she did not want her appearance noticed. They marched along almost in silence, and almost in step, for Cluny's long legs gave her a man's stride; without Roddy to watch and whistle to she looked neither to right nor left, but kept her eyes steadily on the wet road.

"You're a good walker," said Mr. Wilson approvingly.

"I like it," said Cluny.

"It's a healthy and cheap relaxation. With congenial company I ask for nothing better."

"Nor do I," said Cluny.

They reached the village and the shop, and Mr. Wilson let them in with his key. After the freshness outside the faintly antiseptic air smelt cold and shut-up, but as soon as

Mr. Wilson opened the farther door warmth rushed out and enfolded them like a blanket. Mrs. Wilson always kept a good fire. She was sitting close by the hearth, still in her shawl, and as once before, when Cluny came in, she poked out her little brown hand.

This time Cluny took it. It felt hard and knobbly — not a rabbit's paw after all, but a bit of gnarled old wood.

"We're back to tea, Mother," said Mr. Wilson loudly. "Have you got anything for us?"

The question was purely rhetorical: there was the table ready spread, with buns and splits, butter and jam and cream; and the kettle hissed on the hob. To Cluny's mood there was a sort of magic about this; you never saw any one doing anything at the Wilsons', yet everything was done. She asked curiously: —

"Who gets it all ready? Who looks after you?"

"Mrs. Brewer," said the chemist. "A very decent body."

The old lady uttered a loud snort. Her son took no notice, so Cluny didn't either.

"Hilda's a Brewer," she remarked.

"This is her auntie. They're all Brewers round these parts — Brewers or Beers."

"And proper villains they be," interjected Mrs. Wilson. "*I* know. . . ."

"Now, Mother!"

The old lady snorted again, and returned to silence. Cluny rather wondered, as she took off her mackintosh, why Mrs. Wilson had wished to return to Devonshire society. Then she took off her hood and forgot everything else but what she was wearing underneath it.

"I'll hang those in the entry," said Mr. Wilson.

He took the damp garments out of her hands and disposed

of them. He came back and made tea. He pulled out chairs round the table and told Cluny to sit down. Mrs. Wilson did not move, but had things handed to her.

"It's on an afternoon like this," observed Mr. Wilson, "that one enjoys one's own fireside. I took an epicurean pleasure coming to meet you through the wet, knowing there'd be this waiting for us."

"It's all right if you've got a good mackintosh," said Cluny. "And something on your head."

"A raincoat's a very indispensable garment, and not to be economized on. Is Mrs. Maile coughing still?"

"Not much," said Cluny. "Do you like my snood?"

The chemist examined her carefully. He was a very honest man.

"It makes you look considerably neater."

"Yes, doesn't it?" agreed Cluny eagerly. She should have left it at that, but she was always too easily encouraged. "And don't you like the bow?"

"Since you mention it, I should have thought you were too old for hair-ribbons," said Mr. Wilson.

Cluny fell silent. It was her fault, she admitted it: she should have been content with looking intelligent. And neat. That was something. Glancing away from Mr. Wilson, she met the small brown eye of his mother, and surprised there a most unexpected expression: the old lady looked extremely amused. But she said nothing. She had retreated too far into the narrow world of age — in her case bounded by food, warmth, and the villainy of her neighbours — to be bothered with the younger generation. She munched at her creamy bun, eating not very tidily, while Mr. Wilson and Cluny in equal silence finished their tea. There was a constraint between them; the chemist was aware of it, and every now and then gave Cluny an enquiring look, which she would not return. When they finished, however, he fetched a tray and between them they carried the tea-things out to a very neat kitchen, and in that domestic seclusion Mr. Wilson said suddenly: —

"As you will have learnt by now, I'm no flatterer."

"No," said Cluny.

"I shouldn't have made that remark about your hair-ribbon. It's very displeasing to a woman to be told she's trying to look younger than her age."

"I am twenty," admitted Cluny.

"It's just," persisted Mr. Wilson, "that I happen to have conservative tastes. I dare say when I get used to it I'll like it very well."

"I don't want you to get used to it if it doesn't suit me. Oh, dear, I wish I'd never bought it!"

"Did it cost a great deal?"

"No," said Cluny. It had cost half a crown, but she wasn't going to say so, because she was sure he would think it too much. What a failure it had been! Abused by Mrs. Maile and Syrett, jeered at by the Professor — When Cluny remembered the Professor, her cheeks burned again. "I'm silly," she said, with genuine grief. "I try not to be, but I can't help it . . ."

Mr. Wilson opened his mouth to observe that most young women were silly at her age, but for once had the sense to keep quiet. Instead he did what was for him a really imaginative thing: he raised his hands and carefully straightened the scarlet bow, pulling it out, crimping it, so that it set jauntily on Cluny's head.

"There!" he told her. "Foolish or not, you look very spruce. Now we'll get that book I spoke of, and I'll show you a map of this very valley."

It was an odd afternoon altogether. Cluny's spirits were

rising and falling like a barometer in a thunderstorm, and she was glad to sit down at the table and let Mr. Wilson explain his maps. He was exceptionally kind and patient; the old lady slept; gradually peace returned. It deepened and enclosed them; Cluny's first impression of that little room came back stronger than ever. How cosy it was, how warm and safe! How quietly time went between those four bright walls! It was like being inside a warm gay box. . . .

"And here," said Mr. Wilson, "is Exeter, where I was born."

Cluny looked earnestly at the interesting spot, and wondered what he had been like as a little boy. She couldn't imagine him tousled and bare-kneed; he must always have been a serious child, with a precocious eye to scholarships. A steady child, as he was now a steady man. Cluny meditated on this quality of steadiness for some minutes: the lack of it in herself had been so frequently deplored, by Mr. Porritt and the Trumpers, that she had always realized its importance; now, for the first time, she saw its attraction. To be steady was also to be at ease — unswayed by rival passions, undistracted by bypaths, indifferent to the world's weather. . . .

Mr. Wilson folded one map and opened another. They were now in Cornwall. The hands of the clock moved to five, to half past, to six. The room grew hotter. Mrs. Wilson still slept. Cluny began to look about a little, and shift her feet under the table; unused to sitting still so long, she began to feel both restless and sleepy. But she controlled herself until the last map was put aside and Mr. Wilson looked up at her with a smile.

"This has been a quiet holiday for you," he said, "but I hope not a dull one."

"I like it here," said Cluny. "It's so peaceful."

He looked contentedly at the small bright room, at his mother dozing by the hearth. He said: —

"It's always like this, in the evenings."

Why was it that at those words Cluny suddenly felt a pang? Was it the heat of the fire, had she sat too long after eating so large a tea? Had the atmosphere really become oppressive, or was it imagination? For whatever reason she looked at the clock and saw almost with relief that it was half past six.

"I must be going," she said. "I shall be late."

Mr. Wilson made no effort to detain her. He approved her conscientiousness.

"The weather's cleared," he said. "It won't be an unpleasant walk. I'll come with you."

With genuine earnestness Cluny urged him not to leave his mother alone; but the chemist, born organizer that he was, had arranged for Mrs. Brewer to come across in precisely ten minutes. Though the road was safe and plain he had no intention of permitting Cluny to walk home alone through the dusk. And he had moreover a positive intention as well, which he did not reveal until they were halfway up the Friars Carmel drive.

"I believe I'll step in," said Mr. Wilson, "and have a word with Mrs. Maile."

Cluny thought he wanted to enquire after the housekeeper's cough. She had not been at Friars Carmel long enough to realize the extreme gravity of this moment.

## II

For Mrs. Maile was a conscientious woman, as every one knew, particularly the various young men who, over a period

of thirty years, had taken her Floras and Bessies out walking on their afternoons off. Sooner or later in each romance
came the inevitable summons: would Ernest (or Richard, or
Bartholomew) please to step into the housekeeper's room?
Upon which he either made clear his honourable intentions,
or received his *congé*.

There was so much to be said for this system that no Bessie
or Flora ever raised an objection, and Mrs. Maile certainly
anticipated none from Cluny Brown. Her only uneasiness
was with regard to Mr. Wilson. The Ernests and Richards
and Bartholomews were as a rule ploughmen, day-labourers,
perhaps postmen, persons over whom Mrs. Maile had a natural superiority; she wasn't used to so big a fish as a chemist.
Moreover Mr. Wilson, as has been seen, further broke with
tradition by presenting himself unsummoned. Still, duty was
duty, and when Cluny brought in the surprising message,
Could Mrs. Maile spare a moment for Mr. Wilson, the housekeeper reached as it were for her gaff and sent a message back,
"With pleasure."

(Hilda observed this démarche with an emancipated toss of
the head. Her own romance, culminating in Gary, had occurred during a week's holiday at Loo. She gave Cluny a
rather *de haut en bas* look, to which Cluny innocently reacted
by asking what was biting her.)

Mr. Wilson, who had rightly taken no part in this exchange,
made his way unperturbed to the housekeeper's room, which
Mrs. Maile had just had time to adorn with her best antima-
cassars. They greeted each other with mutual respect, and
Mr. Wilson accepted a small whisky, to keep out the cold.

"For the weather," commented Mrs. Maile, "appears to be
turning to the bad."

"I doubt we shall have more rain," agreed Mr. Wilson. 'How's that cough of yours?"

Mrs. Maile coughed to demonstrate it. There was nothing she would have enjoyed more than a thorough discussion of her symptoms (and perhaps a little free medical advice); but her fine manners forbade her to pursue the subject further. Instead, she boldly gave Mr. Wilson his lead.

"It is kind of you to take so much interest in Cluny Brown. She is a Londoner, as you no doubt know, and it is often difficult for them to form acquaintances."

"I think very highly of her," stated Mr. Wilson. "I hope that is your opinion also."

Mrs. Maile paused. For the first time in the long series of these interviews she found herself in the position of one giving, rather than demanding, references. But Mr. Wilson was undoubtedly entitled to them.

"She's a very good girl," said Mrs. Maile. "I can't speak personally, of course, but Miss Postgate, whom I do know, and who saw Cluny in London, tells me she comes of most respectable folk."

"The poor wee lass!" said Mr. Wilson.

Mrs. Maile stared at him. She could hardly believe her ears. That Cluny Brown, five-foot-eight and thinking far too much of herself, could appear in the eyes of a sensible man as a poor wee lass, simply flummoxed her.

"She has great courage," continued Mr. Wilson, "orphaned as she is."

"Perfectly fearless," agreed Mrs. Maile — rather tartly. But she held herself in, for here was obviously the chance of a lifetime for Cluny Brown, and the housekeeper was too good a woman to spoil it. "She is also a hard and obliging worker.

I can't call her truly conscientious, but that may be because she is still a little unsettled."

"Her uncle is a plumber," added Mr. Wilson. "I mention that because many young ladies would have concealed the fact, out of foolishness. Cluny Brown told me at once. There is a great openness about her. One could hardly call her well-educated — "

Mrs. Maile, quite relieved to find that she had not been harbouring a phœnix of all the virtues, readily agreed that in many respects Cluny was as ignorant as a child of six.

"She's young," said Mr. Wilson tolerantly. He finished his whisky and rose. Mrs. Maile too felt that quite enough had been said: she had done her duty, and had certainly no desire to push Mr. Wilson farther than his own good sense judged fit. Indeed, she came very near to changing sides: she felt it was Mr. Wilson, not Cluny Brown, who needed to be protected from an entanglement.

"A plumber may no doubt be a very nice sort of person," said Mrs. Maile, carelessly, "but I don't think you and I, Mr. Wilson, would find much in common with one."

"We should find our common humanity," said the chemist gravely. "Apart from which, I'm no snob."

## III

Cluny's cheerful unconsciousness did not last long. When she came downstairs from changing her dress she was met by another meaning look from Hilda and the information that Mr. Wilson was still on the premises, in the back lobby. Cluny put her head round the door to say good-night, and there, in that very unromantic spot, within the space of five packed minutes, her eyes were opened.

"Come in a moment," said Mr. Wilson.

"I can't stop!" said Cluny — still cheerfully. "It's nearly dinner-time."

"I will not keep you long. I just wish to tell you that I am thinking of going to London."

"What, for a holiday?" asked Cluny, in surprise.

"To pay a visit," said Mr. Wilson. "I shall not be away more than a night." He gave her one of his rare, serious smiles. "So you must tell me the address."

Cluny stood perfectly still. The portentousness of the chemist's manner had given her the most extraordinary idea.

"You're not —" she stammered, "you're not —"

"I thought I would give myself the pleasure of dropping in on your uncle."

Quite overwhelmed, Cluny could do nothing but stare. She could not even think. For no understatement could minimize the importance of what she had just heard: the dropping-in of Mr. Wilson upon her Uncle Arn foreshadowed consequences too tremendous to be grasped. . . . The chemist meanwhile took out pencil and note-book, evidently ready to write down the address.

"Fifteen, String Street," murmured Cluny automatically.

"Paddington?"

"Paddington. . . ."

He wrote it down.

"Maybe you would like to send him some small gift? Fresh eggs are often acceptable."

Cluny saw the point of this at once: a dozen eggs afforded a reasonable pretext for the visit — a non-committal pretext. Eagerly she agreed to a dozen eggs.

"To make sure of my welcome," smiled Mr. Wilson. His manner was nearer to playfulness than Cluny had ever seen it, but she could not smile back. This did her no harm in the eyes of the chemist, who for a moment looked as though he were about to make some more impulsive remark still. However, he refrained. He evidently had his plans cut and dried.

"When are you going?" asked Cluny nervously.

"Probably on Saturday. I dare say, when writing to your uncle, you have mentioned my name?"

"I have, just mentioned it," admitted Cluny. This was indeed all she had done, for as her preoccupation with Mr. Wilson increased she had naturally grown more secretive about him. "He'll be surprised," said Cluny.

Mr. Wilson agreed that this was probable, but shewed no apprehension. Why should he? He could not help knowing his worth. It was arranged that he should get the eggs in the village, and Cluny would pay for them later, and on this business-like note the interview came to an end.

After Mr. Wilson had gone Cluny remained a moment or two longer in the lobby, staring at her own and Hilda's mackintoshes, and Mr. Syrett's boots, and a knitted scarf belonging to Cook. She observed that the boots needed cleaning; but apart from this achieved no constructive thought.

## IV

"Well?" said Hilda, as Cluny returned to the kitchen. "Well, Cluny Brown?"

But for once Cluny was silent. Her own name sounded oddly in her ears. The old question echoed again — "*Who do you think you are, Cluny Brown?*" — and it at last seemed probable that she had the answer.

# Chapter 22

ALL THIS happened on a Wednesday; during the next two days Cluny was afflicted by an extreme absent-mindedness, which Mrs. Maile pointedly overlooked. Too pointedly for Cluny's comfort: happy as she knew herself to be, she wished her affairs could have been conducted with less publicity. Mr. Syrett's astonished looks betrayed discussions in the house-keeper's room; Hilda giggled almost without ceasing. Hilda had expected confidences and been disappointed, so her gig-gling was in fact proof of a warm, unresentful nature, a tribute not withheld, but it got on Cluny's nerves. By Saturday after-noon (when Mr. Wilson had actually started for London) her only desire was for seclusion; as soon as the coast was clear she ran upstairs to her bedroom — and there was Hilda again, ahead of her, with a nightgown of Cluny's in one hand and a tape-measure in the other.

"I'm goin' to make'ee a silk'n!" proclaimed loving Hilda.

Cluny fled downstairs again, back to the kitchen. She knew she was behaving like a fool, and hoped it was natural; but she didn't feel natural. That was the whole trouble: she felt as though this wonderful piece of good fortune wasn't hap-pening to her, Cluny Brown, at all. Sitting at the big scrubbed table, her chin on her fists, Cluny tried hard to think herself into her rightful place. She had no doubt of her feelings towards Mr. Wilson; he was simply the kindest, the cleverest and the best man she had ever known. He was going to give her a place where she belonged, a home she would never leave, and she hoped he would also let her keep a dog. (He liked dogs. He liked Roddy.) And in return Cluny was going to be all that he wished, kind to old Mrs. Wilson, and learning lots of poetry. Put so it seemed easy enough; but on re-examining the point, balancing what each would give and each receive, Cluny thought she had perhaps found the root of her trouble. Perhaps she wasn't worthy of Mr. Wilson. The more she considered it the likelier it seemed, and never can a sense of inferiority have brought greater comfort: for if that was all that was wrong, the remedy lay in her own hands. She had simply to improve. . . .

And this happy thought brought in turn a new and fruitful idea. Who, of all at Friars Carmel, had been her unkindest critic? The Professor. Cluny suddenly felt that a talk with the Professor was the very thing she needed. He would tell her frankly of all those faults which the eye of love (Mr. Wilson's) did not yet, but might later, perceive — so that she could get down to improving without a moment's delay.

Thought and action being ever coincident with her, Cluny jumped up and ran out through the laundry to the stable-yard. It was not certain she would find the Professor there, but Miss Duff-Graham hadn't come that afternoon, there was no tennis, and Cluny hoped that he might for once be doing a bit of work. Emerging into sunshine, she glanced eagerly at the window: no head was visible, but this didn't mean the Professor was not within. Cluny felt sure he was within — and as she crossed the yard she told herself that this time, when he asked her, this time she would go up into his little room, so that they could have a good, long, improving talk.

She reached the foot of the stairs. What happened next was

so unexpected (and yet why should it have been?) that she felt an almost physical shock. From the window above, faintly, came voices: the voices of Adam Belinski and Betty Cream.

Cluny stood a moment uncertain, and then went slowly back through the laundry door.

## II

In designing that small apartment for Mr. Belinski's convenience Andrew had certainly never realized how extremely convenient it might, in certain circumstances, be. Half-secret, secure from household interruptions, it was the very place for intimate or even amorous conversation. Mr. Belinski of course had realized this at once, and of late spent much time and ingenuity in persuading Betty to visit him there. Now he had more than succeeded; Betty brought Andrew with her; and whatever thoughts Cluny took away sprung from a mistaken premise.

"This is nice," Betty was saying. "This is very nice indeed. I believe I could write a book here myself."

"It is yours," said Mr. Belinski promptly — and just as though he owned the place. He shot Andrew a malicious look. "Did Andrew ever tell you why he prepared it for me? So that I might hide away from the Nazis. I am a great disappointment to Andrew: he thought I was a political character, worth saving, and I am not."

Impassioned and unscrupulous, Belinski thus did his best to drive his benefactor away; but Andrew remained where he was on one end of the camp-bed. Betty had curled herself at the other. What a pity it was they were grown-up! As children they could have enjoyed themselves there enormously, safe out of reach from the house, with a horse stamping below;

triumphant — governess evaded, holiday-tasks shirked — at being all together; urgent to hatch plots, tell secrets, concoct strange foods and chemical experiments. Both Betty and Andrew felt something of this, and even Belinski (with childhood memories very different from theirs) recognized that the atmosphere was unfavourable to his original design. He gave Betty one long reproachful look; then with a complete change of aspect pulled a letter from his pocket and flourished it before them.

"This is again from my splendid American publishers!" he proclaimed. "They wish me to go to New York. They wish me to address lunch-clubs. I am famous in the U.S.A.!"

### III

It is a rare guest the cutting-short of whose stay brings no compensation. Andrew heard these tidings with considerable pleasure, and advised Belinski to fall in with whatever plans had been made for him. Belinski turned to Betty Cream: it was for her sake he had held himself in all morning, ever since the letter arrived by the first post; he had hoped to dazzle her with it in private.

"But how perfectly wonderful!" said Betty warmly. "Isn't that just what you wanted?"

"It is undoubtedly a great opportunity," agreed Belinski, enjoying his importance. "I hope they will like me. But I believe they are very unprejudiced."

Andrew, who believed this too, nevertheless hoped that the splendid Americans were not going to get more than they bargained for; he cast a dubious eye on Belinski's shirt. It was the corn-coloured one, worn with an Old Etonian tie, for in his first enthusiasm Andrew had given Belinski the run of his wardrobe, and he remembered how he had grinned to himself at this choice: no Communist was more sardonic than Andrew on the subject of the Old School Tie. But now he felt a reluctance to let Belinski invade America under those particular colours; he thought he would get it back. Belinski could keep his dinner-jacket and his dress shirts, however, and his evening trousers, and his grey flannels — in fact when Andrew came to consider the matter he realized that Belinski would also have to be given a trunk.

"When do you think of making a move?" he asked casually.

"That I am not sure. There is a man I am to see in London. They say at once, but of course I will not go quite at once," explained Belinski, "that would not be polite to your mother. Rather than be in the least discourteous to Lady Carmel, I consign all America to the Atlantic!"

Andrew, trusting this was merely a Polish flower of speech, said he was sure Lady Carmel would understand. But the Professor appeared to be attacked by doubts, and not only with regard to his hostess. He began to look uneasy.

"I hope I am doing rightly," he said. "You do not think perhaps I ought to stay here, Andrew, not prostituting my talent, as you say, but writing good books?"

Andrew replied that all things considered, he thought Belinski ought to go to America and open the eyes of the New World to European culture. He was aware himself of the over-formality of this speech; he was in fact using formality as a dam to a great tide of relief and pleasure. Not until this moment, when relief was in sight, had Andrew allowed himself to admit the force of a dislike which did him so little credit. But for once the old rule, that where we benefit we love, had not held good; Andrew, having benefited the Professor enormously, now wished only to be rid of him. Asked why, he would have taken refuge in sheerest conventionality, and said he disliked the fellow's shirts. . . .

He became aware of Betty's eyes fixed on him in a very thoughtful gaze. Pulling himself together, Andrew said quickly: —

"But would you rather stay in England? Because if so, you know we're only too glad — "

"For how long?" asked Belinski. "For in England I have no other prospects. Friars Carmel has been my Ark." He spoke with great feeling. With him the rule evidently worked in reverse: having received benefits, he was not only grateful, but ready to receive more. "I shall never be so happy again," he said simply. "I have been on velvet."

Already the atmosphere was changed, excitement had given place to doubt, to regret; it was obvious that within five minutes the Professor could talk himself into abandoning America and spending the rest of his life at Friars Carmel. And because this risk was a real one, Andrew felt bound to take it. He remembered all too clearly how he had badgered the Professor into coming; he remembered his very words — "I thought you might stay a few years." Though every instinct urged, he could not go back on them.

Both Belinski and Betty were waiting. Andrew said: —

"We all hoped you were going to make your home here; and of course that still stands. When you say, how long? — my dear chap, I can only say, for ever!"

Out of the tail of his eye he saw Betty bring her hands together, as though in a gesture of applause. Belinski, after one moment's silent, bright gazing, jumped down from the table and caught Andrew by the shoulders.

"You are remarkable, you are magnificent!" he exclaimed. "I am unworthy of such friendship! You give me courage to go to America! — For I believe I shall go to America, after all. . . ."

It was only as they trooped down the stair, happy and excited again, agog to tell Lady Carmel, that Andrew discovered he had been sweating.

## IV

Her ladyship received the news with warm congratulations, and placed no obstacles in the Professor's way. Syrett, overhearing, carried the news below stairs, where Mrs. Maile, who had shown a weakness for the Professor ever since the affair of the silk stockings, blessed her soul and hoped he would do well for himself and not be taken in. Hilda and Cluny were out of hearing at the time, and would have been left in ignorance but for a later remark of the housekeeper's, to the effect that the east room could now be spring-cleaned. "Be Professor leavin'?" asked Hilda carelessly; and passed the news to Cluny that they'd have one less bed to make. Cluny Brown said nothing at all. Why should she? The number of beds in use at Friars Carmel would soon be a matter of complete indifference to her.

In fact, the only person who took Belinski's approaching departure at all to heart was Sir Henry. He wandered in while his wife was dressing for dinner and stood beside her with a troubled look.

"Allie, what's the Professor want to go to America for?" he demanded uneasily.

"Dear, he's had a book published there. That's why we're having champagne, to celebrate. It seems it's a great success, and they want him to go over there and — and what Andrew calls cash in on it."

"Seems a precarious sort of scheme to me," grumbled Sir Henry. "He'd do much better to stay here. I've a good mind to speak to him."

"Do, dear," said Lady Carmel. She was quite certain that Sir Henry's speaking would not affect the Professor's plans, and content that it should be so. There was no doubt that during the last month the Professor had greatly changed; indeed, when she remembered the quiet, dim figure he originally presented, she found it hard to realize he was the same man. "I suppose success has gone to his head," thought Lady Carmel charitably — but at the back of her mind she knew it was Betty Cream, and that this was why his going would be such a great relief. . . .

Alice Carmel looked at her husband, and wondered: he noticed very little of what went on, but was it possible he had noticed nothing? Not even the moments when Belinski, leaning over Betty's chair, held his hand deliberately half an inch, as from a candle-flame, from her golden head? Nor the moments when he discharged a sort of electric shock of emotion as she came into a room? Seeing a small quarrel flare up on the tennis-court, did Sir Henry put it down to youthful high spirits alone? His wife did not. Her constant talk, in the evenings, of gardens and window-boxes, was not undirected; she was well aware of its soothing, almost soporific effect on the lay mind. Like Betty, she had seen Cynthia Duff-Graham's use as a damper. But all this had been wearing, especially at a time of year when her garden needed undivided attention, and Lady Carmel contemplated with gratitude the end of a great nuisance. The Professor, whose coming had created such a stir, was about to go quietly; and as a reward was to be given the best champagne.

Looking at her husband, with these thoughts passing through

her mind, Lady Carmel also observed that Sir Henry had not finished dressing. It was half past seven. (The very moment at which, in String Street, Mr. Porritt opened his door and found a stranger on the step.) She gave Sir Henry an affectionate, dismissive pat, and told him to hurry.

"But the poor fellow's not going at once, is he?" persisted Sir Henry.

"Well, not to-morrow, dear, not on a Sunday," said Lady Carmel. She privately thought that Monday morning would be a very suitable time. That left only two more evenings to get through — "And surely," thought Lady Carmel cheerfully, "surely we can manage that!"

But she was over-optimistic. It was on that Saturday night that everything happened.

# Chapter 23

————— ≫ I ≪ —————

OPENING the door to Mr. Wilson, Arnold Porritt naturally did so in the character of a plumber rather than an uncle. (He had in fact only just cleaned himself up after his last job, and his costume formed a marked contrast to the spruceness of Mr. Wilson.) It was therefore a considerable surprise to him when on admitting his identity, he found a basket of eggs placed in his hands.

"What's this?" demanded Mr. Porritt suspiciously. "I haven't ordered 'em. You've got the wrong house."

"They are from your niece, Cluny Brown," explained Mr. Wilson. "I have just come from Friars Carmel, and she asked me to bring them."

"Oh, aye," said Mr. Porritt, still as much astonished as pleased. "Very good of you to trouble. How is she?"

"She's fine, and sends her love."

"Give her mine," said Mr. Porritt.

So far as he was concerned, the incident was now closed. But the gift bearer showed no signs of departing, in fact it was increasingly obvious that he expected to be asked in. But solitariness had been growing on Mr. Porritt, and he hesitated, until the chemist observed rather firmly that he would no doubt like first-hand news of his niece. At that Mr. Porritt bowed to the laws of hospitality and led the way to the kitchen.

"Sit down a minute," he invited. He himself set the basket

on the dresser and put the eggs into a bowl before turning back to his guest. He couldn't quite make it out: it was natural enough for young Cluny to send him eggs, if any one were coming his way and could look in; but this chap hadn't the air of looking in, he had taken off his hat and opened his coat, and seemed to be settling down for a long spell. . . .

"You'll be wondering who I am," said Mr. Wilson, very aptly, "though I believe your niece has mentioned my name. It is Titus Wilson, and I keep the chemist's shop at Friars Carmel. It is my own property."

This very plain statement, however, rather increased than lessened Mr. Porritt's surprise. He hadn't asked the chap's business, had he? So he merely said, "Aye."

"But Cluny has often spoken to me of you," went on Mr. Wilson, "as being *in loco parentis.*"

It now occurred to Mr. Porritt that Cluny had probably got the sack and this chemist chap was about to break the bad news.

"If there's anything I've got to know, better let me have it," he said grimly; and Mr. Wilson at once did so.

"I'm here to get your permission," he said explicitly, "to ask Cluny Brown to be my wife."

Mr. Porritt's jaw fell.

## II

Only for a moment or two, however, did he stand thus gaping. Astounding as the idea was, he managed to grasp it; and with realization came the dawn of an enormous, an almost overwhelming hope. One look was enough to tell him that here was a suitor worthy of every consideration; dazed as he was, still half-incredulous, Mr. Porritt instinctively went to the cupboard and brought out two bottles of beer. The opening and pouring of them gave him further time to collect himself, and when he spoke again it was with his usual dignified good sense.

"Your health," said Mr. Porritt. "Now let's get this straight. You want to marry young Cluny?"

"I do," replied Mr. Wilson — almost as though he were at the altar already.

Mr. Porritt very nearly asked why. But he restrained the impulse and asked instead: —

"And she wants to marry you?"

"I have not yet asked her. But without being conceited, I think I may say she has a liking for me."

Mr. Porritt, glad to find Cluny had so much sense, nodded encouragement.

"A strong liking," continued the chemist. "We have seen quite a deal of each other, and it has struck me very much how content she has always been with our quiet pleasures. We go fine long walks," said Mr. Wilson enthusiastically, "once or twice she's come home to tea, that's all, yet we always find subjects of conversation. I've never met a young lady so eager to improve her mind."

Like Mrs. Maile, Mr. Porritt could hardly believe his ears. If this was what good service had done for Cluny, it was more, far more, than he had ever anticipated: it seemed almost incredible. But the chemist went even further.

"She is also uncommonly modest — as of course you'll have observed yourself. It's perfectly remarkable."

"Well, she's no oil-painting," pointed out Mr. Porritt.

"Certainly not. But she has a fine intelligent expression and, in my opinion, fine eyes. I would call her definitely attractive."

Mr. Porritt was only too pleased to hear it. Indeed, he began to feel that there must have been more to Cluny than he had realized, if she could fix the affections of so sterling a character as Mr. Wilson. Over the rim of his beer-glass Mr. Porritt considered his prospective nephew-in-law with the closest attention: a steady chap if ever he saw one, well-to-do, practically a professional man and sound as a bell. Also a chap with whom he, Mr. Porritt, could get on very well in a friendly, sensible fashion, without back-slapping or familiarity, but on either side goodwill and solid respect.

"She's a lucky lass," said Mr. Porritt, most sincerely, "and you can tell her I said so."

Upon this encouragement Mr. Wilson immediately gave a brief but highly satisfactory account of his financial situation. He had brought with him on a slip of paper figures showing his turn-over and profits for the last five years: there was a note of what rent he paid, and of the sum annually set aside for future improvements: the whole leaving no shadow of doubt as to his ability to support Cluny Brown, plus a possible family, in every reasonable comfort.

"Moreover," finished Mr. Wilson, "in the changed circumstances, I intend to insure my life for two thousand pounds. You will note a sum set aside for the first premium."

Mr. Porritt warmed to him more and more. This was a sort of talk he understood and appreciated; and the chemist's next words went straight to his heart.

"I want to make her safe," explained Mr. Wilson.

"Ah!" said Mr. Porritt. "That's what I want too. That's what I've always held. That's what every young woman needs: safety. A solid future, with no more worry than's natural, a steady-going husband and a good home."

"I hope I may provide her with all that," said Mr. Wilson, modestly.

"So I believe. And furthermore —" it gave Mr. Porritt deep pleasure to say this, as one substantial, fair-dealing man to another — "furthermore, what I have, Cluny gets. No more than a hundred or two, maybe, but she gets it. And on her wedding-day, she'll have fifty pounds down."

"I call that very liberal," said Mr. Wilson.

Mr. Porritt contemplated himself with satisfaction. It was crossed by a streak of melancholy, for he wished Floss were there too, to approve and admire, as she certainly would have done, the way he was handling the whole business. He sighed.

"I wish my wife was alive," he said. "She'd ha' been pleased."

The chemist met this with a proper look of serious gratification. His practical mind moved forward to a related point.

"There is also the matter," he said, "of where the wedding is to take place. Conventionally speaking, of course, it should be from here; but without womenfolk —"

"There's her aunt," said Mr. Porritt. "My sister. It would be meat and drink to her, no doubt about that." But he pondered a moment. "Would you be going straight back to Devonshire?"

"If we get married as soon as I hope, that would be the case. I could not leave the shop without a proper person in charge. Later on, I would propose a week, maybe two, in the Trossachs." The chemist paused in turn; he perceived Mr. Porritt's mind opening to the more sensible plan. "On the other hand, if Cluny consented to be married at Friars Carmel, where she is already a parishioner like myself, that might simplify matters greatly. It's not as though we want a grand to-do."

"You're right there," agreed Mr. Porritt heartily.

"I don't say it's not a great day for a young woman," went on Mr. Wilson, "and I'd want it to be all as Cluny wishes; but there's a lass at the big house she's made a friend of, and

Mrs. Maile, a very good woman indeed, who I know would stand by her, and I dare say Lady Carmel would come to the church herself: Cluny would be among friends, if not old ones. In fact it's for you to say, sir, whether you can make the journey. I understand you've a business of your own."

"Plumbing and general repairs," supplied Mr. Porritt. "Still, it's not like a shop. I could manage all right, if it's necessary."

"It's essential," said Mr. Wilson positively. "You wouldn't want any one else to give her away, and nor should I. There's a decent bedroom at the Artichoke, and not over-expensive, which I'll be pleased to engage for you."

Strong as was Mr. Porritt's own character, he was aware of having encountered a stronger. He felt, however, no inclination to resist; it was a great relief to find everything so cut-and-dried, in such obviously capable hands. Addie Trumper would no doubt have done all, and perhaps more, than was required — but what a fuss she would have made over it! How infinitely preferable was the calm good sense brought to bear by Titus Wilson! Mr. Porritt thought him the very model of a prospective groom, and brought out two more bottles of beer.

In the end Mr. Wilson accepted not only beer, but also a light supper of corned beef, and stayed talking till half past ten o'clock. It was decided that as soon as he returned to Devon he should get Cluny to fix the day, which would then be communicated to Mr. Porritt; but Cluny was by no means their only subject of conversation. They got on to politics, trades-unionism, the decay of brewing, and found themselves wonderfully in agreement on all points. It was long since Mr. Porritt had had such a good argybargy, and he enjoyed himself mightily — and none the less because all the while, at the back of his mind, he could not cease to marvel at his niece's astonishing luck. He felt fonder of Cluny, now that she was about to be settled for life, than he had ever done before; he felt positively proud of her; he felt proud of himself for having done so well by her in sending her into Devon; and at last went to bed (Mr. Wilson having departed to the station hotel) in a mood most agreeably compounded of thankfulness and self-congratulation, in about equal parts.

# Chapter 24

————— ≫ I ≪ —————

Sober and content went Mr. Porritt and Mr. Wilson to their beds; at Friars Carmel every one was up late, and if the Professor was not intoxicated he should have been, for in the words of Mr. Syrett, he had properly punished the champagne. But in spite of champagne, and in spite of the fact that Cynthia and the Colonel, hastily invited, made it a party, the farewell dinner wasn't exactly gay. Sir Henry was still upset, and Andrew seemed to have something on his mind. (He had: he was trying to conceal an immense pleasure.) Cynthia flinched every time Belinski opened his mouth, and the good Colonel monopolized Betty with interminable canine pedigrees. Moreover, Cluny Brown's waiting was deplorable, it was back to her lowest standard, she scattered cutlery right and left and nearly lost a sauce-boat, and though Lady Carmel, in whose ear Mrs. Maile had dropped a discreet word, tried hard to make allowances, no hostess can feel thoroughly at ease and guide the conversation properly when her guests are in obvious danger from her parlour-maid. Betty Cream helped, but she was wearing white *broderie anglaise;* every time a dish skated over the puff of her sleeve she instinctively froze. To a spontaneously gay party none of this would have mattered, it would have become a joke; as it was, the pauses grew longer and longer, till at last Lady Carmel made a sign to

Syrett, and Cluny went out with the entrée dishes and did
not return.

"What's the matter?" asked Sir Henry. "Girl got tooth-
ache?"

"Yes," said Lady Carmel.

Gloomy and resigned, Syrett carried on alone, and they
were all grateful when the meal ended. Only Sir Henry and
the Colonel sat on over their port, for Belinski followed Betty
out of the room and Andrew came after. It was Andrew who
turned on the wireless and asked Betty to dance; they rolled
up the rugs and pushed back the furniture — and happy was
Lady Carmel to see her drawing-room disarranged, if only
gaiety would result. She caught the Professor's eye and
glanced meaningly at Cynthia. Belinski at once rose, grasped
the girl round the waist, and they began to rumba. It was
perhaps fortunate that Belinski did not know how, for this
gave Cynthia an opportunity to do something she could do
well: she taught him. She was used to difficult pupils — had
she not coerced countless awkward squads through Gathering Peascods? — she was strong and determined, and long
after the other two had sat down the Professor and Cynthia
laboured on. Then Belinski fiddled with the wireless until
he found a Viennese orchestra, and with a menacing look
invited Cynthia to dance again: if he could not rumba he
could waltz, and they circled the room like a whipped top,
Cynthia with scarlet face and set teeth holding up for the
honour of the Guides, Belinski white and tireless. It was less
a dance than an athletic contest, and it ended in a draw.

"That is how we dance in Poland," gasped the Professor, as
the tune ended leaving them both on their feet. "We do not
stand and wriggle our hips, we dance!"

"You've a good wind," approved Sir Henry, who had entered, with the Colonel, just in time to witness the finish. "Ought to go out with the beagles — oughtn't they, Allie?"

This unusual compliment was well received. Cynthia sipped barley-water and looked pleased with herself, Belinski demonstrated a few steps of the mazurka. Andrew and Betty danced again — how differently, thought Lady Carmel! How smoothly and gracefully! It seemed a pity they should ever separate. But Andrew had not yet asked Cynthia, and of course he had to, though the next tune was the best of all, "The Blue Danube." The Professor danced it with Betty.

Even Lady Carmel was forced to admit they made a wonderful couple. Belinski did not grasp Betty as he had grasped Cynthia; lightly his arm touched her waist, lightly her hand lay on his shoulder, as though they had been blown together by the music. Blown by the music her flower-like skirt puffed and swung; blown on the music they floated, not speaking, rapt by perfection. Andrew and Cynthia dropped out to give them room; it was hardly necessary; without taking his eyes from Betty's face, Belinski seemed able to guide their flight like a bat in the dusk; they might have been dancing in empty air. And Betty's eyes, Lady Carmel saw, were closed. And then she saw something else: every time they passed the arch to the smaller drawing-room beyond they wavered towards it, Belinski's arm tightening, Betty, still in perfect rhythm, leaning away; so perhaps her eyes were not quite shut after all. . . .

But they did not know when the music ended. It took the Colonel's hearty clap to bring them back to their surroundings. Betty stood blinking a little, laughing a little, and then dropped down beside Sir Henry in a spread of white skirts.

"My dear, you dance like an angel," said he.

"So does the Professor!"

Belinski, without asking any one's leave, opened a cabinet and brought her a small ivory fan. "My heart," he said politely, and they all laughed. It was a charming little ballroom scene, gay and artificial as the cupids on the fan. Gaiety, indeed, had at last descended: the Colonel insisted on dancing with Betty himself, and they executed a slow waltz to universal applause. That was the last of the waltzes, for now Andrew juggled with the wireless again, and the strains which reached Cluny Brown's ears, as she took round the hot-water bottles, were strictly modern.

"Don't you wish us could have a look?" sighed Hilda, as they went up to bed at their usual time.

"Not particularly," said Cluny.

"It's all right for you, you've seen their dresses," complained Hilda.

"Miss Cream's in white and looks wonderful, Miss Duff-Graham's in blue and looks a mess."

Hilda guessed what was wrong. The humiliation of being sent out of the dining-room still rankled, and no wonder. Even her own splendid breathing apparatus had never brought her, Hilda, so low as that. So she did a kind thing. She slipped down again, to Mr. Andrew's room, and got the hot-water bottle from his bed (he always threw it out anyway) and put it into Cluny Brown's instead.

About midnight Cynthia and her father went home, the party was over, but the Professor's spirits refused to abate. "What shall we do now," he demanded, "with this evening so well begun?" "We'll go to bed," said Andrew. "Impossible!" cried the Professor. But it wasn't impossible at all, at Friars Carmel; Lady Carmel was gathering herself together, Betty picked up her bag and her fan — then looked at the fan and smiled, and went to put it back in the cabinet. At once Belinski intercepted her; as though the thing were his to give, and he had given it her, he seemed to be begging her to keep it. Andrew, from the other side of the room, saw them, and with a sudden annoyance. He walked across, opened the cabinet door so that Betty could lay the fan inside, closed it and turned the key. It was a silly thing to have done, trivial and ungracious: Andrew at once regretted it. For a moment he thought Belinski was going to smash the glass; then Betty laughed and began to say good-night, kissed Lady Carmel, kissed Sir Henry, cried that it had been a lovely party, and disappeared upstairs.

After that, they all went to bed.

## II

But not to sleep. Andrew read two pages of Boswell's *Johnson,* put out his light, and presently put it on again. It was one in the morning, an hour when any unpleasant incident looms larger than by day: he was still cursing himself for his spurt of ill humour. It had been childish — precisely, for he suddenly recollected how once, at the end of an early birthday-party, he had objected to another little boy's taking the last cracker. Then tender age and over-excitement had partly excused him; now he was inexcusable. "Damn!" said Andrew aloud. How idiotic it was to worry, when ten to one Belinski had already forgotten the whole incident! Belinski wouldn't worry, he had too much sense . . . But reason as he might Andrew could not compose his mind to sleep. Discourtesy to a guest, however slight, was a lapse which Friars Carmel did not permit; and presently Andrew thought it would be a good idea if he went along to Belinski's room.

For Andrew had by this time noticed that there was no hot-water bottle in his bed. Possibly there was none in Belinski's either. It would be a most attentive, expiatory act to go and find out.

He got up, put on dressing-gown and slippers, and made his way towards the east corridor. The house always seemed much larger at night: Andrew, sleeping at the extremity of the west wing, passed two empty rooms before he reached his mother's door; then came a dressing-room and bathroom, then Betty's door in the angle before he turned on to the landing. The house was so still that he could hear the tick of the clock in the hall below; so dark that crossing the head of the stairs he blundered against the newel post; he stepped back, groping for the wall, and felt his hand in contact with something hard, smooth, and icy-cold. It was the china swan. Andrew reached behind it (knocking out a bough of lilac) to the curtains of the deep window and drew one back. A little light flowed in, enough to show the angle of the passage. Andrew went on past the service-stairs, turned, and reached the Professor's room. He tapped, gently at first, then louder. Then he opened the door and looked in. The Professor was not there.

## III

About five minutes earlier, indeed, Betty Cream had woken up, switched on the bedside light, and seen Mr. Belinski standing just inside her door. He shut it quietly behind him.

"Please can you lend me a good book?" he asked politely.

Before answering Betty switched on a second light, which thoroughly illumined the whole room. The conjunction of a highly desirable appearance with a great deal of sense had inevitably taught her much that young girls were not commonly supposed to know: for instance, that a strong light is almost as good as a chaperon. Adam Belinski blinked under it.

"No," said Betty.

"I cannot sleep, and I wondered — "

"Mr. Belinski, you're making a fool of yourself. If I scream — "

He looked astonished.

"Scream? But why should you scream?"

"Because I don't like people coming into my room."

"Then why did you not lock your door?" asked Belinski reasonably.

"One doesn't, in private houses."

"Then it is very misleading," complained Mr. Belinski. "If I found a door locked, I would naturally go away again — "

"And I don't want to hear about your experiences in hotel corridors," added Betty. "I want to go to sleep."

"When you danced with me, you were awake for the first time."

Betty sighed. She felt it an unfair paradox that her excellent dancing — an accomplishment so insisted upon by mothers, governesses, and other guardians of the young — should so often lead her, as it did, into this sort of misunderstanding. She said patiently: —

"Mr. Belinski, I don't want to scream, but if I do, do you know what would happen?"

"Nothing would happen. At least nothing that is not going to happen — "

"That's just where you're wrong," explained Betty kindly. "If I scream, you'll be turned out of the house to-morrow. It's an old English custom. Then what will you do?"

"I shall go to America. I *am* going to America. That is what I came to remind you," said Mr. Belinski resourcefully, "since you seem to forget. Soon you will never see me again."

"Good," said Betty.

There was a short pause. (It was while they were thus silent that Andrew as silently passed along the corridor outside.) Then Belinski said earnestly: —

"If you wish to marry me, of course we will get married. But honestly I cannot advise it, I have no income, I am a stranger, your family would undoubtedly and rightly object. I would not advise it at all."

"My dear, I wouldn't dream of marrying you," said Betty.

"You have sense as well as everything else. I adore you. But love is something quite different — "

"Nor am I in love with you. Not in the least."

"Not even while we are dancing? Besides," argued Belinski, "how can you tell, if you will not let me make love to you? How can you tell if you are going to love any one? Such an attitude is ridiculous!"

"In this country, yours is considered immoral."

"In this country, it is a wonder to me how the race survives. Has anything I say sounded shocking to you?"

"No," admitted Betty. "In fact, I've heard it before, and it always sounds like sense. But I'll tell you something I've noticed. Quite a number of people I know keep having casual affairs, and they do it just as you say, to find out if they're in love, and what type suits them, and so on. And they nearly all get rather tatty."

"Tatty?"

"Mothy. Shabby. Like a fur when you keep sending it to the cleaners," explained Betty. "I don't know how it is, but they do. Now look at Andrew's mother and father — "

But Belinski knew too well the dangers, at such a point as this, of rational conversation. Already he had lost the advantage of surprise; Betty, now really interested in what she was saying, became with every moment less vulnerable to reckless emotion. Belinski put his hand to the switch by the door and moved very quickly; but it took even less time for Betty to scream.

## IV

In the great bedroom, and just as Andrew's hand encountered the swan, Lady Carmel sat up and ate a biscuit. She usually woke once or twice in the night, and it did not worry her. As a rule she lay quietly and contentedly waiting for sleep to take her again, enjoying the perfect comfort of the great bed and the familiar warmth of Sir Henry's solid rump. Night-thoughts had no terrors for Alice Carmel: from old habit she often said a prayer or two at these times, because the words were pleasant to her, but the notion that they might penetrate to the Almighty's ear would have distressed her very much. She made no claim on His attention, she prayed as a child hums a hymn. Then she ate a biscuit, being careful not to get crumbs under the sheet, and went to sleep again.

On this night, however, something troubled her. She had the impression that something needed attending to. Had any one tapped at her door? It was possible; possible that Syrett (for instance) still stood without, reluctant to knock again. Perhaps Mrs. Maile, or one of the girls, had been taken ill. . . .

Lady Carmel glanced at her soundly sleeping spouse, and instead of calling out crept carefully from the bed and pattered to the door. No one stood behind it, neither Syrett nor Mrs. Maile in agony; but paddling along the corridor and looking towards the landing Lady Carmel observed, on the floor beneath the window, a vague pale shape like a small cloud. A bough of white lilac had fallen from the swan. "So that's it!"

thought Lady Carmel; and hastened, as to the scene of an accident, to put it back in water. She had just picked it up when some one switched on the light, and there stood Andrew.

For a moment mother and son stared at each other in mutual surprise. Lady Carmel in particular presented an odd appearance: the lilac in her hand gave her a vaguely allegorical look, like a figure strayed out of a pageant. (Sir Henry would have known at once whom she represented: the goddess Flora.)

"Oh, it's you," said Andrew. "Mother, you're not still doing the flowers!"

"No, of course not," said Lady Carmel. "But I heard this fall out. Aren't you quite well, dear?"

"I wanted a cigarette."

"Then be careful of the sheets, for the Professor has made two great holes already. Isn't he quite well?"

"So far as I know. Why?"

"I just thought," explained Lady Carmel, "that as you were coming from the east corridor, and there's no one there but the Professor, and there were two hundred cigarettes in your room this afternoon, perhaps he had been taken ill and you didn't want to worry me. Champagne does sometimes upset the stomach."

"Darling," said Andrew earnestly, "I wish you'd go back to bed."

"I'm going. I just want to hear the house settle down again. . . ."

She turned and looked over the carved railing, into the shadowy hall beneath. Andrew moved to her side, rather touched, rather impatient; so they stood, mother and son, mistress and heir, listening to the clock's tick, the flick of a leaf falling from a flower-pot. There were no other sounds. The old house was solid, and the old furniture. No ghosts walked at Friars Carmel. Its inhabitants, having done their duty in one world, were presumably busy with their duty in the next.

"Andrew," said Lady Carmel, "don't sell it."

"No, Mother," replied Andrew automatically; and then, still staring down into the hall, he added, "But I'm going to join the Air Force."

There was so long a silence that he wondered whether she had heard; but when he turned and looked at her, her face told him that she had. She said: —

"Does your father know?"

"Not yet. I'll talk to him to-morrow. You don't mind, Mother?"

"No," said Lady Carmel steadily. "I suppose it's logical . . . Thank you for telling me just now, Andrew, when we are so by ourselves. Now get back to bed, dear, or you'll catch cold."

Andrew laughed and put his arm round her shoulder; below them the clock struck the half-hour, leaving a deeper silence after the chime, a silence that held them there one moment longer; and in that moment, Betty screamed.


# V

Immediately the scene was one of complex animation. Andrew, rushing towards Betty's door, collided with Mr. Belinski bolting out. (It was an awkward moment for the Professor; expecting darkness and a clear field, he emerged into bright light and company.) Andrew grasped him by the arm; Belinski, with great presence of mind, as promptly grasped Andrew. Betty Cream appeared in the open door, saw Andrew, saw his mother, and disappeared to get her dressing-gown. Cluny Brown appeared on the service-stairs, looking, with long white nightdress and dishevelled locks, rather like Lady Macbeth. In the darkness behind her a low but continuous squeaking indicated the presence of Hilda. Lady Carmel still agitated a spray of lilac. They all spoke at once.

"Has there been a murder?" called Cluny Brown.

"Good God! It is Andrew!" cried Mr. Belinski.

"Brown, go back to bed immediately," said Lady Carmel.

"What's happened?" demanded Andrew.

Betty, now dressing-gowned and composed, very distinctly informed them.

"I'm so sorry, Lady Carmel: I heard my door open and thought it was a burglar, so I screamed."

"What *happened?*" repeated Andrew stubbornly.

"I mistook the door," explained Belinski. "Coming back from the bathroom, in the dark."

Since every person present knew that his bathroom, like his bedroom, was situated in the other wing, this explained a good deal too much. Lady Carmel glanced hastily towards the service-stairs: the two girls were no longer in sight, but she suspected their presence on the upper landing. She said swiftly: —

"How very tiresome, but that does happen in a strange house. No wonder Betty was alarmed, they had a burglar at the Hall last year. Andrew, I don't want your father disturbed if he is still asleep. Dear me, what an exciting evening this has been! Good-night again, Professor; Andrew will turn off the lights."

## VI

Like a good hostess, Lady Carmel accompanied Betty into her room and saw her get into bed again. (She also placed the lilac in a vase of tulips, where it would do very well till morning.) Betty made no further reference to her burglar story, and Alice Carmel expected none; they were both aware that it had served its purpose and could now be forgotten. But the elder lady did not immediately leave, and Betty sat up against her pillows with an attentive air — not as though expecting a scolding, but as though the time and place were well suited to conversation. In her blue gown, neatly curled for the night, she looked like a very sensible child.

"You know, dear, you'd better get married," said Lady Carmel.

"Yes, Lady Carmel," said Betty meekly.

"Are you going to marry Andrew?"

"Yes, Lady Carmel."

"Then I think you should tell him so. He's getting quite nervous."

"I'll tell him to-morrow."

"Thank you, dear." Lady Carmel nodded in a satisfied manner and turned to go. But Betty stopped her.

"Lady Carmel, you — you haven't always been sure about me, have you?"

"No, dear. But my opinion has changed."

"Will you tell me what changed it?"

"I think it was the way you screamed," said Lady Carmel meditatively. "When I was young, I think girls screamed a great deal more — at mice, or ghost stories, or the sight of blood. And one could always tell — at least, another girl could — whether the scream were genuine or put on. You screamed as though you meant it. Now go to sleep, Elizabeth, and to-morrow we'll have a long talk. Especially about the gardens," added Lady Carmel, "because they're all planned three years ahead."

## VII

The conversation between Andrew and Belinski (for Andrew too conducted a guest back to his room) was far less satisfactory. Andrew was in a pugnacious mood; he had acquiesced in his mother's handling of the situation, but it had left him still full of undischarged energy.

"Look here," he said baldly, "all this tale about the wrong door — I don't believe it."

"I am so sorry," said Belinski, with a disarming smile. "And of course, it is not true. But I had not time to think of anything better."

"If you admit that, you're admitting a good deal."

"How can I help it? You were there," said Belinski simply.

Andrew leant back against the bureau and stared. His attitude, his expression, were full of unconscious arrogance — the first defence put up by his kind against an unknown quantity.

"Did you go into Miss Cream's room deliberately?"

"Of course. And if you ask me why, I warn you that the answer will embarrass you very much. However, let us call it an overwhelming impulse. An overwhelming impulse is by definition irresistible."

"Right," said Andrew. "At the moment I've an overwhelming impulse to hit you."

Mr. Belinski at once did the most sensible thing possible. He got into bed. Andrew continued to glare down at him, but he was baffled, and he knew it. Belinski (actually wearing a pair of Andrew's pyjamas) turned very comfortably on his side and closed his eyes — abandoning himself, defenceless, to his host's chivalry. And his trust was justified: even in a blind rage Andrew would hardly have hit a man when he was down; nothing on earth could have made him hit a man in bed. To exhort Belinski to get out and put his fists up was equally beyond him: even as he stood scowling, a nursery rhyme of his youth ridiculously crossed his mind. "*One fine day in the middle of the night, Two blind men went out to fight. . . .*"

"I'm too damn civilized," thought Andrew furiously.

Belinski appeared to sleep. The charming room, filled with every luxury for a cosseted guest, was peaceful and still. It annoyed Andrew very much that he could not even slam the door, since the noise might have aroused his father.

# Chapter 25

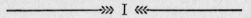

THERE is always something soothing about a fine Sunday morning in the country: its influences (at the opposite pole from those of a Saturday night) conduce to orderliness and tranquillity, good sense and forbearance. And this Sunday, at Friars Carmel, had especially the quality of being a new day — partly owing to the excellent staff-work of Mrs. Maile, who by nine o'clock had the drawing-room in order again, the wireless closed, the rugs replaced: looking into it, a stranger might have thought, "How long since any one danced here!" Out of doors too all was particularly well-organized: birds sang, the sun shone, dew-drops sparkled: an immaculate early-summer morning confidently offered itself to Divine inspection.

There was also something soothing in Sir Henry's complete ignorance of all that had happened after he went to bed. He had slept through everything. This made him very grateful company to Andrew, who, breakfasting alone with his father, soon began to see matters in their proper perspective, that is, with his own affairs in the foreground. He had a very important communication to make, and the occasion seemed suitable. As soon as they were both supplied with sausage, kidneys, toast and coffee, Andrew said cheerfully: —

"By the way, Dad, I've decided what I'm going to do. I'm going to join the Air Force."

Sir Henry received this statement with the blankest surprise. He was not nearly so quick as his wife, he lacked the sensitive ear which always warned Lady Carmel when Andrew's casualness was assumed.

"Now, where did you get hold of a notion like that?" marvelled Sir Henry.

"It isn't a notion, sir; you know I belonged to the University Air Squadron — "

"And a mad break-neck affair I always thought it," put in Sir Henry. "However, your mother said so was hunting, so I gave in. But you hadn't any idea of joining the Air Force — had you, now?"

"No, sir," admitted Andrew. "I suppose, as you say, it was rather like hunting. But I've since thought things over — "

"Join the Air Force!" reiterated Sir Henry, as though the words themselves were astonishing. "But, my dear boy, we're not at war with any one!"

"We soon may be."

"If there's a war, of course you'll go. I'd expect it. But there isn't," reasoned Sir Henry.

Andrew tried a rather foolish grin.

"I think I'll get in on the ground-floor."

"You'll do whatever you please, of course," said his father, beginning to take umbrage. "You know what my hopes are — and your mother's. Have you told *her* yet?"

"Yes, sir. Last night."

"What's she say?"

"She approves."

"She'd approve if you wanted to join a circus," grumbled Sir Henry — most unjustly. He drank some coffee, looking at his son over the rim of the cup with puzzled eyes. Andrew felt unreasonably apologetic.

"I think the point is, Dad, I believe there's going to be a war and you don't. We've both got to act up to our beliefs. You've always done your duty — "

"I hope I have. I know I've always done what the country's asked of me — even when some ignorant feller tells me to plough up permanent pasture, I've done it. *You* think you know better than the country."

"You knew better about the ploughing, sir."

This put Sir Henry in something of a quandary. Moreover he did at the bottom of his simple heart believe that his son was cleverer than himself — as Allie was wiser than the pair of them. If Allie approved, perhaps it was all right. He sighed.

"If you've made up your mind, Andrew, I dare say you know best. Give me time to get used to the idea, that's all." And he added irrelevantly, "I remember last time, they took the horses."

"That must have been a great blow," said Andrew sincerely.

"It was." Sir Henry looked up with sudden humour. "I'm not comparing you to the nags, my boy; I'm just rambling."

Upon that they both felt much happier; the silence that ensued was friendly. Both were preoccupied with their thoughts — by comparison with which Belinski, who just then appeared, was so unimportant that neither took any notice of him. " 'Morning," grunted Sir Henry; "Hello," said Andrew, and Belinski was thus able to insinuate himself, so to speak, upon the scene again, on his usual footing. After a wary glance at the two Carmels he quickly helped himself from the sideboard and sat down at the other end of the table. The Sunday papers did not reach Friars Carmel till noon, so that he could not conceal himself behind an *Observer* — but within a very few minutes Belinski realized that concealment was unnecessary: Andrew no longer wished to hit him.

With growing cheerfulness Belinski re-filled his plate, and in the end ate a rather larger breakfast than usual.

It was indeed quite remarkable how completely the Professor's misdoings were not only forgiven, but forgotten. This was partly of course because he was in any case leaving the next day; but also because to Friars Carmel as a whole he was in sum an irrelevance. Betty later in the morning greeted him with her customary good humour, and so did Lady Carmel. (Her ladyship's attitude was coloured throughout by the fact that Belinski was a foreigner. As a foreigner he had surprised her by his good behaviour; his bad surprised her much less.) For the first time she took him to church with her, and this left Andrew and Betty with the house to themselves.

## II

They did not stay indoors, however, they went wandering in the garden, and at last into an old orchard where the blossom was at its height; and there Andrew told her what he had already told his father, and a good deal more.

"You're quite right," said Betty. "I'm glad, Andrew. We all talk so much — "

She broke off, contemplating a spray of blossom on a level with her face. A bee clung in it, easing his furry body from cup to cup. She said, what he once before had said to her: —

"Suppose nothing happens? Suppose there isn't war?"

"I might get out. I don't know. The point is, life's going to be rather different. I shan't be much at Friars Carmel."

"You know," said Betty thoughtfully, "I'd begun to think you were attached to it."

"I am. That's also the point. Whenever I come here I feel it belongs to me. I feel like a damned Lord of the Manor. I don't mean to, but there it is. All right, I'm a survival. But if I accept that," said Andrew, very slowly, "at least I know what I ought to do. Fight for my damned manor. Am I talking like an utter ass?"

"No," said Betty.

"Will you marry me?"

"Yes."

They kissed each other. The sensation was exquisite, and very soon perfectly natural. Presently they began to walk through the orchard, pausing often, turning to look back where the chimneys and gables of Friars Carmel showed beyond apple blossom and darker trees. They felt watched, not from any window, but by the house itself.

"It's too big," said Andrew regretfully. "I don't suppose we'll ever live here."

"It wouldn't be too big if we had a large family."

"Would you like a large family?"

"Seven," said Betty at once. "I know we shan't be rich, darling, but you can bring up children very cheaply in the country, if you've got a house."

"You start sending seven boys to Eton —" began Andrew.

"Only four boys. And they needn't go to Eton."

Andrew halted to look at her.

"That cuts out London and going abroad, and we probably couldn't even run a car. Darling, do you really want to spend the rest of your life in Devon bringing up children?"

"Yes," said Betty. "It's something I shall be very good at. I think I've had enough fun."

Andrew suddenly recollected a conversation he had once had with John Frewen, on the subject of Betty's future: never, they agreed, could she hope for any kind of a career. He thought their definition of a career had been too narrow.

And remembering those uneasy, unsatisfying days in London, he said suddenly: —

"I want to know something. When you told me you came here simply because you liked the country, was it the truth?"

Betty gave the matter earnest thought.

"Yes, it was. At least, it was the top layer of truth. I should have come even if you hadn't been here. But I also felt — and this is as near as I can get to it, Andrew — that I wanted to be in — in your vicinity. We saw a lot of each other in London, when we both happened to be in London, but it was all patchy. We had fun. . . . When you asked me to marry you before, it didn't seem exactly real."

"I behaved like a prig and a boor," said Andrew violently.

"No, you didn't. I knew how you felt. But it was *not* the way," said Betty primly, "in which I wished to be proposed to. I mean, not if I were going to accept."

"Oh, darling — " cried Andrew — uttering the eternal lover's cry — "how have I got you? When I think of all the others — "

"You needn't," said Betty serenely. "You're my only one, Andrew. For ever and ever, amen."

"Amen."

### III

Andrew went to find his mother as soon as she got back from church. ("We shall now wallow in sentiment," he told Betty. "Then let's," said she.) Lady Carmel however behaved very well, without pretending to astonishment, and without any references to Andrew's infancy. She was most deeply pleased, especially when he told her they proposed to marry very soon.

"As soon as possible," urged Lady Carmel. "If you're going into the Air Force, dear boy, you will no doubt live in dread-

ful furnished lodgings, but at least that saves bother. Though
when Elizabeth — if Elizabeth — " She paused, delicately; no
need to go into that *yet,* thought Lady Carmel. . . .

"I expect you'll see Betty a good deal," said Andrew. It was
rather odd: he and Betty, like so many modern young couples,
had agreed that they wouldn't live in each other's pockets; but
the reason was in fact Betty's extremely old-fashioned preoccupation with a large family. When Andrew had pointed
out, in this connection, that it might be years before they had
a permanent home, Betty said it wouldn't matter in the least,
because there was always Friars Carmel. Andrew suspected
her of some vague plan for spending the week at Friars and
the week-ends with him — but of course it would be many
years, added Betty reassuringly, before all seven young Carmels
were clamouring for her attention . . .

"Indeed, I hope so," said Lady Carmel. "Now I must write
to her mother at once, at least we've always sent Christmas
cards. Have you thought where you'll go for your honeymoon?"

"Well, Betty would rather like to come here."

"*Here?*"

"Yes, she likes the house, and she wants to see the gardens
in summer — now, don't get sentimental, Mother," said
Andrew hastily. "I know Dad hasn't moved off the place for
twenty years — "

"He will," said Lady Carmel energetically. "My dear
Andrew, nothing has ever pleased me more! I shall love you
to have your honeymoon here, and I'll tell your father at
once."

This was, however, the only aspect of Andrew's marriage
that did not give Sir Henry complete satisfaction. Apart from
his dislike of moving about, he appeared to take the view

that Andrew's and Betty's honeymoon, an obviously delightful event, was one which it would be a pity to miss. He agreed that he and his wife must clear out of the house; but need they go far? "There's a very decent inn at Carmel," suggested Sir Henry hopefully. "You'd be quite comfortable, Allie."

"No, dear, I shouldn't," said Lady Carmel firmly. "We must go at least as far as Bath."

"I dare say the Colonel would put us up at the Hall."

"Or London," said Lady Carmel. "It's a long time since we had a trip to London — and I could give Betty's mother some really practical help with those window-boxes. Don't be difficult, dear."

Sir Henry continued to fight a rear-guard action for some time; but Bath, or London, was his destined fate.

## IV

They also, of course, told Belinski — after Mrs. Maile. He showed so much pleasure that Andrew could not make up his mind whether the man were an exceptionally good loser, or merely exceptionally short-memoried. In either case he felt very friendly towards him, especially when Belinski spent the afternoon packing his own and many of Andrew's belongings in Andrew's best suitcase. Andrew was now particularly glad that he had done the Professor no physical violence: it would have marred the day to see him with, for example, a black eye. Nothing marred the day. Without, the sun continued to shine, birds to sing; within, all was bathed in the sentiment Andrew had foreseen (and which he now found he rather liked), even to the kitchen. Mr. Syrett was in his glory, his prophecies fulfilled; Mrs. Maile, in the pleasure of seeing her household established to another generation, generously forgave him for being right. All united in praise of Miss Cream's beauty and breeding — and though Cook rather unexpectedly came out with the remark that she'd never be such a one as Lady Carmel, Syrett wittily capped this by saying that Lady Carmel was just what Miss Cream *would* be, and no mistake about it.

They drank the young couple's health in a bottle of port, Hilda and Cluny partaking with their betters; and in the general atmosphere of rejoicing and congratulation the other four all turned to Cluny with their raised glasses, as much as to say, "You're next."

# Chapter 26

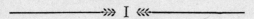

## I

MONDAY was a day of bustle, with an early lunch, for Belinski was leaving by the two-o'clock train; the housekeeper also prepared, with her own hands, an elegant little snack to sustain him on the journey. But even in the kitchen they had more to think of than Mr. Belinski, for immediately after breakfast there arrived Mr. Wilson's errand boy with a note for Cluny Brown. (Mr. Wilson himself had of course got back the day before, and very properly spent the evening with his mother.) The note was brief, but very much to the point: he had seen Mr. Porritt, who was in good health and sent his love, and he, Mr. Wilson, proposed, with Mrs. Maile's permission, to call at Friars Carmel that evening at six. Cluny stared at it so long that Hilda, through whose hands it had first passed, quite lost patience and at last simply read it over her shoulder.

"Well, Cluny Brown!" she exclaimed. "Well, Cluny Brown!"

"I suppose I'd better answer it," said Cluny slowly.

"Certain sure you had. The boy's waiting."

Hilda began to giggle uncontrollably. Cluny shot her a repressive glance and stalked into the housekeeper's room to lay the missive before Mrs. Maile. Her behaviour was indeed quite admirable; there was not the least secrecy about her, no reluctance to display what was after all her first love-letter. Mrs. Maile read it with approval.

"Certainly, my dear," she said. "Six o'clock is a very convenient time — and you may see him in here."

Cluny nodded dumbly. The housekeeper was pleased to see she looked properly impressed by the gravity of the event. And what an event it was! Casting her mind back over thirty years, Mrs. Maile could not remember one of her girls doing better than the postmaster at Carmel: and here was Cluny Brown (quite untrained, thought the housekeeper automatically) about to be cocked up in a chemist's shop!

"You may offer him a glass of port," said Mrs. Maile.

Cluny nodded again.

"If you haven't any suitable paper," finished Mrs. Maile, quite carried away, "you may write the answer here."

Cluny sat down and wrote it, under the housekeeper's eye. Mrs. Maile read it over for her, altered the spelling of the word "receive," and herself sealed the envelope. The officious Hilda, hovering outside the door, snatched it and ran with it to the boy. Every one was as helpful as possible — and Hilda especially, who even in the midst of this excitement did not fail to remind her friend that Professor was goin', and they ought to be on the look out for'n. "Where is he?" asked Cluny quickly. "In the garden," said Hilda. "Now's too soon, silly, us'll catch'n just before he departs." But whether or not Cluny took this in, Hilda could not be sure; for her friend was evidently (and naturally) in a proper miz-maze.

## II

Despite her impatience to show Betty Friars Carmel from top to bottom, Lady Carmel was taking the Professor for a last walk round the gardens first.

"It *is* such a pity," she lamented, "that you won't see them in the summer!"

"Who knows?" responded Belinski brightly. "I may come back."

For one moment Lady Carmel had a dreadful vision of him turning up just in time for the honeymoon — and having to be taken to Bath or London by herself and Sir Henry. She said hastily: —

"I expect you'll like America very much. It must be such a wonderful country, I've always quite longed to go there. They say, of course, that one can't judge it for at *least* three months, or preferably six. . . ."

Belinski halted between the box borders (in the very spot where she had instructed him to borrow Andrew's dinner-jacket) and spoke with great earnestness.

"Of one thing I am sure, Lady Carmel: nowhere in America, nowhere in the world, will I find people so good and gracious as you. It is not possible. When I think how you received me, and of all the trouble I have given you — "

"Oh, no!" cried Lady Carmel. "You've been no trouble at all!" This was practically true; he hadn't been, until the last few weeks; and now, when he was about to go — when he was about to go three thousand miles — Lady Carmel's soft heart quite melted. "It's been a great pleasure," she said sincerely, "we've all enjoyed your company so much. My husband is really distressed at your leaving us. You must write to us often, and tell us all you do."

"I will write to you every week, on Sundays," promised Belinski.

They finished the tour quite mournfully, and with many more expressions of mutual regard. Belinski then sought out his principal benefactor, Andrew, not only to thank him in the warmest terms, but also to find out how much he should give in tips. "I wish to give largely," explained Belinski. "I am probably the only Pole they will ever see, and I wish to leave a good memory." But he had been at Friars Carmel over three months, and valeted by Syrett all the while; when Andrew mentioned an appropriate figure, remembering Cluny and Hilda as well, Belinski looked uneasy. He had only his hundred pounds, not intact, and he was going to America; for a few moments prudence and generosity strove painfully in his breast. But he was a man of great resource and no inhibitions; and in the end solved the dilemma very happily, by borrowing from Andrew himself. "I will pay you back in dollars," explained Mr. Belinski, "and thus you will probably gain on the exchange."

Andrew's ideas of tipping were generous, and when the interesting moment for disbursement arrived Belinski made as good an impression as he had desired. Syrett's best wishes were heartfelt, Hilda went puce with pleasure — and then bolted off to look for Cluny Brown. For Cluny was nowhere to be seen, she was going to miss the Professor after all. The last moments were passing, the last farewells drew to a close in the hall — still Hilda rushed about looking for Cluny Brown. She found her in, of all places, their bedroom, just standing by the window, doing nothing, not even looking out.

"He's goin'!" cried Hilda. "He's given I five pounds — run, Cluny, or you'll miss'n!"

Cluny gave her a quick, startled look, and ran.

## III

Of the extraordinary events that immediately followed Ernest Beer was the only witness; for the car was halfway down the drive when Mr. Belinski suddenly told him to stop. He did so; a moment later Cluny Brown ran up and stood panting as the Professor opened the door. "Nearly missed'n," thought Ernest Beer — his mind working on the same lines as Hilda's. But no tip passed. Nothing seemed to be happening. Mr. Beer squinted over his shoulder and saw the Professor lean forward and remain motionless — no movement of hand to pocket. "Mean," thought Mr. Beer. And Cluny also remained quite still, staring back at the Professor: they might both have been struck by lightning. Then Mr. Belinski spoke.

"Oh, get in," said Mr. Belinski.

That was all. As Ernest Beer afterwards reported, Cluny got in and sat down without a word. He thought she was stealing a ride to the village, and if it got her into trouble, that was her look-out. However, when he stopped outside Wilson's, the Professor told him to go on, which he did. He couldn't hear what was said inside the car, and his impression was they didn't say anything. On reaching the station Cluny Brown got out as well, and went on to the platform — and that was the last Mr. Beer saw of her. Not till the London train had come and gone did he call out to the stationmaster to hurry her up; learning that she had gone off in the train he ejaculated "Good riddance," and drove stolidly back. Such was his meagre account of the vanishing of Cluny Brown, and Lady Carmel was completely bewildered by it.

"Andrew," she said, "ring up the station at once. There must be some message, and Beer's too stupid to remember. She can't just have *gone!*"

But it appeared that she had. Andrew talked to the stationmaster for five minutes, and received a very curious impression. The man had seen them both; he found the Professor an empty first-class carriage and put him in with his bags; for a few moments while the train waited he had noticed Cluny Brown standing by the carriage-door, over which the

Professor leant out. They were not talking to each other. Then just as the whistle was blown the Professor opened the door and Cluny Brown got in. She hadn't taken a ticket, and she had no luggage. She had, in short, just gone. . . .

"I don't understand," said Lady Carmel. She looked anxiously at her son. "Andrew, was there — was there anything between them?"

"Not that I know of," said Andrew. "There couldn't be. He was making a fool of himself over Betty."

"And Mrs. Maile told me she was as good as engaged to Mr. Wilson, and was most in earnest about it! She must be mad!"

Andrew shrugged his shoulders. In spite of his greater worldly experience, he was just as much at a loss as his mother; but it was not he who would have to write to Mr. Porritt, and he could regard Cluny's departure with comparative equanimity. Lady Carmel, seriously troubled, had a long talk with Mrs. Maile, and then one with Hilda; neither of whom could give her the least help. Cluny Brown had apparently been happy in her work, happy, above all, in the attachment of Mr. Wilson. On this point the housekeeper laid particular stress, not scrupling to describe it as a stroke of luck as splendid as astonishing. "And she never seemed to take any . . . special interest in the Professor?" asked Lady Carmel helplessly. "No," sobbed Hilda, "her just baited he a morsel, dear soul!"

Lady Carmel went upstairs to the girls' room. There bewilderment finally overcame her — bewilderment and distress, for she found Cluny's little floral arrangements, the jam-jars filled with moss, the flowers in the cracked vases, inexpressibly touching. They spoke such a simplicity, such an innocence of mind. "A child!" thought Lady Carmel. And everything was in its place, brush and comb and face-cloth, all Cluny's clothes, her cotton nightgown, lovingly offered by Hilda, folded on the pillow. Indeed what Lady Carmel was seeing was no more than a cast skin, sloughed as easily; or the white shards of a hatched egg; but this she did not know. She turned to the mantelpiece, and there — the final mystery — met the stolid gaze of Mr. Porritt, and Aunt Floss, and Mrs. Brown. They were exactly the photographs one would expect, and hope, to find in a parlour-maid's room; but not in the room of a parlour-maid who had just fled with a Polish Professor. At Mr. Porritt in particular Lady Carmel gazed for several minutes, perceiving in him the very type of a class she knew how to prize: respectable, respectful, and self-respecting. She would have employed him without hesitation. She had employed his niece, and this was what came of it.

"I *cannot* understand," said Lady Carmel aloud.

She wasn't the first, and she wasn't the last. As far as Friars Carmel was concerned, they never did understand. Cluny Brown had come, and was gone; as Cook said, she had always seemed rather pro tem. Hilda at least mourned her sincerely, and for a long while after certain exotic phrases, lingering in her speech, were a memorial to her friend. She taught Gary to say "Oh yeah." Mrs. Maile wrote Postgate's a rather reserved letter, and engaged through them a parlour-maid of sixty who was at least thoroughly trained. To save him worry, Sir Henry was told that Cluny had suddenly been called to her uncle's sick-bed. Andrew and Betty wondered a little, and in their own preoccupations soon forgot all about Cluny Brown.

As for Mr. Wilson, he arrived that evening at six and was received by both Lady Carmel and Mrs. Maile. After hearing what little they could tell he went away again so silent, so forbidding in either grief or anger — for they could not guess which — that neither dared ask whether he intended to pursue Cluny Brown to London, or whether he had blotted her name from the human register.

# Chapter 27

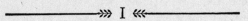

## I

CLUNY, jumping into the train just as it started, was thrown into the seat opposite Belinski's; he reached out and slammed the door; and there they were, alone, together.

Some minutes passed before either spoke. Cluny looked slightly dazed, as though her body had moved more swiftly than her mind, and she hadn't yet had time to catch up with it. She leant her head against the cushions and shut her eyes, presenting the remarkable picture of a girl in a parlour-maid's uniform, hatless, apparently asleep in a first-class carriage. Belinski stared at the sweep of her dark lashes on her white cheeks and for a moment saw nothing else. It was a moment that came to all who ever considered Cluny Brown beautiful: a moment of revelation. If it didn't come, she remained plain. (Mr. Ames had had it, Betty Cream almost; and they alone of her early acquaintances could understand the reputation she later acquired.) So Belinski gazed, with something like astonishment, because here had been beauty, and he had not perceived it. It had not influenced him. He had acted under a compulsion which he was only beginning to name.

Cluny opened her eyes and gave him a tentative smile. She said: —

"I haven't a ticket."

"We can pay at the other end," said Belinski.

"I can't. . . ."

"Well, I can."

This brief and practical exchange brought them both as it were to the surface; almost immediately Belinski spoke again.

"I suppose you know I'm going to America?"

"No, are you?" said Cluny.

"Where did you think I was going?"

"I don't know."

"Do you know why you are here?"

"You told me to come," said Cluny reasonably.

"Well, I could scarcely leave you behind," argued Mr. Belinski. "At any rate, take off that idiotic apron."

Cluny stood up in the swaying carriage, removed her apron, rolled it up, and tossed it into the rack. Then she sat down again, not beside him, but opposite. They looked at each other earnestly. Beneath the surface constraint a deep current of ease and understanding had begun to flow between them, a sense of naturalness as strong as sweet. For a moment they gave themselves up to it without question. Then Belinski said abruptly: —

"Something will have to be decided."

"Yes," said Cluny.

(But it was decided. It had been decided as she stood by the car, in the drive at Friars Carmel.)

"Do you want to come to America with me?"

Cluny nodded.

"That means we get married. They are very particular about that kind of thing."

"All right," said Cluny.

They sat looking at each other almost solemnly. Belinski reached across and took her hand, and at once the current flowed stronger and sweeter still.

"I think it is all right," he said consideringly, "because I have never felt like this about any woman before. I have made love to so many, and I have not made love to you at all, but I have never felt them to be necessary. I could not have gone without you."

"You got started," pointed out Cluny — not reproachfully, but because every detail was of such absorbing interest.

"Yes, but I was already wondering what it was I had left behind. I should have come back for you. Perhaps sometimes you will have to run after me again, because I do not yet know how my constancy is. But I have a feeling that I shall be quite constant to you. It's fine," said Mr. Belinski.

He regarded Cluny with deep satisfaction, and she nodded gravely.

"I'll always come after you."

"As I say, perhaps there will be no need. Perhaps you have just witnessed my last . . . excursion." He released her hand and leant back and grinned at her. "Cluny Brown, what have you been thinking about me?"

"About you, or — ?"

"You know what I mean. About me and Miss Cream."

"Well," said Cluny carefully, "she *is* so beautiful. . . . I mean, I didn't wonder you lost your head. But I never thought anything would come of it."

"You weren't jealous?"

"No. Because she's so beautiful," explained Cluny again. "Besides, I didn't know then. I mean, I didn't know about us."

"You were too much taken up with your Savonarola. My darling, you have had such a narrow escape it is quite appalling to think of. You'd have married him."

"No, I shouldn't."

"You would. You were in love with your prig of a chemist. You learnt pieces of poetry for him — and made me help you. If I can put up with that," exclaimed Mr. Belinski irrationally, "no doubt I can put up with anything, and you have got me under your thumb. Cluny Brown, I forbid you to see him again!"

Cluny looked rather worried.

"Well, I've got to write to him. . . ."

"Why?"

"I've got to send him a postal order. I never paid him for Uncle Arn's eggs."

All at once, at the mere mention of his name, it was as though Mr. Porritt had entered the carriage. Cluny sat up. None of her recent actions had seemed in the least reprehensible, or even unusual to her, until this moment, when she suddenly saw them through Mr. Porritt's eyes. There was no doubt that Mr. Porritt would view them very unfavourably indeed. Cluny was still unaware of what exactly had passed between him and Mr. Wilson; but the fact that anything had passed at all was enough to alter the whole character of her home-coming. . . . She put out her hand again, this time in a gesture of appeal.

"What is it, my love?" asked Mr. Belinski.

"Uncle Arn," breathed Cluny.

"But there is no need to see your uncle at all, if you do not wish it."

"Isn't there?"

"None in the world. We will go and stay at an hotel somewhere until we can get married, and then we will go to America."

Cluny hesitated. So much in this plan appealed to her, chimed with her longing to embark at once on her new life, without fuss, without the handling and petty rubs of an argument which could end only one way, and so, like so many domestic arguments, would be futile as well as hurtful. And why not? Wouldn't it be better, after all, to present Mr.

Porritt with a *fait accompli* such as his stern sense could not reject? Why not? She was indeed under certain obligations to him: she owed him, putting the matter at its lowest, for eighteen years' keep; but with a detachment as complete as it was unresentful Cluny realized that if Mr. Porritt had done his duty by her, it was because he was a man to whom duty was the root of self-respect, and self-respect the condition of a tolerable life. The affection he had given her was largely passive, but probably quite as much as she deserved, for there was no doubt that she had often been a great nuisance to him; for the affection Cluny could have given Mr. Porritt he had simply no use. He had as it were no place for it, the death of his wife had closed too large a portion of his heart. "He won't miss me," thought Cluny sadly. "He'll just worry a bit. . . ."

So why go to String Street? Why not just cut it out?

Cluny hesitated. It was, though she did not realize it, a moment of testing; but as she sat with her hand in Belinski's the current between them flowed ever stronger, filling her with confidence, with kindness. She couldn't go off and leave Uncle Arn just like that. She wasn't going to start her new life by running away from the first difficulty. Better to take things as they came and deal with them as best she could, and (if she could) leave Uncle Arn with his sense of duty unimpaired.

"We'll go to String Street," said Cluny, on a long sigh. "I dare say it won't be so bad. I dare say we'll quite enjoy it."

Adam Belinski drew steadily at her hand, drew her on to the seat beside him.

"You are my brave dear," he said. "I can see you are going to be very good for me."

He would have kissed her, but at that moment the train

stopped, and some people got in. But Adam and Cluny did not mind. They had entered upon such good fortune that kissing was relatively unimportant.

## II

Cluny got out at Paddington feeling extraordinarily happy. She did not feel different: on the contrary, she felt more like herself, as though she had at last stopped acting a difficult part. There had been no conscious play-acting in her relations with Mr. Wilson — but she had played up to him. She would never have to play up to Belinski; anyway she couldn't, because he was too clever. Nor would he ever ask her who she thought she was, because to him — and to him alone, so far as Cluny could see — everything she did, thought or said appeared perfectly natural. . . .

She looked slightly different, however, for Belinski had pulled a dark red scarf from his suitcase for her to wind around her head, and it became her. She looked taller than ever, just as odd, but striking: a porter said "Taxi?" to her in the most natural way. But they didn't need a taxi to go to String Street, they left Belinski's luggage in the cloak-room and turned out of the station on foot. Cluny sniffed appreciatively at the familiar London air.

"Devon was beautiful," said she, "but I couldn't have stayed there always."

"Of course you could not. Shall we ever stay anywhere always?"

"I don't know. It doesn't matter," said Cluny Brown. "Wherever we are — "

She paused, and stopped dead. They were passing a public-house, on whose threshold stood a weazened old man with a mug of beer in one hand and a dog in the other. The animal was so small that it fitted quite comfortably into his palm: it was black and fluffy, with a neatly curled plume of tail and very bright eyes.

"Mr. Belinski!" said Cluny, pulling at his sleeve.

"You had better begin calling me Adam," said Mr. Belinski. "What is it?"

"Adam, look at that puppy!"

The old man, observing their interest, at once set it down on the pavement. It staggered a few steps, and sat. Even after four months' association with a well-bred dog like Roderick, Cluny was able to gaze on it with rapture.

"Do you want it?" asked Belinski casually.

"Yes, please!" gasped Cluny. "Ask him if it's to sell. . . ."

It was; its price was one pound. This wasn't much, indeed, for a pure-bred male Pekingese and the companion of a man's declining years, but even Cluny felt doubtful. The puppy she had once, so briefly, owned already cost but half a crown.

"Offer him ten bob," she whispered.

But Belinski said he would not haggle over the first present he had ever made her, and offered fifteen-and-six, and at this figure the animal changed hands. It was all done so swiftly, so simply, that Cluny could hardly believe her good luck: even with the little creature tucked safely in her arms she kept stopping to marvel and exclaim; she might, thought Belinski, have been given the moon.

"But why should you not have a dog, if you want one?" he asked. "That was what I never could understand."

Cluny shook her head gravely.

"I couldn't understand why I couldn't do half the things I wanted to. There never seemed to be a proper reason: it was just because people didn't want to do the things themselves. Look at Uncle Arn."

The thought of Uncle Arn impelled Cluny to shift the puppy to one arm and take Belinski's hand. They walked hand in hand down String Street, and knocked on the door. Mr. Porritt was at home, and very much surprised to see them.

# Chapter 28

## I

"It's ME, Uncle Arn," said Cluny Brown.

For some moments Mr. Porritt simply stood and looked at her. His mind never worked very swiftly, and the unexpected appearance of a niece presumed to be in Devonshire gave him almost too much food for thought. (It was characteristic of him also that he got down to these thoughts at once, there on the doorstep, without even telling her to come in.) Only four days ago he would have supposed that she had got the sack; the very recent visit of Mr. Wilson offered an alternate explanation, that she had come to ask his consent to her marriage—wasteful, indeed, when you looked at the train fare, but right and proper at that; what absolutely stumped him was the presence of a strange man who (if number two held good) ought to have been Mr. Wilson or no one, and wasn't Mr. Wilson. So Mr. Porritt stood and turned all this over in his mind, until Cluny grew impatient.

"Let's come in, Uncle Arn!" she cried; and gave him an affectionate shove.

Mr. Porritt moved back; Cluny pulled Adam Belinski in after her and shut the door. Under the bright light the plumber gave him a close look; his first and damning thought was that he couldn't place him. Cluny meanwhile kissed her uncle heartily, and with a backward jerk of the head performed the necessary introduction.

"That's Mr. Belinski, Uncle Arn, and we're going to be married."

"You've got the wrong chap," said Mr. Porritt.

These, the first words he had spoken, had at least the merit of putting the whole matter on a sound, argumentative basis. Having uttered them almost without thought, Mr. Porritt found himself on firm ground, and Cluny for her part saw exactly what she was up against. As for Mr. Belinski, he wisely held himself in reserve.

"Well, you might say you're glad to see us," remarked Cluny irrelevantly.

"What's that dog doing?" asked Mr. Porritt.

"He's mine. We've just bought him. You can help think of a name."

Cluny held the puppy up, his four short legs dangling from her palm, and gently approached him to her uncle's face. The puppy hiccuped.

"Going to be sick," prophesied Mr. Porritt gloomily. "Don't you take him into the kitchen."

"If I don't go into the kitchen, how can I get us anything to eat?" asked Cluny reasonably; and marched through the door leaving the two men behind.

The extreme narrowness of the hall gave them a forced air of intimacy, as though they were there for some common domestic purpose, such as shifting the hat-stand. Mr. Porritt continued to fix the stranger with an unwinking gaze, to which Mr. Belinski returned a genuinely sympathetic look. He already knew far more about Mr. Porritt than Mr. Porritt was ever to know about him.

"I am sorry that this is such a shock to you," he said at last. "Indeed, it happened very suddenly. My name is Adam Belinski, I am a Pole, and a writer. But we are going to the United States."

These statements had the effect upon Mr. Porritt of a mild concussion. They sounded wonderfully clear and plain, but he could attach no meaning to them. He therefore ignored them altogether, and harked back to his original line of thought.

"Where's the other chap?" asked Mr. Porritt.

"Mr. Wilson, the chemist? I imagine he is back at Friars Carmel."

"I suppose he *was* a chemist?" said Mr. Porritt uneasily.

"Certainly. Of the highest standing." If it seemed odd to Mr. Belinski that he, as one suitor, should be required to supply the credentials of another, he did not show it. Indeed, he understood very well Mr. Porritt's urgent need for some solid ground. He added helpfully, "Mr. Wilson is probably the best chemist in the neighbourhood, and studied at Nottingham University."

"Well, then. . . ." Mr. Porritt fetched a deep snort of breath. "Two days ago comes this other chap, saying he wants to marry her. I tell him to go ahead. Two days after, you come saying you're going to marry her. It don't make sense."

"We can only offer Mr. Wilson our sympathy."

"Furthermore," continued Mr. Porritt, getting into his stride, "if Mr. Wilson's all you say, and it agrees with what I've seen of him, she'd be daft to change her mind, and what's more I won't allow it. Stay and have a bite if you like, but if you don't, no one will take it amiss."

Before Mr. Belinski could reply to this very fair proposition, however, they were interrupted by Cluny putting her head round the kitchen door.

"Uncle Arn, you've never eaten eight eggs in two days!"

"I gave half a dozen to your Aunt Addie."

"Well!" cried Cluny. "Mr. Wilson takes all that trouble to

bring you fresh country eggs, and you go giving them away! Now there's only one each, and one over."

"You have it," said Mr. Porritt.

"Well, you might open some beer while I boil them."

"I don't feel like beer," retorted Mr. Porritt. "I'm too put out."

"Then give Mr. Belinski a glass. I bet you gave Mr. Wilson beer," said Cluny stubbornly.


## II

It was extraordinary how Mr. Wilson had somehow managed to join the party. Cluny, having absently boiled the fourth egg, put it too in a cup: it looked like a fourth place. After all, as she pointed out, if it hadn't been for Mr. Wilson they'd have had nothing to eat. Moreover, he had evidently left a great impression on Mr. Porritt, who delivered what was practically a speech in his praise. Cluny's tender conscience forced her to join in, and Mr. Belinski had at least nothing to say against him. There *was* nothing to say against him. From whatever angle one approached, Mr. Wilson was perfect.

"He told me," mourned Mr. Porritt, "his turn-over was up ten per cent every year. That's what I like. That's steady."

"He *is* steady. And he's wonderful to his mother."

"He said, 'There's some object to living over the shop.' What I said was, 'If you've got a shop, stick to it.' There's nothing like trade."

"You did get along well," said Cluny. "Go on, have his egg."

But Mr. Porritt waved it aside.

"We had quite a long chat. I don't know I've ever met a

chap I liked better, not at first go. We got everything settled — "

Cluny offered the fourth egg to Belinski, and on his refusal ate it herself. She was quite untroubled, for she had still
a child's capacity for contemplation: deep inside herself she
was brooding quietly and continuously on the infinitely rich
sensation of being at last where she belonged. She belonged
with Adam Belinski. Were they in love with each other?
Cluny could only have answered, she supposed so. All she
knew consciously of love were its preliminaries as taught by
the movies, and these she and Belinski had skipped: they
had met at the centre of the maze, not on its outer rim: they
accepted each other simply and finally as the basic fact of their
joint lives.

Mr. Porritt talked on. They did not mind him, they did not
even wish him to stop. The untidy supper table, the over-
heated kitchen, suited them very well. They were never to
pay much attention to their material surroundings. Raising
her head, Cluny met Belinski's eyes fixed on hers in a look
of great peacefulness: it was a look she was to meet again
and again in the diverse circumstances of their erratic, turbu-
lent, haphazard existence. In shabby lodgings, in luxurious
borrowed penthouses, travelling steerage or by air-liner, eating
off gold plate or out of paper bags, peace would be theirs —
not as a shield against the world (for they always welcomed
the world, whether it pursued them in the shape of duns or
disciples) but rather as a warm cloak, a travelling cloak, against
the world's weather. Mr. Porritt's obstinacy was no more than
a light mist; however he might talk, thought Cluny easily, he
would soon come round. She was sorry for his disappointment,
because Mr. Wilson was so obviously Uncle Arn's cup of tea,
but he would get over it. . . .

She stooped down to see if her puppy was eating his supper. She had prepared him a saucer of bread and bovril; he had consumed about half and fallen asleep in the middle. Cluny picked him up and tenderly wiped his ears; through his soft fur she could feel the warm supper inside him. He put out his tongue and licked her hand.

"He knows you," said Mr. Belinski.

Cluny nodded, feeling almost unbearably happy.

"What shall we call him?" she asked.

But before any one could make a suggestion, there was a loud knock at the door.

### III

How various were the emotions with which each heard it! Cluny Brown turned pale: across her happy confidence shot a feeling of something very like guilt, and certainly like apprehension; Belinski, with his strong literary background, immediately thought of the knocking in *Macbeth;* Mr. Porritt turned on them both a look of sombre complacency, as of a man who sees Nemesis approaching, but not for him. It was he who answered the door, and he alone who felt a pang of disappointment as he returned not with Mr. Wilson but with only a telegram from him.

It was addressed to Mr. Porritt, and reply-paid. The boy waited; he was, for the time being, Mr. Wilson's errand boy. Mr. Porritt left him in the hall and shut the door on him while, very deliberately, he read the message through twice. Then with a solemn gesture he laid it flat on the table between Belinski and Cluny Brown.

IF CLUNY BROWN IS WITH YOU [said Mr. Wilson] TELL HER I WILL MEET THE 3.15 TRAIN LEAVING PADDINGTON 10.40 TOMORROW

TUESDAY STOP IF SHE IS NOT ON IT I WILL MAKE NO FURTHER COM-
MUNICATION STOP IF SHE IS NOT WITH YOU ADVISE YOU TRACE
ADAM BELINSKI POLISH PROBABLY KNOWN TO POLICE STOP YOU
HAVE MY SYMPATHY WILSON

Cluny slowly raised her dark head.

"It must have cost shillings," said she.

"All of five bob," agreed Mr. Porritt. "See what he says? I
have his sympathy."

"He is undoubtedly a very magnanimous man," declared
Mr. Belinski.

They all paid Mr. Wilson the tribute of a moment's silence.

"What are you going to say?" asked Mr. Porritt at last.
"It's for young Cluny to answer."

Cluny slowly fetched the big diary, with pencil attached (in
which she had once written the address of Mr. Ames), and
sat down with it at the table. She knew her uncle was right:
it was for her to answer. Under the eyes of the two men she
wrote, crossed out, chewed her pencil and wrote again; and
at the end of ten minutes silently drew back to let them read.

DEAR MR. WILSON [Cluny had put] PLEASE DO NOT TROUBLE TO
MEET THAT TRAIN STOP I AM VERY SORRY TO BE A DISAPPOINTMENT
TO YOU BUT BETTER NOW THAN LATER ON STOP I SHALL NEVER FOR-
GET YOU STOP POSTAL ORDER FOLLOWS ALL THE BEST FROM UNCLE
ARNOLD MR. BELINSKI AND CLUNY BROWN

If no one was quite satisfied with this production, no one
could suggest any improvements — or none that Cluny would
admit. Belinski felt he had been rather dragged in, but she insisted that this was a delicate way of publishing their intentions. Mr. Porritt wanted to send sympathy in return, which
Cluny considered impolite to Belinski. She was not perfectly

satisfied herself, but at least the message had one great merit, that of length; it was going to cost a lot more than Mr. Wilson had allowed for, thus showing they weren't mean. She took it out to the boy, and it was a solemn moment when they heard the gate close behind him and his footsteps diminish down the road.

"That's that," said Cluny Brown. "Cheer up, Uncle Arn; we're nct dead yet."

She caught Belinski's eye, and wordlessly indicated that he had better take himself off. He bade his future uncle-in-law good-night, adding that he would come round in the morning (to which Mr. Porritt replied that he would be out on a job) and Cluny took her lover into the narrow hall, where for the first time he kissed her. They had been sure of each other already, but it was with a sweeter assurance still that Cluny returned to the kitchen and after a moment's hesitation sat down in her old place, opposite her uncle, across the Porritt hearth.

## IV

It felt queer to be back; not quite real. She had been away only four months, but after Friars Carmel the familiar room seemed smaller than she remembered it. Cluny was glad to see it so clean and well-kept, yet its very neatness made her feel like a stranger. She had used to leave bits of sewing about, magazines, books from the twopenny library; now not a tea-cup was out of place. The spun-glass bird no longer adorned the clock, and her collection of calendars had all been taken down. Well, perhaps Mr. Porritt had never liked them. . . .

Cluny considered her uncle. He didn't look any smaller, but

he too had changed. As he sat before the hearth, staring into the grate, he gave the very definite impression of a man used to living alone. He didn't look unhappy, but he looked remote. Cluny suddenly felt a great desire to recapture, if only for five minutes, if only for the last time, something of their old companionship. She said softly: —

"Been busy, Uncle Arn?"

"Fair," said Mr. Porritt.

"Been getting along all right without me?"

"Well enough," said Mr. Porritt. "Well enough. . . ."

Cluny paused. She did not really want to hear that he had missed her, for that would make it too hard to leave him and go to America; but she wanted him to say something affectionate. She wanted to say something affectionate herself, but could not find the words.

"How's Aunt Addie, Uncle Arn?"

"She's all right."

"And Uncle?"

"They're both all right," said Mr. Porritt.

"Do you still have dinner there on Sundays?"

He nodded impatiently, and silence fell again. Cluny began to wonder how long her sojourn in String Street was going to last: whether there would be many evenings spent like this; how long, in fact, it would take to get married. For want of something to do she rolled Mr. Wilson's telegram into a ball and offered it to the puppy to play with; but the puppy was asleep. Cluny involuntarily yawned. She was just about to say she would go to bed when Mr. Porritt turned and fixed her with a long, troubled look.

"I suppose you know what you're doing," he said heavily.

"Yes, I do," replied Cluny, waking up. "I'm going to be very happy. I'm going to have a wonderful time. I'm sorry it's not what you wanted, Uncle Arn, but it's what suits me. That's the great thing, isn't it?"

"In my day," said Mr. Porritt, "it wasn't what suited you, it was what you got."

Fortunately Cluny had not to take this remark at its face-value. She knew perfectly well that whatever he might say, Mr. Porritt had always liked being a plumber, he enjoyed the position and importance it gave him. But she didn't want to argue. Standing up, she said, very earnestly: —

"Uncle Arn, before I go and get married, I want you to know I'm grateful. You've done an awful lot for me, that I'll never forget. I'm very fond of you, Uncle Arn."

She stooped and kissed him. He turned his head and rather clumsily kissed her back.

"That's a good lass," said Mr. Porritt.

# Epilogue

―――――――――≫≫≪≪―――――――――

THE REPORTERS had just come on board. They had several
people to interview, a famous bridge player, a Balkan prince,
a minor British film star, and Adam Belinski. The prospect
did not appear to excite them at all unduly; they advanced
along the deck in a small, business-like group, five men, two
women, with looks alert but reserved. They would have liked
to find their celebrities in a bunch, lined up and ready for
them; but it was their experience that celebrities, when about
to be interviewed, rarely bunched.

"Now, there's some one who looks like somebody," observed Miss Beebee.

The others followed her glance. Leaning against the rail
stood a very tall young woman with a red scarf round her dark
head and a small black dog under one arm. She returned their
combined gaze with interest and complete ease.

"The film star?" suggested Miss Beebee.

"Too tall," objected a colleague. "Also the film star's a
blonde."

"She's some one, anyway," asserted Miss Beebee.

Detaching herself from the group she advanced purposefully
on Cluny, née Brown, now Belinski. Cluny watched her approach with extreme admiration, thinking she had never in
her life seen any one so beautifully dressed.

"Pardon me, but are you Miss Deirdre Foster?"

"Certainly not," said Cluny. "I'm Mrs. Adam Belinski."

"Lead me to him," urged Miss Beebee. "I represent a whole row of women's papers, who are thirsting for an interview."

"Oh, are you the Press?" asked Cluny. She had indeed been stationed there by Belinski to catch the Press as it came aboard, and before the edge was taken off its enthusiasm by the bridge player, the film star and the Balkan prince; but Cluny's ideas of the Press were gathered solely from films, and she had expected a far tougher, cigar-chewing, hat-on-back-of-head company.

Miss Beebee, returning Cluny's stare with interest, nodded. Mrs. Adam Belinski was certainly some one; and she looked almost as though she might be some one in her own right. . . .

"Then he's in the bar," said Cluny. "He says he always meets journalists in the bar."

"And a very good idea too," agreed Miss Beebee warmly. But she hesitated. Turning to her colleagues, she said, "Boys, Mr. Belinski's in the bar. I'm just going to have a talk with *Mrs.* Belinski. . . ."

For a moment the others hesitated in turn; they had a great respect for Miss Beebee's acumen, and she looked as though she were on to something. However, the husband had to be dealt with at some point; they nodded, and went on.

"I believe," continued Miss Beebee, returning to Cluny, "we'd like a picture of you with that cute little pup. I guess it's a bit early to ask your opinion of American women —"

"Are they all like you?" enquired Cluny seriously.

"Well, I naturally consider myself a piece above the average, but you can take me for a fair sample."

"Then I think they're beautifully dressed, and very friendly."

"Go on," urged Miss Beebee. "Keep it up. Tell me something about yourself. How long have you been married?"

"Three weeks."

"Then this is your honeymoon? Look," said Miss Beebee, "why don't we go into the saloon or some place, where we can talk comfortably?"

Cluny was only too eager to do so. She was longing to talk, longing to tell some one how enthralling it was to be yourself, Cluny Belinski, invading America with your husband. And she had more to tell than even that; at last she had found some one willing to hear about Cluny Brown. She couldn't wait; she began at once.

"Well, I've had a very interesting life," said Cluny joyfully. "I used to be a parlour-maid — "

"For goodness' sake!" exclaimed Miss Beebee, really startled.

"But I wasn't very good at it," added Cluny, "because I didn't know my place. My husband says that won't matter so much in America."

"He's probably right," agreed Miss Beebee, considering Cluny very attentively. "May I ask where you were a parlour-maid?"

Cluny pulled herself up. After all, Lady Carmel had been very kind. . . .

"I don't think I'll tell you that," she said. "They mightn't like it. I mean, so long as domestic service survives, the convenience of the employer naturally comes first."

How strangely it sounded, that phrase of Mr. Wilson's, on the deck of the *Queen Mary!* How remote seemed those employers, Lady Carmel and Sir Henry, and Syrett and Mrs. Maile! Cluny cast them a final backward look as she followed the fascinated Miss Beebee into the saloon, and dismissed them for ever. She thought of Mr. Porritt and the Trumpers: less remote, but still dim, already fading. "Good-bye, Uncle Arn!" thought Cluny with a last flicker of regret; and sat down beside Miss Beebee, and opened her heart to the United States.